The Training of a Marquess

by

Sandra Owens

This is a work of fiction. Names, characters, places, and incidents are either the product of the author's imagination or are used fictitiously, and any resemblance to actual persons living or dead, business establishments, events, or locales, is entirely coincidental.

The Training of a Marquess

COPYRIGHT © 2013 by Sandra Owens

Contact Information: info@thewildrosepress.com

Cover Art by *Tina Lynn Stout*

The Wild Rose Press, Inc.
PO Box 708
Adams Basin, NY 14410-0708
Visit us at www.thewildrosepress.com

Publishing History
First English Tea Rose Edition, 2013
Print ISBN 978-1-61217-931-5
Digital ISBN 978-1-61217-932-2

Published in the United States of America

"I asked if you have come for another kiss."

"Yes," she whispered.

He spread his legs. "Come here then."

Thank you, she wanted to say, but it seemed silly. She stepped into the embrace of his body. Heat enveloped her as muscled arms circled her waist. She laid her head on his chest. His heart pounded in her ear, and it thrilled her to know it beat rapidly because of her.

His hands pressed against her spine and she snuggled closer. He curled her hair around his fist, gently pulled her face away from his chest and peered down at her, his eyes the blue of an agitated ocean—dark and stormy.

"Claire," he murmured as he lowered his head.

His mouth moved over hers in a playful tease. Wanting to taste him, she licked his bottom lip. A low hum vibrated deep in his throat, and the teasing turned into a kiss so deeply carnal her legs lost their ability to support her. His arm tightened around her back, the only thing holding her up.

He broke the kiss, picked her up and carried her to a lounge partially hidden by several tall potted plants. Claire slid her arms around his neck and buried her face against his skin. The scent of bergamot, milled soap, and the male musk that was him drugged her senses.

No words had passed between them since he had whispered her name, but none seemed needed to identify this fire burning inside her. Did he feel it, too?

For tonight, he would belong to her.

Also by Sandra Owens

THE LETTER
(available from The Wild Rose Press, Inc.)

~Winner of the 2012 Golden Claddagh~

Dedication

In my book, *The Letter*, I thanked my family, and I still do—for their love, their patience, my husband's tolerance for burnt dinners.

Now, I want to send very special thanks to all those who helped me make it this far. My critique partners—Jenny Hall, Gina Miel Heron, Sandy James and Erika Olbricht (no, you didn't critique this particular book, but I'm thanking you anyway).

To the many authors who answered my endless questions or cheered me on, I wish I could name you all. The support and encouragement I've received from the writing community is amazing, and I am humbled by it.

Then there's my editor, Cindy Davis—she of the evil grins. Thank you, Cindy, for helping to make this process as painless as possible.

Chapter One

London, 1809

Chastain Warren, the Earl of Kensington, sat by his dying wife's bedside and wondered if it was possible to hear the sound of his heart breaking into pieces. He had promised to love, cherish and protect her for the remainder of their days. Except her time was at an end and he couldn't save her.

Teresa looked at him through fog-filled eyes. "Harry?"

No, dammit, he wasn't Harry. The pain was as sharp as a knife blade that he'd never held his beautiful wife's heart. This woman he would die for had never been able to let go of Harry's memory. Chase held her hand and gently rubbed his thumb over her palm. "Yes, love, Harry is here," he said, giving her the only gift he could.

"Harry?" Her gaze swept past him. Such joy lit her eyes that he turned, half expecting to see Lord Hollingsworth. The life faded from her eyes. He had lost her to Harry forever. Chase bowed his head, closing his eyes against the burning tears falling down his unshaven cheeks. Placing his hand over her stomach, he said farewell to his unborn child. After kissing Teresa's still-warm lips, he walked to the door and opened it.

Teresa's mother, the Dowager Duchess of Aubrey, sat in a chair in the hall. Teresa's doctor knelt in front of her, quietly talking. There was such pain in Her Grace's eyes that Chase couldn't bear it.

"She is at peace now." He walked past her, down the stairs, out the front door and disappeared into the night.

****

Chase woke sprawled on a bench in the middle of Hyde Park. He had a vague recollection of being in a tavern. From the queasy rolling in his belly, it appeared he had consumed copious amounts of liquor. Leaning his head against the bench, he closed his eyes and attempted to get his spirit-soused brain up and working. It proved impossible. He was drifting back to oblivion when he felt a slight tug on his coat. In a reflexive speed he didn't know he possessed at the moment, his hand wrapped around a small, boney wrist. He slid one eye open and looked into the dirty face of a street urchin.

The boy tried to pull his hand away, but Chase held tight. "What are you about? Think to steal my watch, do you?"

"Wot?" the boy said with the innocence of angels on his grubby face.

"What's your name, boy?"

The lad clamped his mouth shut and glared at Chase.

"Come now, this isn't a good day to try my patience." The child was bone thin and dressed in rags. Chase would learn his name, give him a coin and send him on his way.

"Wot ye care, guv?"

It was a good question. "This is your last chance before I call the Watch. Your name, please."

His voice sullen, the boy said, "Harry."

Chase stilled. *Harry.* His heart pounded as his hand tightened on the boy's wrist.

"Ouch!"

"Sorry." Chase loosened his hold. "Where are your parents?"

"Don't got none. I told ye my name, guv. Ye gonna let me go now?"

Of course he was.

"Guv?"

Christ, what was happening to him? His hand refused to let go of the boy. He didn't register the presence of another until Christian Fallon, the Duke of Aubrey, spoke. "What have we here?"

Chase turned to his closest friend and brother-by-marriage. "Not sure, says his name is Harry."

Pain flashed in Aubrey's eyes. "Harry, you say? Why are you holding onto him?"

Why, indeed? Clearly, he wasn't thinking…well, clearly. Aubrey had lost his sister, but God help him, Chase couldn't bear his own grief, much less that of another.

"Don't really know. Scrawny little thing, isn't he?" Go away, he silently begged his friend.

"Indeed, he is. What do you plan to do with him?"

"I think he needs a bath and some food in his belly."

"Who's that?" the boy asked.

"That is the Duke of Aubrey," Chase said, happy to delay talk of Teresa.

The boy's eyes widened. "Ain't never saw a dook

afore."

Chase's battered heart peeked out from its hiding place and, in that moment, claimed the boy as his. What the bloody hell was happening to him? Not letting go of the lad's wrist, he stood. "Come along. You desperately need a bath."

The child pulled in the opposite direction. "Ain't never had me a bath, guv. Don't think I wants one."

Chase caught the pitying look from Aubrey and shrugged. "He's filthy and he stinks."

Aubrey, friend that he was, nodded as if that made sense in a world gone awry.

"When did you arrive?" Chase asked, towing the reluctant boy along.

"A few hours ago. Mother said you left the house last night and didn't return, so I have been out searching for you. Chase—"

The familiar use of his nickname carried too much sympathy. "Don't. Just don't." His wife's brother laid a comforting hand on his shoulder, and they returned to Kensington House in silence.

"Cor," the boy breathed.

He glanced at the dirty urchin to see him staring—mouth agape—at Angel House. Chase tried to see his home through the lad's eyes. Rising five stories high, the gray stone structure sat on almost a half city block. Under the flat roof featuring a cupola, an angel, wings spread wide, graced every third dormer window of the fifth story's attic. The house would be impressive to a child who lived on the streets. Hell, Chase was impressed.

He started up the steps still dragging Harry. "Did Her Grace and the children come with you?" he asked

Aubrey.

"Megan and the twins are at Rosemont with their nurse. When I left, Mother and Katie were hugging and crying. I couldn't bear to stay and used the excuse to go find you."

Aubrey's voice wavered and Chase understood. Pain lent a trembling effect to one's words. God, he didn't want to walk through the door. His efficient staff had covered the knocker in black and he pretended not to notice, turning his attention to Harry. If he concentrated on the boy, he just might be able to enter his house and go through the motions everyone expected of him. His butler opened the door.

"Tell Mrs. Jenner to ready a bath in the kitchen, Stillwell."

The butler glanced at the boy. "Certainly, my lord."

Harry tried to pull his hand away. "I don't wants a bath, guv."

Before Chase could respond, Aubrey knelt. "Would you be willing to make a trade? You agree to a bath in return for a meal?"

"Is there cakes, dook? I never had a cake, but Bensey says cakes is the best ever."

"Who's Bensey?" Chase asked.

The boy clamped his lips together and refused to answer.

"Yes, there is cake," Aubrey assured him. "So, do we have an agreement?"

"Does I have to have the bath to have the cake?"

Aubrey nodded. "I'm afraid so. No bath, no cake. And Bensey's right, cakes are the best ever."

The boy heaved a great sigh. "Aye, I wants the cake."

They led the child to the kitchen where Mrs. Jenner was heating water for a bath. Chase pushed the lad in front of him. "This is Harry, Mrs. Jenner. Do you suppose you might find something for him to wear after he is clean? These rags he has on need to be burned."

"I'm sure I can come up with something, my lord."

"Take your clothes off, Harry, and let's get you clean."

The boy looked around the kitchen, his gaze taking in Mrs. Jenner, the cook and scullery maid. "I ain't taking my clothes off with them ladies looking ats me."

After the tub was filled, Chase cleared the room of all the women. "Into the bath with you."

Harry eyed the hipbath as if it was a living thing that would devour him. Chase almost smiled. He turned and walked out of the kitchen, angry that he would allow a dirty boy to take his mind off his wife. The walls closed in on him, and he had to get out of the house. Not caring where he went, he ended up in the stables. Mischief poked his head out of his stall and nickered.

"We lost her," he told Mischief. Tears welled and he rested his head on the horse's sleek neck.

Where did he go from here? From the moment he had seen Teresa he'd wanted her. When she fell in love with Lord Hollingsworth, Chase buried his love for her deep inside.

When Lord Hollingsworth was killed, Chase had been given a second chance to win her. Though she cared for him, she had never fallen in love with him. He had decided he could live with that. He would love enough for both of them. And if he were very lucky, perhaps the day would come when she would say the three words he longed to hear. Her death had cheated him of that possibility.

Chase had been elated when he learned she was carrying his babe, praying that a child would help her forget the past. Instead, she turned melancholy and fearful, having tormenting dreams of the day Harry was killed and the baby she had lost that day. He could do nothing but watch helplessly as her health declined.

Now, any hope he might have had at seeing love in her eyes had died with her. And the worst thing of all—the very worst thing—she had taken his child with her. He could almost hate her for that. And with the near hate, came guilt for even thinking such black thoughts.

Mischief nuzzled his neck. "How are we supposed to go on without her, Mischief?"

"One day at a time."

Chase turned. He hadn't heard Aubrey come in. "She never loved me, you know."

"I know, and I'm sorry for it."

Chase bristled. "You are sorry? Is that supposed to help? How would you feel if you knew your Katie didn't love you, while you only took your breath because she lived? Tell me, Your Grace, how would you feel?" A part of him understood he wasn't being fair, but Chase couldn't stop the anger.

Aubrey lifted a hand and scratched Mischief's muzzle. "I would feel just as you do. The thought of being where you are now, knowing Katie was lost to me forever, I think I would tear England apart with my bare hands."

"Then you do understand." Chase walked out of the stables. The sound of Aubrey's footsteps following came to him, but he didn't slow. Coming to a crossroad, he didn't know which way to go. Should he go left, or maybe right? God help him, he didn't know.

"The boy was having meat pies and cake when I left. What do you plan to do with him?"

What did he care about a dirty boy? *Keep them*, Teresa's voice said in his head. So now she wanted to talk to him. How was he supposed to feel about that? And what did she mean by them? Chase turned and retraced his steps to his home.

"The boy stays with me," he said. "He needs to put some meat on his bones, and he won't do that living on the streets."

"No, I daresay, he won't. Does he not have any family?"

"He says not, and if he does, they should be beaten for their lack of care for him."

"Well then, it seems as if you have a ward," Aubrey said.

Was that what he wanted? Not really.

****

Chase stood next to the hole in the ground staring down at the box that housed his wife's body. The vicar's words were but a buzz in his head. He wished he could ask her why she couldn't love him. Take care of her and my child, he silently told Harry.

Chase returned to London. The three days he spent at his estate had been as smothering as he had feared. His mother and sisters had overwhelmed him with their attentions, and he'd fled at the first opportunity.

Entering his townhouse, he nodded to his butler. He had intended to go to his chamber, but changed direction at the top of the stairs. Was there still a street urchin living in his home? At the door into the nursery, he stilled.

"Mother of God, you've multiplied!" he exclaimed upon seeing two of Harry. He had no idea which boy he had dragged home. Cleaned up, they were handsome lads with their pale hair and dark brown eyes. Thankfully, someone had found them decent clothes. Likely Anders.

Chase had left his valet behind to keep an eye on Harry. It had been a welcome excuse. The man would have fussed over him as annoyingly as Chase's mother. Maybe worse.

Anders gestured at one of the boys. "My lord, meet Harry's twin brother, Bensey."

Ah, the expert on cakes. One of the boys stood and gave a perfect bow. "My lord, I hopes," he darted a look at Anders. "I mean, I hope Bensey can stay with me. We promise to be good."

Based on the boy's improved speech, Anders had performed a miracle in the three days Chase had been gone. "You are Harry, I presume?"

"Aye, my lord, I be—" Another quick glance at the valet. "I am Harry."

"Anders, may I see you for a moment in private?"

Reaching the hallway, Chase closed the door to the nursery. "How did we come to acquire Bensey?"

His valet gave him a wry smile. "The first morning after you left, Harry disappeared for half the day. Thought he was gone for good. Just in time for luncheon, however, he reappeared in duplicate and wanted to know if his brother could have some cake. I made the same agreement His Grace made with Harry. No bath, no cake. You should know, my lord, as smart and quick as Harry is, Bensey is almost the opposite.

9

There is a strange innocence and simplicity about him."

"What in the world have I got myself into?" Chase muttered.

Returning to the nursery, he pulled up a chair, turned it to face the twins, and straddled it. "How old are the two of you?"

Harry shrugged. "Mum used to tell us that, then she died. I don't remember what she said."

Chase glanced away from the child's soulful brown eyes. A man shouldn't have to watch his wife die, a child shouldn't lose his mother. Teresa's words came back to him. *Keep them.* Dear God, she knew. Shaken, he turned back to Harry. These children belonged to him now. He cleared his throat.

"I see. Well, I would estimate you are about eight years. So, as of now, today is yours and Bensey's birthday. Next year on this date, you will be nine."

"Does we get cake for our birthday, my lord?"

Chase decided he could get Harry to do anything if cake was the prize. "If you wish it."

"Does we get one cake or two, since we are having two birthdays?"

This was the one to watch. "It's up to you to decide."

There was no hesitation. "We wants two cakes, my lord, one for Bensey and one for me." He stood and bowed deeply. "Thank ye ever so much, my lord."

Christ, the little devil was clever. He was going to have to keep an eye on him or the child would soon be running circles around him and his entire staff. Harry's twin didn't seem to be paying any attention as he busied himself drawing a beautiful garden of flowers.

"Do you like flowers, Bensey?" Chase asked.

Bensey shifted his gaze from the picture to his brother, his eyes wary. Harry moved to block his brother from view. "I tells him not to draw flowers, my lord, but he likes the way they look. Ain't nothing wrong with him."

Chase leaned around Harry to see Bensey's reaction to his brother's words. His attention back on his drawing, the boy didn't seem to understand the undercurrents flowing through the room.

Chase studied Harry's posture as he stood protectively in front of Bensey, anger radiating from every pore. Chase had a sinking feeling in his belly. "Have men tried to hurt Bensey?"

Harry tensed, and Chase had his answer. What would it be like to be that young, living on the streets, having to steal for survival and having a brother like Bensey to protect? Somehow, his problems seemed to pale in comparison.

"You and your brother will always be safe with me," he gently said.

Harry's smile was beatific.

Chase's heart found a new home.

Chapter Two

One year later

Chase glared at the stack of invitations Stillwell had left on his desk. He should have considered society's hostesses would have marked the date his mourning officially ended—wasn't ready to face the matchmaking mamas and their daughters, didn't have any desire to attend their balls and musicals. He would not marry again. His brother, Robert, could produce the next Kensington heir because it was not going to be him.

He scribbled a note to his secretary to regretfully decline all invitations until otherwise notified. A knock sounded on his study door. "Enter."

His butler stepped into the room. "My lord, you have a visitor."

"I am not at home, Stillwell."

"I'm sorry, my lord, but he is most insistent." Stillwell handed Chase an embossed card. "Lord Bennet."

What the devil could the man possibly want with him? "Very well, you may show him in. If you see Harry, tell him to meet me in the stables at ten, please."

"I believe that is where he is now, your lordship."

"Of course, it is. If you ever catch him trying to move his bed there, notify me immediately."

"My lord, if Harry decides to relocate his bed, no one will know about it until after the deed is done."

Chase chuckled. "Right you are." He waved a hand in the air. "Show Lord Bennet in."

The man who entered his study was small, bookish looking and held a satchel in his hand. He pushed his spectacles up on his nose. "My lord. Thank you for seeing me."

Chase nodded at a chair in front of his desk. "Have a seat and tell me what brings you here."

Lord Bennet sat and placed the satchel on his lap. "I am here on behalf of the House of Lords to deliver a writ of summons. Do you know Thomas Tremaine, the Marquess of Derebourne?"

"I believe he is a very distant cousin, but I have never met the man. What does he have to do with me?"

"As of eight months ago, my lord, quite a lot."

"What happened eight months ago?"

"He died, my lord."

This conversation grew stranger by the moment. "I confess I'm perplexed. Perhaps you should start at the beginning."

"First I should tell you the pertinent result of his death. You, my lord, are the new Marquess of Derebourne."

Well, the devil. "I suppose that is something I should have been aware of, but I guess it just proves how distant a cousin he was." Nor had he been out in Polite Society this past year, thus missing all the latest gossip. Actually, he hadn't missed a bit of it.

Lord Bennet handed Chase the summons. "You are his cousin, six times removed, and closest living male relative on your father's side, thus making you his heir."

"Do you know how he died?" Chase asked.

"Lord Derebourne took a fall from his horse and hit his head on a rock. His family home, Hillcrest Abbey, is located in Kent and is a profitable estate. He's well known for his stables."

The marquess was said to breed some of the best stock in England. Chase gave an inward sigh of relief. It had taken years to repair his family's fortunes after his father had taken them to near ruin. He had no desire to have the responsibility of another failing estate.

"He had no other family?" When Lord Bennet squirmed Chase was sure he wasn't going to like the answer.

"His lordship was racing to the village to fetch the doctor for his two-week-old son. The child died the same night."

"What of Derebourne's wife?"

"She is in seclusion at Hillcrest Abbey."

Chase sighed. He didn't need this. "Does the marchioness have family?"

"No, my lord. She was an only child, and her parents were killed in a carriage accident after she married."

"So she has no place else to go?"

"To my understanding, no."

Chase would like to go back to bed and start this day over. He would have to travel to Kent, and had no idea what to do with a grieving widow with no place to go. Profitable or not, he would give it all back without a second thought. The title meant more responsibility. He didn't need a despondent widow on his hands and didn't need the income from the Derebourne estates.

Ten years ago, he would have welcomed it. He was one and twenty when his father was killed in a duel and he inherited the earldom. There had been times when he worried he would lose everything not entailed. He had been young and frightened by the responsibility of seeing his family fed and clothed. Creditors had lined up at the door upon his father's death, and there had been no money to pay them. But he had dug in and persevered, making a promise to himself to never follow his father's example.

"Is there anything else I should know?"

"Other than to deliver the summons requiring you to appear before the House of Lords for the announcement, I have nothing further."

Thank God. He needed time to assimilate this turn of events. "Very well, my butler will show you out."

Lord Bennet stood and bowed. "Thank you."

"My lord," Chase called as the man walked out the door of his study. "Do you know the Marchioness of Derebourne's name? Her Christian name?" The deuce. Why had he asked that?

"Claire Tremaine, my lord."

****

Claire Tremaine, the Marchioness of Derebourne, read the missive from Lord Derebourne and seethed. It had been three months since he had been informed he had inherited the title and he was only now getting around to visiting Hillcrest Abbey. Granted, he had sent his steward to the abbey a month ago, but only to go over the ledgers. Apparently all the new marquess cared about was the income from the estate.

She had heard rumors about his profligate ways. The vicar's wife had delighted in passing on the letter from a friend in London detailing the man's many sins. Never mind the letter was several years old. Once a rake, always a rake, Mrs. Fisherman claimed.

Claire paced the room in agitation. What was going to happen to her horses? Although, they were no longer hers. True, but that didn't keep her from worrying about their welfare. If nothing else, her husband had, after an ugly scene, given her free rein with the stables. She had put her heart and soul into making a name for the business. Claire couldn't imagine the new marquess agreeing to let her stay and manage the stables.

She mourned the loss of her son for many reasons. When he died, she hadn't been sure she could go on living. If Andrew had lived, Hillcrest Abbey would have been his and she wouldn't be faced with losing her home. She would have been able to stay and raise her son the way she wanted and life would have been lovely for the two of them.

Tears fell down her cheeks as she thought of the baby boy she would never see grow up. She didn't even have a portrait of him and her greatest fear was that there would come a day she would forget what he looked like. Shortly after he died, she tried to draw a picture of him, but she wasn't an artist and the effort had been in vain.

She crushed Derebourne's letter in her fist. She wouldn't make it easy on him to take the only thing left that was important to her. He could have Hillcrest Abbey; it was his by rights. But the horses were hers and she wouldn't hand them over without a fight.

Surely, the marquess wouldn't evict her upon his arrival—could only hope he wasn't so heartless. She needed to observe him, learn his weakness and come up with a strategy. Feeling better for having the beginnings of a plan, she walked to the bell pull and tugged the rope twice.

When the housekeeper answered the summons, Claire instructed her to ready the master's chamber. "Also, he writes he is traveling with two young boys, their tutor and his valet. He doesn't say the children's ages, but prepare the nursery and adjoining rooms." She resented the idea of strange boys occupying what should have belonged to Andrew.

"Yes, my lady."

"Please move my things to the yellow guest room in the east wing."

Mrs. Smithfield gave her a pitying look and left. Claire had no intention of staying in her bedroom as it was attached to the master's chamber. By all accounts, the man was a rogue and she wanted to be as far from him as possible. Perhaps she should sleep with her pistol under her pillow. Wouldn't he be in for a surprise if he tried to enter her room in the middle of the night? She knew right where she would shoot him. Smiling at the image, she headed for the stables.

****

Chase halted Mischief a half-mile from Hillcrest Abbey. Aptly named, the abbey stood in magnificent glory atop the hill. Below the front of the great red stone structure a terrace had been cut into the hill, and grazing sheep dotted the landscape. Below and across from him, a sparkling blue lake covered several acres.

"It's beautiful here, Father," Harry said from beside him. "Will you teach me and Bensey to swim?"

Chase was still getting used to being called Father. The twins had come to him a month ago and shyly asked if they could call him Father. He had been honored they wished to do so. By the relief in their eyes, he realized that, even after a year of living with him, they had been unsure of their permanence in his life. He hadn't thought about it because they belonged to him. To them, it appeared being their father meant he would keep them.

"If you wish. We shall take a rest here and wait for the carriage so we can all arrive together."

They dismounted and walked to the grass, allowing Mischief and Victory to graze. He had let three months pass since inheriting the title, not wanting to intrude on Lady Derebourne's time of mourning.

He had, however, sent his steward. The man reported that the ledgers were in good order, the current steward competent, and lastly, that he hadn't set eyes on Lady Derebourne. Nor had his solicitor been able to learn much of the widow. It seemed she led a quiet, private life, never leaving Hillcrest. Chase had an image of a mousy, fragile, and possibly ailing widow.

After much consideration, he had decided on what he considered a brilliant plan. He would take her to London so she could find a husband. Having lost her husband, child and soon her home, he had great sympathy for her and would happily offer whatever necessary to see her settled with a decent man. He would treat her gently and with compassion.

The carriage arrived and he and Harry mounted their horses, leading the way up the hill. Liveried footman in forest green and gold, and servants in starched black and white lined the steps. Grooms waited to take the horses. It occurred to Chase that the place must be awfully expensive to maintain, and he felt fortunate the estate could afford the upkeep. He climbed the steps to where a butler waited.

"Lord Derebourne, welcome."

Chase caught himself before he looked behind him. He supposed in time he would get used to being addressed as Derebourne. "Thank you."

"I am Smithfield, my lord, and this is the housekeeper, Mrs. Smithfield." He indicated the woman standing next to him. "I imagine you would like to be shown to your rooms to freshen up. Lady Derebourne will meet you in the family parlor for tea at four, my lord."

"Very good." Chase pulled Harry and Bensey to his side. "The one on my left is Harry and on my right, Bensey." He put a hand on each of their heads. "Go with Mr. Edwards and I will find you after I meet with Lady Derebourne."

"Yes, Father," they said in unison, following their tutor and a maid into the house.

Mrs. Smithfield led Chase and Anders to the master's chamber.

****

"They called him Father?" Claire asked.

"Yes, my lady," Mrs. Smithfield said.

Claire had watched from the window as the marquess approached with a young boy riding by his side. When another boy alighted from the carriage, it was obvious the two were identical twins. Mrs. Fisherman had told her Derebourne had been briefly married before losing his wife. The boys were too old to be from that marriage, which meant they were his bastards.

She didn't know whether to be appalled or

impressed he would publicly claim the boys. It just wasn't done, yet she thought gentlemen who carelessly sired bastards and left them to uncertain fates to be the lowest of men. After one look at the man standing on the steps, she could imagine how women would swoon at his feet.

She wouldn't be one of them.

"Thank you, Mrs. Smithfield. Have tea and cakes brought in promptly at four. We will keep country hours unless his lordship instructs otherwise."

Which she was sure he would promptly do. The man probably slept until noon and spent his nights carousing. Perhaps she should send a warning to the village fathers to hide their daughters.

Claire sighed. She was feeling nasty and possibly not being fair to the man, but she had seen the proof of his perfidy standing on the steps next to him. If he were a careless reprobate, would that not serve her purpose?

Surely, all he cared about were the monies she would pay, enabling him to continue his dissolute ways. Yes, he had only just arrived and she had him figured out.

Claire had no doubt things would go her way.

****

Chase entered the family parlor at precisely four. He stopped on the threshold and studied the woman standing at the window. She was as pale and fragile as he had imagined. Seeming to sense his presence, she turned. He had visited Greece on his Grand Tour—had stood on sand as white as sugar and marveled at the shimmering blue of that ancient city's sea. The color of her eyes took him back to that moment in time.

She curtseyed. "My lord."

Her gaze raked over him, her expression clearly meant to let him know she found him lacking. The skin on his neck bristled. Who was she to judge him?

"Lady Derebourne." He bowed. "It is a pleasure to make your acquaintance."

"Is it?"

Startled, he quirked a brow. "Of course, why would you think otherwise?"

"I might think otherwise because you find me a burden. I might think otherwise because you don't know quite what to do with me."

He'd always been at ease around women, but this one confused him. He didn't want to start off on the wrong foot, but apparently, without understanding how, he had.

"Lady Derebourne, please forgive me. It's not my desire to upset you. You are correct, however. This was your home, yet no longer. So, you tell me, what am I to do about you? I do have some thoughts on the matter, but welcome your opinion. I'm all ears, my lady."

She stared at him with those deep blue eyes and he waited, surprisingly curious to hear her response. She gestured at the tea tray. "You are correct, my lord. This is my home no longer. Shall we sit and have tea and some honest discussion?"

"As you wish." She chose the sofa and he settled in a chair facing her.

"How do you like your tea, my lord?"

"Only a small amount of milk and sugar, please." Chase watched her perform the ritual, his gaze resting on her slim, elegant fingers as she stirred in the milk. He followed the line of her arm up to her pale, delicate face.

The lady wasn't at all what he'd expected.

Her black widow's weeds were not flattering and drained the color from her face, but he'd once been a connoisseur of women and saw her potential. With the right color of gown and artfully styled hair, she would be quite striking. He breathed an inward sigh of relief. It shouldn't be difficult after all to find her a husband, especially with the dowry he planned to offer.

He glanced at her neck searching for any loose hair that would tell him its color, but no strands escaped the ugly lace cap. She caught him studying her and raised a questioning brow. Embarrassed, he shifted his gaze away, noticing the painting above the fireplace.

His breath caught in his throat. The portrait was of her, and the man standing behind her must be Derebourne. She was exquisite—a fragile, pale beauty that made a man want to cherish and protect her.

The rose-colored gown she wore brought color to her cheeks and lips. Her hair was the color of moonlight and her eyes—her best feature—looked back at him in amusement. In his rogue days, she would have been a woman he would have been determined to possess. The man standing behind her had to be at least thirty years older.

"Was that Derebourne?" he asked.

"Yes."

There was no affection in her voice, and he found himself curious about their marriage. Ill at ease, he sipped tea and waited for her to set the tone of their conversation.

"I know this must be awkward for you, my lord. What does one do with an unwanted guest? I have the right to the dower house, but I don't want to live there, and I doubt you much like the idea. So, do you give me time to make other living arrangements or do you show me to the door? Perhaps you think I might be desperate enough that I would agree to be your mistress. If it is the last, I assure you I am not. Desperate or agreeable, that is."

Chase couldn't find the words to respond. She had a sharp tongue and obviously blamed him for her circumstances. If she treated all men as she did him, it might not be as easy to find her a husband as he had thought. She had gone beyond the pale in insinuating he would be crass enough to take advantage of a grieving woman.

"Well, have you nothing to say, my lord?"

"Oh, I have much to say, Lady Derebourne," he said, finding his voice. "You don't know me, yet you feel free to malign my character. It is my understanding you have no family to turn to. I have no intention of showing you to the door without knowing you are safely settled elsewhere."

His anger was so great he carefully set his cup down lest he spill the contents. "As for considering you for my mistress, it never entered my mind, nor will it. You are not my type of woman, Lady Derebourne. Your tongue is too bitter for my taste. Have I said enough, my lady? Yes, I believe I have."

He stood. "I wish to spend some time with my boys and think it best if we continue this conversation tomorrow. Perhaps by then you will be in a better frame of mind."

"As you wish, my lord. We keep country hours. Dinner is served at six."

"Please have a tray sent to me and my sons. I find I

23

prefer their company tonight." He walked out of the room and asked the butler to direct him to the twins' rooms.

Claire fell back onto the sofa and buried her face in her hands. Bells in hell. She had handled that badly. From the moment the marquess entered the room her resentment had simmered. It wasn't his fault she was going to lose her home and most likely her horses. It hadn't helped that she had to force herself not to stare at him, and that had unnerved her. She had never met a man before that she would apply the word beautiful to. His hair was golden, his skin also golden as if he spent much time outdoors, and his eyes were the violet-blue of woodland bluebells.

What had possessed her to suggest he might want her as his mistress? A man like him would never want someone as inexperienced as her. She had never learned to control what came out of her mouth when she was angry, but this time, she had gone too far.

There was nothing for it. She would have to apologize. At least, he didn't plan to immediately evict her. Had he meant it when he said he would see her safely settled somewhere? If she could work out an agreement with him allowing her to keep her horses, she could support herself and make a life that held some meaning.

Claire had no intention of marrying again. She had been seven and ten when Thomas saw her walking down a lane in her village. Before she understood what was happening, she was married and carried off to Hillcrest. More of a child than a woman, she found herself living in a home she still sometimes got lost in, married to a man who could have been her grandfather and with nothing to do.

The servants, long used to answering to Thomas, virtually ignored her. What they ate, when they ate, the activities of the household—all operated to the preferences of her husband. She only saw Thomas at dinner or when he visited her bed in the dark.

One day, feeling miserable and sorry for herself, she wandered into the stables. The stable master and several grooms were gathered around a stall and she peered in to see what had caught their interest. They didn't notice her, and she watched a mare deliver her colt.

The miracle of the birth and the moment the baby horse stood on wobbly legs touched something deep inside her. From then on, at every opportunity, she went to the stables. In the beginning, the men were uncomfortable with her presence in their territory. She made sure not to get in their way, just listened and learned.

When Thomas discovered where she spent her days, he had ordered her to stay away. She'd pleaded, begged, bargained and outright refused to obey. It was the only time in their marriage he had struck her. The force of his hand across her face had knocked her backwards.

She had gathered herself and faced him. "Hit me a thousand times, sir, it will not change my mind on this."

His hand fisted as if he wished to do just that but then he'd stalked out of the room. No more was ever said on the subject. Eventually, she had taken over management of the horses and made a name for Hillcrest Stables.

There came a time when Thomas realized what she

had accomplished, but he never acknowledged her efforts, instead taking the credit. She didn't care. Let him have the glory, she knew in her heart the truth.

She would not allow the marquess to take away everything she had worked for. She had lost her son, endured a loveless marriage and was going to lose her home. As far as she was concerned, she had sacrificed more than any one person should.

The sound of male voices floated into the room, drawing Claire to the window. Derebourne walked toward the stables, a son on each side holding his hand. Her gaze slid over the man's back noting the difference in his long muscular legs, taut buttocks and broad shoulders from those of her husband's. Her mouth turned down into a frown, an attempt to quell the pace her heart insisted on setting at the sight of him.

She turned away and went to find Mrs. Smithfield to inform her of the change in dinner plans. Then she had better go see what Lord Derebourne was up to.

Chapter Three

"Why did the farmer get sent to the gaol?" Bensey asked.

Chase, having heard the riddle before and knowing the answer, allowed his mind to drift to Lady Derebourne. His instincts said there was more to the woman than what he had expected. She had eyes a man could get lost in. She also had a temper and a biting tongue. Not at all the biddable mouse he had imagined. It would be best if he avoided her as much as possible until her mourning ended and he could proceed with his plan.

"I give up," Harry said.

"He was caught beating an egg."

Harry roared with laughter, and Chase grinned upon seeing Bensey's wide smile at besting his brother. It didn't happen often.

As they approached the stables, Chase studied the huge structure and was duly impressed. The building covered an acre of ground and was freshly painted white with forest green trim. High across the front, the letters Hillcrest Stables were painted in the same green color, and then outlined in gold. The wide, double doors were open and he let an eager Harry pull him inside.

The floors were wood planks—scrubbed clean. The stalls on each side of the long aisle were generous in size and each had a wood plaque on the gate indicating

Sandra Owens

the horse's name. He inhaled, smelling hay, horse and leather. Several horses stuck their heads out and eyed the newcomers. From what he could see, they were prime horseflesh. Derebourne had certainly known his business.

Next to him, a wide-eyed Harry giggled. "Is this all yours now, Father?"

Chase feared he might giggle himself. "I suppose it is. What say you we find Mischief and Victory?"

"Oh yes, please."

An older man approached, pulling on his forelock. "May I help you, my lord?"

"Yes, young master Harry and I are looking for our horses."

An uncomfortable expression crossed the man's face. "The black one won't stay in his stall. He keeps turning up here and there."

Chase grinned. His horse hadn't been named Mischief without reason. "A terrible habit of his, to be sure. Do not fret, my good man, he won't run off. He's a curious one and likes to poke his nose into things that do not concern him."

"As long as you don't mind, my lord."

When they reached Mischief's stall, it was—unsurprisingly—empty. Chase found his errant mount in Victory's stall, contently munching Victory's hay.

"Mischief, you idiot," Chase said. "What are you doing in here?" His horse trotted merrily back to his own stall.

"An interesting stallion you have there, Lord Derebourne."

Her voice, coming from behind him, was unexpected and disconcerting. He turned and sketched a

28

bow. "Yes, my lady, he is that, if nothing else."

She walked to Mischief's stall, her black skirts swirling around her legs, and he thought of the rose-colored gown she wore in the portrait. When they arrived in London, he'd make sure she ordered at least one rose-colored gown.

He frowned. What the devil did he care about the color of her gown?

Mischief stuck his head out—all innocence, as if to say, *I've been here where I belong, all along.* Lady Derebourne held out her hand offering her palm for Mischief to lick. She stepped closer. Horse and woman touched noses, inhaling each other's scent.

Chase narrowed his eyes. The lady knew horses.

"Aren't you just the sweetest thing?" she cooed. Mischief snuffled her neck, causing her to chuckle.

Chase suddenly envied his horse. Watching her eyes slide closed as Mischief nuzzled that pale, smooth skin caused his blood to heat. He could imagine his lips on that very same soft, sweet spot.

Bloody hell. "Harry, Bensey, come along. It's almost time for dinner."

Bensey stood on his tiptoes and whispered into Chase's ear.

"Bensey would like to know if you have a conservatory, Lady Derebourne."

She smiled at Bensey. "We do. Would you like to see it?"

Bensey nodded.

"All right. Meet me tomorrow for breakfast. After we eat, I'll show it to you."

Bensey once more stood on his toes and whispered to Chase.

29

Chase relayed the message. "He would like to know what time you expect him."

Again addressing Bensey, she said, "What time would suit you?"

Chase realized he hadn't presented the boys to her. "I have been remiss in not introducing my sons, Lady Derebourne. The one so interested in your conservatory is Bensey and the horse mad one is Harry." He liked that she acknowledged each boy personally.

"What would be a good time for you, Bensey?" she asked again.

"Oh no, my lady, you don't wish to leave it to him," Chase said. "He will have you agreeing to meet him long before the sun even considers rising. Would nine suffice?"

She directed her answer at Bensey. "Perfectly."

His son gave her his sweet smile, and her eyes softened. *Be warned, Lady Derebourne, you will be his slave if you are not careful.*

A young man hurried over. "Lady Derebourne, I have the report—"

"Not now, Gordon. I'll sit down with you later."

Chase's curiosity kicked in. "If you have things you need to do, my lady, please feel free."

"No, it's nothing important. If you have a moment, my lord, may I have a word with you?"

"Of course. Harry, why don't you take Bensey and say good night to Mischief and Victory."

They scampered off and he turned to Lady Derebourne. "You have my attention."

Her gaze skimmed across his face and settled on a spot over his shoulder. She seemed nervous, chewing on her bottom lip, drawing his attention to her mouth.

And a very nice mouth it was. He jerked his eyes up to find her watching him. Her cheeks flushed pink, bringing color to her face. For some reason, it pleased him that he could unsettle her.

"What is it you wish to say, my lady?"

"Yes, well...I want to apologize for this afternoon," she told his chest. "I was rude and you were right. I don't know you and should not have said the things I did."

He had never been one to want to cause a lady discomfort. "Apology accepted. Perhaps we should take a few days to allow me to settle in before we continue any serious discussions."

"As you wish, my lord."

"I think I wish you would stop lording me. I suppose Chase is too familiar, but Derebourne should do for now. You can return my gesture of goodwill and give me leave to address you as Lady Claire."

"I wasn't born a lady, so it doesn't seem appropriate."

"Unless you're agreeable to just Claire, I think we can dispense with the rules while at Hillcrest."

She studied him as if he were up to some kind of trick.

"I only wish to ease the tension between us, my lady. It is difficult to hold resentment toward another when you think of that person as a friend."

"Are we friends, my lord?"

"Not yet, but we could make an attempt."

She gave a curt nod. "Very well. Derebourne and Lady Claire it is."

The regret she hadn't agreed to just Claire was disturbing. He needed to put some distance between him and those blue eyes. He called the boys.

"Your sons are lovely. How old are they?"

"I haven't the slightest idea, probably around nine." He collected the twins and herded them into the house.

****

Claire had started to think she had misjudged him until she asked the ages of the twins. What kind of father didn't know the ages of his children? He probably saw very little of them, likely leaving them in the care of their tutor. Why couldn't men be as easy to read as horses?

Disappointed, she went to find Gordon. It was time to go to work. She spent two hours with him going over the breeding charts and the background reports he had prepared on two potential buyers. One she had no problem with, but the second concerned her. On the surface, the viscount seemed acceptable, but there were rumors of races where he had pushed his mount to near collapse.

"Write Lord Daventry and arrange a visit, but I'm uneasy about the viscount. See if you can learn more about him before we respond to his request," she told Gordon.

It hadn't taken her long to understand that the men who came looking for a horse were not comfortable doing business with a woman. Several outright refused. So, she had hired Gordon to act as her business manager and voice in all transactions. Through Gordon, she had cultivated several contacts, men who had purchased horses from them to whom they could ask for insight on potential buyers.

Perhaps it wasn't good business sense to not sell

her horses to just anyone, but they were her babies and she had to know they were going to a good home.

Walking out of the office, she came face to face with Mischief. "Silly horse, what are you doing out of your stall?"

Her stable master came up beside her. "His lordship said he lets himself out and likes to nose around. I'll take him back, but don't think it will do much good."

Claire scratched Mischief's nose. "So you like company, do you? Leave him be, Clyde. He can visit with me for a while."

She began preparations for feeding time and as she worked, Mischief followed her around. "So, Mischief, tell me what your master is truly like. He puzzles me and I don't like puzzles." She smiled at Mischief, who had his nose in a water trough, blowing bubbles. Claire didn't know what she thought about his lordship, but she very much liked his horse.

"Not talking then? You could at least give me a hint as to his true nature." Mischief lifted his head, water dripping from his muzzle.

"Obviously, you are loyal to your lord and your refusal to speak ill of him is admirable. I'll reserve judgment, my friend, and give him time to show himself one way or the other."

Mischief shook his head as if agreeing with her good sense.

****

Claire entered the breakfast room to find Bensey standing beside a chair, his eyes trained on her. "Hello, Bensey. Have you been waiting long?"

The boy darted a glance to a far corner where Lord

33

Derebourne leaned against the wall—a golden angel, impeccably dressed in fine English clothing. Or perhaps he was a devil in the disguise of an English lord.

"Always assure a lady, Bensey, that she has not inconvenienced you." When confusion crossed the boy's face, he added, "The proper answer, son, is 'No, my lady, I only just arrived'." He grinned and added, "Even though you knocked on my door this morning before the cocks crowed and asked if it was time yet."

Bensey eyed to the floor. "No, my lady, I only just arrived."

"Splendid. Let's you and I have some breakfast, and then off to the conservatory we will go."

She purposely left out the angel holding up the wall, hoping he would take the hint and go away. He didn't, pushing himself up and sauntering toward her. Her breathing changed it cadence.

Bells in hell, what was wrong with her?

Turning away from the man who currently overwhelmed her senses, she asked, "Why are you interested in my conservatory, Bensey. Do you like plants and flowers?"

His eyes lit with a fervor she recognized. It was the same as the passion she felt for her horses. "I like plants and flowers very much."

"Then I think you will like my conservatory."

The devil lord settled beside her as if invited to this party. She almost giggled. Angel or devil? Make up your mind, she chided herself. She attempted to keep her attention on the boy. "What plants and flowers do you like best, Bensey?"

Lord Derebourne groaned. "Now you've gone and done it," he muttered.

She learned what he meant when Bensey talked her through breakfast. He told her of his favorite plants—their Latin names flowing off his tongue like smooth running water. He told her of their origins, their life span and whether they attracted butterflies, bees or birds. He was animated and exuberant and charmed her down to her toes. There was such an otherworldly innocence to him that she wanted to touch him to see if he felt real.

When he finally took a breath, she said, "I'm impressed with your knowledge. If you're finished, let's go see what you think of my indoor garden."

In the blink of an eye, he was up and around the table. She joined him and when they exited the room, he stopped to pick up a satchel from the hall table. She gave it a curious look.

"His art supplies," a deep male voice said from close behind her—too close. She could feel the heat from his body. Flustered, she quickened her pace.

"Do you like to draw?" she asked Bensey.

He bestowed a blissful smile on her and nodded. "Would you like to see my drawings?"

"I would like that very much."

He came to a sudden halt and unlatched his satchel.

"Not here, Bensey," Lord Derebourne said, coming up beside the boy and placing his hand on his son's shoulder. "You can show her when we reach the conservatory." He grinned. "You have shown an interest in his plants and his art. He is now your devoted servant."

A dimple appeared on his right cheek, and something fluttered in her belly. Disturbed by the unsettling feeling, she turned her attention to the boy.

"You are full of surprises, aren't you? Come along, we're almost there."

When they arrived, she stepped aside and watched Bensey's face. Hillcrest Abbey's conservatory had been the pride of Thomas. Not that he cared about the plants. He liked showing it off and impressing guests.

There were two full-time gardeners assigned to the conservatory. There was a section of exotic plants from Africa, an area filled with fruit trees from around the world, lush ferns, flowering plants that she could not name and had no idea where they came from, and even a section featuring desert plants.

Bensey's expression did not disappoint. His satchel fell from his grasp as he wandered off into the dense foliage.

"Bensey," Lord Derebourne called, "weren't you going to show Lady Derebourne your art?"

"You may show her, Father," he said and kept going.

"Well, if he ever goes missing," Chase said, "we'll know where to look for him."

She kept her gaze on the path Bensey had disappeared down. "He's an amazing boy."

"He is that. If you're amazed now, wait until you see his drawings."

Bending down, he picked up the satchel and pulled out a sketchpad. When he stepped next to her, Claire smelled bergamot and fine milled soap—a combination of scents she didn't know before now she liked. His arm touched hers when he opened the sketchpad causing her belly to do that funny thing again.

He slowly turned the pages, his arm brushing hers each time. It was only the material of his coat touching the sleeve of her gown, so why was the skin on her arm tingling? She forced herself to lean away so that he no longer touched her when he turned a page. She mustn't forget he was her adversary, come to take her horses and her home.

He was not her friend.

Claire focused on the drawings, each page an exquisitely rendered flower or plant. "My God."

"Exactly. Hard to believe a boy drew all this, but I assure you he did."

"Does he only draw flowers and plants?"

"With one exception, yes."

He flipped to the back to show her Mischief standing tall and proud as if he knew he was being put on paper. The marquess turned the page to a picture of the horse with his nose buried in a rosebush, and she could almost smell the scent of the red roses. The last drawing was of Mischief's face as he stared crossed-eyed at a fat bumblebee buzzing over his nose.

"Incredible. I wonder if I can get him to draw some of my horses."

His lordship's eyes lit with curiosity when she laid claim to the horses. She needed to be more careful around him. He had a way of making her forget to guard her secret. Until she decided her approach, she didn't want him to know she was the one responsible for the stable's success.

And first, she needed to understand him better. Was he like Thomas, the kind of man who thought a woman should have no interest beyond producing an heir and her embroidery? She would study the marquess and learn him in the same way she learned a horse. Observe and formulate a plan that best suited him.

Sandra Owens

"You're welcome to try. However, if he doesn't wish to, there is nothing you can do to change his mind."

What was she welcome to try? Bells in hell, the man muddled her mind. "He's an unusual boy."

"He is, but I would use the word special to describe him. I think he's not of this world. I should warn you he doesn't like to be touched. The first time he let me hold his hand, I almost wept. He doesn't mind when Harry touches him, and he is only now getting used to mine, but he won't allow it from anyone else."

There was love in his voice when he spoke of his son. The man was more complicated than she'd first thought.

"And what of Harry?" she asked. "I've yet to have the opportunity to talk to him, but he seems like a typical boy."

"In many ways, yes. Certainly more so than Bensey. Harry has a quick mind and will run circles around you if you let him." He chuckled. "And sometimes manages it despite all your efforts to outwit him. He loves horses above all things, so if he ever goes missing, just look for him in the stables. He would sleep there if I let him."

"I'll keep that in mind." A sliver of fear coursed through her. She didn't want him or his son to covet her horses. "Perhaps you should not allow him free rein of the stables. I don't think it's a safe place for a young boy."

Chapter Four

Chase frowned at Claire's change from pleasant to brusque in the blink of an eye. She had seemed to be warming up to him, but the curtness of her voice just now was that of the woman he'd met yesterday. He mentally reviewed the last part of their conversation, but couldn't find anything that should have angered her. Perhaps she was a woman whose moods changed from hot to cold for no reason.

By joining Bensey on this visit, he'd hoped to establish a friendly relationship with the lady. He wanted to tell her his plans for her, but was hesitant to do so until he knew her better and was certain she would be receptive to his intentions. It was the perfect solution. Didn't all women want a husband and children—a home of their own?

She still had several weeks of mourning left before he could present her to Society. Although, as a widow, she wouldn't need a chaperone, he would still ask his mother to attend her in London. As the Dowager Countess of Kensington, and the mother of the Marquess of Derebourne, Lady Anne could ensure Claire's acceptance by the ton.

When had he started thinking of her as just Claire?

If she—Claire—needed new gowns, they should leave for London soon so she could visit the modiste and get the process started. She'd be pretty in something besides the black bombazine. His experienced eye raked over her, and his fingers itched to pull the ugly lace cap from her head. He wanted to see the woman in the portrait, not this washed out, pale replica. Did she ride and if so, did she change into a riding habit? The urge to find out was irresistible.

"Wait here a moment, please. I'll be right back."

Chase strode down the hall and found the butler. "Smithfield, please tell my valet I have need of him."

When Chase returned to the conservatory, he stopped in the doorway, taking in the sight before him. Bensey held a flower, Claire's head bent close to him as they admired the plant. For the first time since the boys entered his life, he wondered if they needed a mother. He shook off the unwelcome thought and approached them.

Bensey glanced up and smiled. "Look, Father, it's from Africa. Do you want me to tell you its name?"

If he said yes, he would hear not only the name but its history, growing needs and more. "I do want to hear all, but can it wait a while? Harry's chewing at the bit to ride, and you know how that is. Anders is on his way and will surely die of pleasure to be invited to share all this with you."

Bensey's eyes lit up. His son and valet shared a love of botany and had formed a bond over tables of dirt and potted plants.

"My lord?" Anders entered the conservatory with the same awe on his face Bensey had shown on first seeing it.

"Anders, I think Bensey would like to spend the day here exploring. I thought you might wish to join him."

"Oh my," Anders said. "Bensey, have you ever seen such as this?"

The two wandered off, and Chase turned to Lady Claire. "If we don't come to collect them later, they won't remember to appear for their dinner. Do you ride, my lady?"

Her eyes sparkled with amusement. Why did the question amuse her?

"I do."

"Good. I promised Harry a ride this morning and would appreciate it if you would join us. I'd like a tour of the estate."

She chewed on her bottom lip in obvious indecision. He wished she wouldn't do that.

"Come now, Lady Claire, there's no reason to refuse."

"All right. Shall I meet you at the stables?"

"Yes, in thirty minutes. That will give you time to change into your riding habit. I'll collect Harry." He left before she could change her mind. Would she don a riding habit or appear in her widow's weeds? A lightness invaded his body, and he took the steps two at a time.

"Harry!" He burst into the room. "Put your boots on."

Harry jumped up from his desk. "Are we going riding, Father?"

"We are. Sorry, Mr. Edwards, to interrupt his lessons, but I promised him we would ride this morning."

"You didn't say we were riding this morning," Harry pointed out.

"Didn't I? I am certain I meant to. I'll come back

41

for you in a few minutes."

Chase strode to his room and quickly changed into a loose linen shirt. He chose a bottle green coat from the clothespress and slipped it on. Since Anders wasn't available to arrange a cravat, he decided to do without. He was in the country after all, and as the lord of the manor, he could damn well set the rules.

He collected Harry and they arrived at the stables ahead of Lady Claire. Harry headed for Victory's stall while Chase instructed a groom to saddle Lady Derebourne's horse. Not having any idea where Mischief might be at the moment, he whistled. Mischief poked his head out of his stall nickering a greeting, then stretched his neck over the gate, unlatched it with his muzzle and trotted up to Chase.

"For once, you were where you were supposed to be," Chase commented and Mischief snorted. "I know, don't get used to it. Let's get you saddled. A lady is going to join us on our ride."

The groom led an Arabian mare as white as new fallen snow to the hitching post. Chase and Mischief gave the mare appreciative looks. Mischief loudly exhaled, and the mare turned her head away.

Chase chuckled. "I think you have received the cut direct from the lady, my friend."

Movement caught his eye and he peered over Mischief's back to see Lady Claire approaching. He suppressed his smile. She had changed into a royal blue riding habit, and in place of the white cap she wore a pert straw bonnet trimmed with blue ribbons. Her moonlight pale hair was pulled into a twist low on her neck, and he idly wondered if her hair touched her waist.

The compliment on the tip of his tongue died at the warning in her eyes. Instead, he praised her horse.

"Mischief and I have been admiring your Arabian," he said. "I think Mischief is in love, but the lady is having none of it."

Claire had fretted over changing into a riding habit. Finally, she justified the habit by telling herself the wind would blow the loose skirts of her gown, revealing her ankles. She refused to consider that she wanted Lord Derebourne to see her in something other than her widow's weeds.

Mischief stretched his neck toward her and she obliged him with a scratch under his chin. "Poor boy. I'm afraid Amira is a princess with very high standards. Even if she encourages you, you would be wise to forget her as in the end she will only break your heart."

"No surprise there," Derebourne murmured.

Had a woman broken his heart? Her gaze drifted to his neck. He hadn't donned a cravat and the V of his shirt revealed a glimpse of the top of his chest. She wanted to place her fingers on that spot of golden skin and learn its texture. She lifted her eyes to find him intently watching her. Her skin rippled and her breath caught in her throat.

What in blazes was wrong with her?

Harry trotted up on Victory. "Are you ready to go, Father?"

The spell broken, she jerked her attention back to Mischief. After giving him a final scratch, Claire briskly walked to Amira. The groom held the Arabian beside the mounting block while she stepped up and settled onto the sidesaddle. It wasn't her preferred seat, but she could hardly ride the mare astride in front of the marquess. She gave Amira a slight tap with her foot and led the way out of the stables.

"Do you have a preference where to ride, my lord?"

He came alongside her. "I thought we agreed you would not 'my lord' me."

"So we did. Is there anything specific you wish to see, Derebourne?"

"Take me where you will, Lady Claire."

She would like to take him back to London and deposit him there where he would be far away from Hillcrest Stables and her horses. She would like him to go far enough away so he no longer unsettled her. She would like to touch his neck. As nothing was going as she liked, she decided to take them to the lake.

She turned to Harry. "Do you swim, Harry?"

"No, my lady, but Father has promised to teach me and Bensey."

"Then I shall show you the best place for it."

As they rode, Harry chatted away while Derebourne stayed silent. "Your mare is splendid, Lady Derebourne. She's an Arabian, is she not?"

"She is. Your horse is splendid as well."

The boy gave her an impish grin. "I chose him myself, and then Father allowed me to bargain with the owner over the price."

"Truly?" She couldn't imagine Thomas allowing a child to bargain over the price of a horse.

"Oh yes." Harry leaned toward her and confided, "I paid much less than he was asking, and I don't think he was pleased. The owner, that is. Father was quite pleased."

Claire laughed, delighted with this boy. "I imagine

you're correct on both of them. Your father said you love horses, and I'm impressed with your knowledge."

"I know a lot, but still have much to learn. Father brings me books about horses to read."

"Does he?" She glanced at Derebourne. He was a much different father than Thomas had been. "I have a large number of books on horses. You're welcome to borrow them whenever you wish."

What was she thinking? The books no longer belonged to her, but to the man riding silently beside her. Had he taken exception to her misspeak? He still seemed to be lost in his own thoughts.

"Oh, I would like that ever so much," Harry said.

"When we return to the Abbey, I'll show you which shelf they're on in the library."

She was uncomfortable offering books that no longer belonged to her. If she had been alone, she might weep. What was going to happen to her? If Derebourne refused her offer for the horses, where would that leave her?

Rage at Thomas welled inside her. He had given no thought to her future should something happen to him. He had died leaving her flapping like a trout on a line with no hope of rescue.

"With your conservatory and your horses, you have endeared my sons to you, Lady Claire. It begs the question, what have you to offer me?"

His question confused her. Was he asking for something she wasn't willing to offer? There was a teasing glint in his eyes and she realized he was playing with her. No man had ever teased her in fun.

She had never learned how to flirt, had never learned how to coyly converse with a man. No Season in London for her to learn the art of accepting or deflecting a man's attentions. Did she want to deflect his attentions?

Except to enter her bedroom—always in the dark—and do the minimum necessary to sire his heir, Thomas had never touched her.

No man had ever kissed her.

How would it feel to have Derebourne kiss her? She didn't doubt he would be quite the expert at the thing. Something wild and foreign inside her took hold, and she gave him a half smile.

"What have I to offer that would please you, Derebourne?"

Chase blinked. Bloody hell. What had possessed him to ask such a question? He'd apparently lost all good sense. And what did her answer mean? Was she flirting with him? Once he would've known, but his skills in that area were rusty.

Tuning out her and Harry's banter, he'd been considering what her extensive knowledge of horses meant. It could mean nothing, but he didn't think so—not after he had watched her working in the stables and the way she handled the feisty Arabian.

How should he answer her question? "Do you play chess?" Well, that sounded witless.

"I do, and I must warn you, I'm very good at it."

She was very good at it? His mind went to images it had no business conjuring up.

"I get to play the winner," Harry piped up, capturing Lady Claire's attention. Chase could have kissed the boy in gratitude.

"Are you any good?" she asked.

The little imp gave her an evil grin causing Chase

to chuckle. Harry loved chess almost as much as horses and was a worthy opponent in the game.

Suddenly, Lady Claire spurred her horse. "Catch me if you can."

They galloped down the hill, Amira and Victory pulling ahead. Mischief preferred a lazy run which suited Chase. He was able to observe Lady Claire as she and Harry raced ahead, laughing like children let out to play.

Her laugh was low and sensual—a courtesan's laugh. The woman was a constant surprise, and he determined to learn her secrets.

They reached the bottom of the hill and turned their mounts to face him. "Mischief, you are a lazy boy," she chided.

At the edge of the lake, they allowed the horses to drink. Mischief kicked at the water, playing with it. Lady Claire grinned at his idiot horse's antics. The lady was very pretty when she smiled.

"Come, I'll show you the best place to swim," she said.

He and Harry followed until they came to a stand of trees. "If you would help me down, my lord, it would be best to walk from here."

Chase dismounted and dropped Mischief's reins. Easily lifting Claire, he held her until her feet were firmly planted on the ground. Blue eyes met his and he had to command his hands to let go of her waist. He quickly stepped back, putting distance between them.

She blinked, glancing around as if she had forgotten where she was. Thank God Harry was with them because Chase wasn't sure he would have let her go otherwise. The beginnings of an attraction simmered between them and if he wasn't careful, the heat would soon cause the pot to boil over. He needed to get her to London and find her a husband. Soon.

She led them through the trees on a regularly maintained path. After a ten-minute walk, they came to a large boulder jutting out into the lake. On the other side of the rock, a sandy shore edged the water.

"The bottom doesn't drop off sharply here, so you won't have to fear the boys stepping into a hole," she said.

Harry climbed onto the boulder. "Will you teach us today, Father?

"Not today. If the weather is clear tomorrow, we will begin your lessons." It was a beautiful, secluded spot—perfect for teaching the twins to swim.

"What do we wear when we swim?" Harry asked.

Chase glanced at Lady Claire and deviltry took control of his tongue. "Your drawers, Harry." Pink strained her cheeks, but she didn't look away.

Claire tried to form a vision of his lordship in his drawers, but having never seen a naked man she had nothing to build from. From the time she had wondered what it would feel like to be kissed by him, she hadn't been able to get the thought out of her head.

All she wanted was one kiss so she could stop thinking about it. Then she would be able to stop staring at his mouth and would be able to ignore his dimple. She wanted this unsettled feeling to go away so she would feel normal again.

Yes, one kiss would do it.

When he had lifted her from Amira, the heat of his hands on her waist had birthed butterflies in her belly. Thomas had never affected her like this, and she didn't know if it was normal. Did other women ever feel this way? There were no female friends she could ask, and she wasn't about to ask Derebourne.

"A sovereign for your thoughts," he said with a grin.

Her eyes focused on his dimple, and she forgot to listen.

"Lady Claire?"

"Yes?"

"I asked what you were thinking."

Good heavens. As if she could tell him. She hadn't thought her cheeks could get hotter, but they did. "I don't know."

His grin widened. "You don't know what you were thinking? How singular."

"Look, Father!" Harry yelled.

Derebourne's grin disappeared. "Come back from the edge this instant!"

Claire's heart raced at seeing Harry perched precariously on the edge of the boulder. "Oh, my."

Harry gave them a cheeky grin. "I wasn't going to fall."

"The boy is going to be the death of me," Derebourne muttered.

When Harry reached them, Derebourne placed his hands on the boy's shoulders. "Harry, you are not to stand on the edge like that until you know how to swim. If you had fallen into the lake, I would have had to get my boots wet to rescue you." He flicked a finger under Harry's chin. "And you know what Anders would have to say to that."

"Yes, Father, I won't do it again. But when I learn to swim, can I jump off into the lake?"

"When I'm satisfied as to your ability to swim and after I show you how to jump so you don't hurt yourself, then yes, you may."

"Splendid," Harry exclaimed.

His handling of the boy fascinated Claire. There had been fear in Derebourne's eyes, and she'd expected him to berate his son—perhaps even punish him in some way. But he seemed to understand the ways of a boy and how to manage them without hurting or humiliating them. A yearning invaded her to be a part of a family that laughed and loved as Derebourne and his sons did. A feeling of loneliness seeped into her heart.

They returned to the horses and rode for another hour. Claire showed them the fields of wheat, corn and cotton. She pointed to a large building in the distance. "There is the dairy and beyond, the tenant's cottages. I'll take you there on another day and introduce the tenants to their new lord."

Derebourne listened attentively and asked intelligent questions. Her concern for the tenant's welfare under their new lord eased. Harry also asked questions, impressing her with his quick mind.

Riding with the two of them, listening to their banter and answering their clever questions, she again longed for something she would never have.

But she had made up her mind on one thing. She wanted her first kiss and the angel riding beside her was the one she wanted it from. How did one go about getting a man to kiss her?

Would he even want to?

Chapter Five

Chase covertly observed the woman riding next to him. The blue riding habit brought out the deep blue of her eyes, and her cheeks were rosy from the wind and exertion. Strands of pale hair had come loose, curling around her neck. In his rogue days, he would have reached over and twirled a lock around his finger. Would it feel as silky as it looked?

His gaze moved to her mouth, one entirely too kissable. She nibbled on her bottom lip—something she really needed to stop doing. An image of taking that lush, plump lip between his teeth and...bloody hell.

"Race you home," he called and spurred Mischief.

Back at the Abbey, Chase sent a note to Lady Claire asking permission to bring Harry and Bensey to dinner. He didn't trust himself alone with her. She replied that she would be delighted to have the twins join them. When Anders arrived to help him dress, he fussed over what to wear.

"I don't know which of you is more difficult tonight," Anders commented.

"Which of whom?" Chase discarded the coat Anders had chosen. "And I'm not being difficult, I just don't want to wear this one."

"That is the third one you don't wish to wear, my lord. You are going to run out of choices soon. Harry was as particular as you when I helped him dress. He said he must be perfect for the lady." Anders gave him an amused smile. "I don't suppose that's your problem?"

"I have no idea what you're going on about. And wipe that irritating smile off your face."

Anders' smile transformed itself into a smirk. "Is this better, my lord?"

"No, it's not better." Chase picked up the forest green coat of superfine. "I'll wear this one."

"Ah, of course, the one I first chose and you rejected."

Chase held out his arms so Anders could put the snug coat on him. "I know you believe yourself to be entertaining, Anders, but truly, you are not."

His insolent valet laughed. Chase would have made Anders redo his cravat, but the man was entirely too amused as it was. So he was being more particular than usual. It didn't mean anything. He merely wanted to make a presentable appearance.

He strode down the hall to the boys' room and found them in an argument—the first he had known them to have. "What is the meaning of your raised voices?"

"I want to escort Lady Derebourne into dinner and so does Bensey," Harry said. "But I said it first, so I should get to be the one."

"I'm the oldest, so it should be me," Bensey countered.

That was news to Chase. He'd never thought to ask which was the firstborn. The twins glared at each other. Well, it seemed his boys were experiencing their first infatuation. His had been with a governess at least ten years older.

"This is easily solved," he said, suppressing a chuckle. "You may both escort Lady Derebourne, one on each side."

Identical smiles formed on their faces. "Splendid," Harry said.

"Thank you, Father," Bensey said. "I knew you would have the answer."

Ye gods, he loved these boys. Taking their hands, they descended the stairs. Chase ushered the twins into the family parlor.

Seated on the sofa, Lady Claire stood when they entered. She wore a lavender half-mourning gown—her hair styled in an artful weave of twists and curls. Harry and Bensey stopped, staring in awe. Chase stepped around the boys and bowed. The twins came to their senses and followed his example, giving her their little boy bows.

"My lady, allow me to compliment your lovely gown," Chase said. It might not be the height of London fashion, but it was certainly an improvement over her widow's weeds.

"You look ever so splendid, Lady Derebourne," Harry said.

Not to be left out, Bensey added, "You are as pretty as a flower."

She curtseyed. "Aren't I the fortunate one to have such handsome gentlemen joining me for dinner?"

The boys beamed and Chase made a mental note to thank her for her kindness in treating a pair of street urchins as if they had every right to be in her presence.

She sat and patted the space on each side of her. The twins looked to him for approval and Chase nodded. They took their seats and he settled into a chair facing them.

"I hope you enjoyed your day in the conservatory, Bensey," she said.

"Oh yes, lady, it was the best ever."

Harry leaned around Lady Claire and said in a whisper meant for Bensey, but loud enough for all to hear. "It's 'my' lady, Bensey."

Bensey turned distraught eyes his way. "Is she his lady, Father?"

Lady Claire's lips twitched, and Chase was hard pressed to prevent his own lips from twitching. Before he could respond, Harry spoke up.

In a gentle voice he often used with his brother, he said, "No, I only meant you are supposed to say, 'my lady', not just 'lady'."

"If she is not his lady or my lady, why are we supposed to say, 'my lady'?" Bensey asked.

Lady Claire's eyes sparkled with humor. "Yes, Lord Derebourne, why is that?"

Three pairs of eyes focused on him, one blue-eyed pair entirely too amused. How did one explain to a brilliant boy something too simple for his comprehension?

"It's the same as when you used to call me 'my lord', Bensey. It's the way the thing is done."

"I called you my lord, Father, because you were mine and a lord."

Harry rolled his eyes. "You're not explaining it to him right, Father."

"Then let's see how well you can explain it."

Lady Claire pressed her lips together. If this went on much longer, she was going to lose the battle to hold in her laughter. Chase exchanged an amused glance with her. His heart did a little bounce at the warmth in her smile.

Bloody hell. This lady wasn't for him, and he needed to remember he had other plans for her. He didn't want her turning those blue eyes his way.

Harry cleared his throat. "A long time ago, maybe a thousand years even, the king made a rule that all the lords must call the noble ladies 'my lady' so the lords would know which lady they could marry. Think about it, Bensey. What if a lord married the butcher's daughter by mistake because he thought she was a lady? No one calls Bettna 'my lady', so a lord knows he can't marry her."

Chase turned to Harry in wonder. Where did the boy come up with these things? Apparently, this made perfect sense to Bensey because he nodded his agreement.

Lady Claire suddenly stood. "Excuse me, please," she said, a suspicious tremble in her voice. "I need to check on…" Her words trailed off and then Chase thought he heard her mumble "refreshments" as she exited the room.

Claire made it as far as the library before she gave way to the merriment. Sweet heavens, she had never laughed this hard. The thought sobered her. This was what had been missing in her life. Laughter and the love of a family. For surely, Lord Derebourne and his sons were a family. She had seen the truth of it in his eyes when Harry spun his tale. Derebourne loved his boys, and, oh God, why hadn't Thomas loved Andrew like that?

"Lady Claire?"

She spun. Lord Derebourne stood in the doorway.

"I was just..." Just what? She was lost in her own misery and didn't want him to be a witness. He approached her the way she did a wild horse—cautious and slow.

"I had thought to come and share a moment of amusement. Instead, I find tears in your eyes. What makes you sad, Claire?"

The intimacy of his use of her name was too much to bear. Tears she couldn't stop flowed down her cheeks. He pulled her into an embrace, and she foolishly allowed him to hold her.

"Tell me." He gave her back a few awkward pats.

The words flowed from her mouth. "Andrew...my son. I'll never be able to laugh at his funny stories, will never see him dressed like a little gentleman. I'll never be able to tell him how much I loved him."

"Ah, Christ, Claire. I'm sorry." He offered no other words, only held her close and she found comfort in the warmth radiating from him. When her sobs ceased, he leaned back and caught a tear with his thumb. "The boys are missing your company. Are you well enough to return, or should I make your excuse?"

"No, I want to stay. I'm fine, truly. It was strange. They were so very amusing, but I didn't want to laugh in front of them and have them misunderstand. I'm sorry, I didn't mean to cry."

"Don't apologize for loving your son." He pulled a handkerchief from his pocket. "Here, wipe your eyes. I'll tell the boys you're right behind me. They're in the throes of their first infatuation and will be watching the door for your return. They had their first ever disagreement tonight—the heart of it being who would escort you into dinner. I hope you don't mind, but I solved the dispute by telling them they could both do the honors."

She looked into eyes as blue as a robin's egg and smiled. "I would be honored, my lord."

"Chase," he said and left.

Chase. The name suited him. She said it aloud to see how it sounded on her lips. She would never call him that, of course, except perhaps in her mind. When she put the handkerchief to her face to wipe her tears, she smelled him. Bringing the square of cloth to her nose, she inhaled the scent of bergamot.

Would he notice if she didn't return the handkerchief? Slipping it into the sleeve of her gown, she reached the door of the drawing room as Mrs. Smithfield rolled the teacart in.

Chase stood when Claire entered and flicked his hand at the boys. They shot to their feet, but their attention was on the cart. She smiled. They might be infatuated with her, but at the moment, they only had eyes for the plate of cakes.

"Have a seat, Lady Claire, and allow me to do the honors."

Derebourne's concern touched her. Not even her father had shown much regard for her in the seventeen years she had lived in his home. Yet, this man she had only known a few days offered to take care of her. Her heart took a little tumble.

He pulled a small table over to the sofa and placed the glasses of lemonade and a plate of cakes on it. "What do you like above all things, boys?"

"Cakes!" they exclaimed in unison.

Whenever he grinned, his dimple appeared. Her butterflies apparently liked dimples very much.

"Milk and sugar, my lady?"

"Yes, please." Her voice sounded odd to her ears—breathless, as if she'd just ran up the stairs.

He put an assortment of cakes on a plate and set them and the teacup on the table next to her. After pouring himself a brandy, he sat in the chair closest to her. "I discovered the use of cakes as a bribe the first day I dragged Harry home with me."

"Father made me take a bath," Harry said. "I didn't want one, but he gave me cakes, so I didn't mind so much." His gaze fell. "Now, I like baths," he added, giving her his cheeky grin.

"I like baths, too," Bensey said around a mouthful of cake.

Dragged Harry home with him? What did he mean by that? And why had the boys once called him my lord? She wanted to ask, but didn't know if she should. He took a sip of his brandy and her eyes followed his hand as he brought the drink to his lips.

Long, elegant fingers held the glass, and the sapphire of his signet ring reminded her of his eyes. She lifted her lashes to see that his attention was on her. Blasted butterflies. Would they ever go away? His attention shifted to the twins and the air swished out of her lungs.

"Harry, did you tell Bensey the two of you are going to have a swimming lesson tomorrow?"

"Yes, Father. He wants to know how he's getting down to the lake."

"I saw a pony cart in the stables. If Lady Derebourne is agreeable, we'll borrow it."

"It is your cart and the pony to pull it, Lord Derebourne. You needn't ask me to borrow what is yours, my lord. Excuse me, please. I need to see if dinner is ready."

Once out of his sight, she leaned against the wall inhaling deep breaths. She was flustered and it was his fault. One minute he made her feel fluttery inside and all she could think about was kissing him, then in the next, she wanted to rail at him for the unfairness of it all. Pushing away from the wall, she went to check on dinner.

Chase narrowed his eyes on the back of the confusing woman. What had he said to rile her?

"You made her angry, Father," Harry accused.

Yes, apparently, he had. It had to be because of all she had lost. Although he wasn't to blame for the circumstances that brought him here, she had no one else to take out her anger on. Her little champion glared at him. He'd never been anything but a hero to Harry before, and this was new ground.

"I think she's only worried about our meal being ready on time." By the boy's fierce scowl, Harry wasn't buying it.

She returned and announced dinner. By her smile, it appeared she'd gotten over her little snit. Relieved, he nodded at the twins. "You may escort Lady Derebourne in to dinner."

Trailing along behind them, Chase inhaled the faint scent of violets. He liked violets. Instead of the formal dining room, she led them to a small, intimate room where a square table was set for four.

All during dinner, she chatted cheerfully with the boys, but ignored him unless he asked a direct question. Apparently, she wasn't over it—whatever it was—after all. When they finished their meal, Lady Claire excused herself for the evening. Chase took the twins to Mr. Edwards and then returned to his room. After Anders left, he tried to read the horse breeding book he'd found in the library. When he caught himself staring off into space for the third time, he tossed the book aside.

The picture of Claire shedding tears for her son played in his mind. It had been a mistake to hold her in his arms even if it had only been to comfort her.

Several times tonight, he had caught her watching him, the desire in her eyes obvious. If he knew women—and he did—she didn't understand what was happening to her. That alone would unsettle her, but add the loss of her son and home into the mix, and it was not surprising she was easily riled.

What had her marriage been like? He didn't think she grieved for Derebourne, so he guessed it had been a loveless union. Even so, why hadn't the man made any arrangements for her? Chase had carefully read the will and the marquess had made no provisions for his wife. What kind of husband left his wife's wellbeing to the whims of another?

"Bloody bastard," he told the dead Derebourne.

The clock struck twelve. Sleep wasn't coming anytime soon and with a sigh, he slid his legs over the side of the mattress and stood. Restless, he slipped on breeches and a shirt. He remembered seeing an inner courtyard during his tour of the abbey. With a brandy and cheroot in hand, he slipped out of the room and made his way barefoot through the quiet house.

The abbey was U-shaped, wrapped around a slate courtyard, the main feature being a bubbling water fountain. The moon was half-full, providing enough light for him to find his way to a four-foot-tall stone wall. He placed the brandy on the ledge and hoisted himself up. When his eyes became accustomed to the pale light, he surveyed his surroundings.

The stone wall he sat on ran from one side of the open U to the other, sealing in the courtyard. A tree on the outside of the wall rose above him, draping him in shadows. A comfortable breeze blew in, ruffling his hair. Benches and lounges were scattered about, and blooming flowers scented the air.

If he wasn't feeling lazy, he might retrieve his pillow and counterpane to make a bed on one of the lounges. With a flick of the flint, he lighted his cheroot, and then cradled the glass in his hand to warm the brandy.

His thoughts returned to Claire.

As if he'd conjured her up, the lady wandered into the courtyard. Lowering the cheroot, he rested his hand behind the wall so she wouldn't see the glowing tip. She aimlessly roamed the courtyard, stopping now and then to smell a flower. Occasionally, she sipped from the glass of wine in her hand.

She wore a white silk dressing gown over her nightdress, the moonlight giving it a silvery sheen. Her hair fell straight and long down her back. Like him, she was barefoot. The breeze picked up, fluttering the silk around her legs and her hair moved in shimmering waves. She raised her face to the stars, lifted her arms as if a partner stood with her and began the steps of a waltz.

An angel danced under the stars just for him. God save him from beautiful moonlit women dressed in sheer silk.

Her dance over, she ambled his way. He supposed

it would be impolite to continue to allow her to think herself alone. Bringing the cheroot to his mouth, he took a deep drag causing the tip to glow brightly. She stilled and squinted into the shadows.

"Lord Derebourne?"

"I am he, although I thought we agreed you would stop lording me."

Her mouth curved in a smile. "So I did. What are you doing here, Derebourne?"

"Chase," he said. "The same as you, I suppose. Couldn't sleep and thought to enjoy some fresh air." He held the cheroot out for her inspection. "And to enjoy a smoke."

She inhaled. "I have always liked the smell of them."

Who could resist a woman who danced under the stars and liked the smell of a cheroot? But he must. She stepped closer. If he were smart, he'd warn her off, tell her to run away as fast as she could.

She leaned her head to the side and peered at him. "If I asked you to kiss me, would you?"

No. Yes. "Why would you ask me such a thing?"

"Because I have never been kissed and just once in my life, I would like to know how it feels to have a man kiss me."

His traitorous cock stirred with talk of kissing her. "How is that possible? You were married for how long?"

"Four years."

Mother of God, what kind of fool had Derebourne been? "Why me?" he asked in desperation.

She lifted her face as if the answer might be written on the moon. Her eyes drifted back to him. "Because it seems to me you would be good at kissing."

Yes, he would. "How old are you?"

"I recently turned one and twenty."

He sucked in a breath. "You were married at seven and ten? Good God, you were a child."

"True, I was a child then but I'm a woman now, married four years, yet never kissed. Does that not sound pathetic? I want you to give me my first kiss."

He crushed the end of the cheroot on the wall. God save him from himself. "Claire."

"Yes?"

"Come here."

Her eyes trained on his, she moved forward, stopping when she reached his knees.

"Claire."

"Yes?"

He spread his knees. "Two more steps if you want to be kissed. But you should walk away. No. Run. To your room and lock the door. Your choice."

Two steps put her between his legs. He was doomed. She leaned against him and placed her glass on the wall next to his. The scent of violets filled the air. If he licked the skin below her ear, would she taste as good as she smelled?

He held out his hands, palms up. "Place your hands in mine."

She did as he asked, and he placed them on the sides of his waist, then cradled her face with his palms.

"Close your eyes, Claire."

Her lashes lowered as he touched his lips to hers. She tasted of berries from the wine, and he had clearly lost his mind.

Chapter Six

This was how Claire had imagined a kiss—like the soft wings of a butterfly fluttering over her mouth. She sighed in pleasure. Chase groaned and the kiss changed, his mouth descending over hers in a firm and consuming possession.

Sweet heavens. This she had never dreamed—had never known a kiss could cause her to forget her name or make her legs tremble. She pushed her hands under his shirt, and when her palms touched his heated skin she thought she might swoon for the first time in her life. He wrapped her hair around his fist and gently tugged.

"Open for me, Claire," he said against her lips.

When she opened her mouth to ask what he meant, he slid his tongue inside. If not for his legs pressed against her waist she would have gone down in a boneless heap. She hadn't known a man's kiss—this man's kiss—could sear her down to her toes. His tongue explored the inside of her mouth and she shyly touched her tongue to his. He tasted of brandy and his cheroot. A low noise came from his throat and she grew bolder, teasing him with her tongue while her hands roamed over his chest.

"Chase," she whispered.

Abruptly, he pulled away and let go of her hair. "Go to bed, Claire. You've had your kiss and you need to leave now."

If his chest wasn't heaving, she would have thought the kiss hadn't affected him. She stepped away from the warmth of his legs.

"Good night, Chase." She was halfway across the courtyard when he spoke.

"Claire."

She glanced over her shoulder. "Yes?"

"Lock your door."

Chase picked up his brandy and drained it in one swallow, then picked up the wine she had left behind and finished it. If the lake were closer, he would go and jump in. Perhaps the water would be cold enough to put out the fire in his loins.

Just one kiss, she said. Ha! Naïve girl. She had almost gotten more than she'd asked for.

When her tongue touched his and her soft, delicate fingers trailed over his chest, he came close to climaxing like a green boy. If he were in London, he would slip out and go straight to the Pink Slipper. Unfortunately, the only thing available to him tonight was his hand.

He slid off the wall, picked up the two glasses and returned to his room. He would not kiss her again—would avoid her as much as possible until he could put his plan for her in motion. Resolved and feeling better because of it, he removed his clothing and climbed into bed.

The taste of Claire lingered on his lips as he fell into a restless sleep.

****

Claire stared at the canopy of her bed and relived the moment Chase's mouth touched hers. She slid a finger over her lips and smiled. Her first kiss had been beyond her wildest imagination. She was glad now that Thomas had never kissed her. If he had, she would have never asked Chase to do so.

Chase. His name struck a chord in her heart. Would he kiss her again? Claire grinned. How foolish to think one time would satisfy her. She fell asleep and dreamed of kissing an angel.

When the early morning sun on her face woke her, she rang the bell for her maid, performing her absolutions and dressing with a bounce in her step. Not wanting to wear her black bombazine, she settled on a lavender day dress suitable for half mourning.

She arrived in the dining room and, ravenous, piled her plate high with food. As she ate, she watched the door. When Chase hadn't appeared by the time she finished breakfast, she went searching for Mrs. Smithfield. Claire found the housekeeper in the kitchen.

"Has Lord Derebourne come down to breakfast, yet?"

"No, my lady, he asked that a tray be sent up to him and the boys."

Disappointed, she went to the stables and spent several hours closed up in her office with Gordon. When she returned to the house for luncheon and there was still no sign of him, she asked Smithfield if he had seen the marquess.

"Yes, my lady, he left not long ago to take the twins to the lake for a swimming lesson."

Alone for luncheon, she nibbled on her food, her excitement waning. Was he avoiding her? No, he had promised the twins he would take them to the lake today. Harry's question from yesterday popped into her head. Chase would be swimming in his drawers. The thought refused to leave her mind and she gave up trying to eat. Returning to the stables, she learned he had saddled Mischief and Victory, and had rigged up the pony cart for Bensey.

The marquess was at the lake wearing only his drawers. There was a spot where she could go and see him swimming, and he would never know she was there. No, she mustn't. Even as she swore to herself she wouldn't do it, she returned to her room and changed into a green riding habit that would blend in with the trees.

Claire tied Amira to a branch and made her way through the woods. When she arrived at the place from where she could see the lake, she stopped. The most amazing view of a man she had ever seen stood before her. Chase walked out of the water wearing only his drawers. His hair was wet, and water ran down his muscled chest and long legs. He laughed and said something over his shoulder to the boys, but she was too far away to hear.

Sweet heavens, he was beautiful. She chewed on her bottom lip as a battle waged in her mind. She should leave. It wasn't proper to spy on a near naked man. Oh, but she wanted to see more. And she might never have another chance to see a man's body as beautiful as this one. If she slipped through the trees just a few more feet, she'd have a closer view. He would never know.

****

Chase stood at the edge of the boulder preparing to dive into the lake. The twin's lessons had gone well, both of them taking to the water like baby fish. They had learned to stay afloat by paddling their feet and thought it grand fun to hold their noses and sink under. As their reward, he'd agreed to jump off the boulder. Just as he lifted off, he saw a flash of moonlight-colored hair before it disappeared behind a nearby tree.

The minx!

The surprise of catching her spying almost caused him to hit the water on his belly. At the last second, he pulled up his knees, wrapped his arms around them and made such a big splash that when he came to the surface the boys yelled their approval.

"Jolly good, Father," Harry yelled.

"Do it again," Bensey said.

So, she wanted a show. Well, he would give her one. He sauntered out of the water and climbed back onto the rock. This time, instead of jumping, he dived—his legs together, his toes pointed and his arms held straight out from his sides. When he neared the water, he swung his arms forward and followed his hands into the lake with the barest of ripples. When he surfaced, the twins madly clapped their hands.

"That was the most splendid of things," Harry said. "Will you teach us how to do it?"

"When I'm confident you're good swimmers I'll teach you how to jump first, then how to dive."

Satisfied, Harry and Bensey started a splash war. Chase glanced up at the trees from the corner of his eye and caught a sliver of pale hair flash in the sun. He grinned. Prepare yourself, my sneaky little minx, you haven't seen anything, yet.

He waded out of the lake and picked up a drying cloth. Turning his back to her, he leisurely rubbed it over his body. When he bent over to dry his legs, he stole a peek from under his arm. Claire leaned out from behind the tree, her eyes wide and staring. He stifled a laugh and called to the boys to come dry off. She disappeared into the forest.

"Happy to oblige," he murmured.

Riding back to Hillcrest Abbey, his mind was full of Claire Tremaine. Again. He couldn't help but to be amused by her antics today. Had she never seen a man's body? She had been married four years, for God's sake. How could one be married that long, yet never been kissed or seen a man without his clothes?

Clearly, Derebourne had bedded her as she had given birth to a son. Chase had heard there were men who bedded their wives in the dark, only lifting their nightdress enough to do the thing. He might understand if she was hard to look on, but Claire was far from unsightly. *You were a fool,* he told the dead Derebourne.

If she were his wife...he ruthlessly shut the thought down. He'd avoided her for most of the day for his own peace of mind. Kissing her had been a monumental mistake, even if it had been a kiss he couldn't stop thinking about.

****

Claire rushed into her room, closed and locked the door. Sweet heavens. When Chase had bent over with his back to her, she hadn't been able to look away. Even though she should have, because what kind of woman spied on a naked man? His lean, muscled body was a piece of art and should be in a museum on display. Although the mere idea of other women looking at him in appreciation didn't settle well.

And oh, the sight of his buttocks outlined by the

wet linen of his drawers—all firm and rounded—and his powerful legs had caused her mouth to dry.

She would die if he knew she had been hiding in the trees and watching him. This couldn't continue. She had her kiss. Now, she needed to concentrate on her goal of convincing him to give her the horses, or make an arrangement to purchase them.

She rang the bell for her maid and unlocked her door. Maggie arrived and helped her into her widow's weeds and white lace cap. The sound of carriage wheels on the gravel drive floated up. Claire glanced out the window and groaned at seeing Mrs. Fisherman, the vicar's wife, and her daughter step out. She pushed the last strands of hair under her cap and waited for Smithfield to send word she had visitors.

In the drawing room, Mrs. Fisherman droned on as she importantly disclosed the latest village gossip. Claire's thoughts strayed to Chase and the way his wet body had looked when he emerged from the lake—the droplets of water on his skin glistening in the sun. She had touched that muscle-hard chest and wanted to do it again.

"Lady Derebourne!"

Claire blinked. "My apologies. I just recalled something I need to tell my housekeeper. You were saying?"

Mrs. Fisherman gave a small tsk. "I was saying, if you had been listening, my lady, that I understand the new marquess is in residence. Is he available for introductions? I'm quite certain he would wish to make the acquaintance of my dear Rhonda. As soon as I heard he had arrived, I knew we must have an assembly to welcome him. The ladies planning committee agreed and we have set aside a week from Saturday."

Oh, no. Mrs. Fisherman couldn't possibly think Chase would be interested in her daughter. Rhonda was one and twenty, and for the past two years, Mrs. Fisherman had desperately tried to find her a husband. The unfortunate girl was horse faced with teeth a rabbit would envy, as thin as a stick and as shy as a mouse. Her overbearing mother constantly pushed men at her.

Once, Claire had found the girl in the lady's retiring room in tears. When Claire comforted her, Rhonda had admitted she had feelings for Bobby, the blacksmith's son, confiding that Bobby had asked Mr. Fisherman for her hand. Mrs. Fisherman had refused the offer as she expected her daughter to make a better match than the son of a blacksmith.

Between sobs, Rhonda said she couldn't bear the embarrassment of her mother's matchmaking efforts with men who would never consider her for a wife. In Claire's opinion, Rhonda and Bobby were a perfect match. He was homely and as shy as Rhonda. It likely took years for the two to get up the courage to greet each other, but they suited so well.

Chase would give the poor girl the vapors. Already, Rhonda was shrinking into the sofa as if she could become invisible. Claire wanted to slap some sense into Mrs. Fisherman.

"Lady Claire, Bensey would like—forgive me, my lady. I didn't realize you had guests."

His golden hair still damp from his swim, Chase stood in the doorway alongside Harry and Bensey.

"Mrs. Fisherman, Miss Fisherman, the Marquess of Derebourne and his sons, Harry and Bensey. My lord, allow me to introduce Mrs. Fisherman and her daughter, Miss Fisherman."

Chase pushed the twins into the room ahead of him and bowed, Harry and Bensey following his example. "A pleasure, Mrs. Fisherman, Miss Fisherman."

"My Lord Derebourne, it is such an honor to make your acquaintance," Mrs. Fisherman gushed. She gave the boys a dismissive glance. "I didn't know you were married, my lord."

"I am a widower, madam."

"Oh, well good. I was just telling my darling Rhonda it was our Christian duty to pay a call and welcome you. In your honor, my lord, we are holding an assembly a week from Saturday. My daughter's dance card fills up quickly, Lord Derebourne, but I'm certain she will save you a dance."

Claire cringed at Mrs. Fisherman's reply to Chase being a widower. By how his eyes turned to ice at the woman's tactless response, Mrs. Fisherman was not endearing herself to the marquess.

"Please excuse my sons, Mrs. Fisherman," Chase said. "Their tutor is waiting to start their lessons."

The relief on the twins' faces was almost comical. Claire gave them credit for not running from the room.

"Charming boys," Mrs. Fisherman said. "My dear Rhonda loves children."

Dear Rhonda had practically disappeared into the sofa. Claire felt great sympathy for the girl.

"Indeed," Chase said.

He glanced at Claire, a brow slightly raised. She shrugged. Did he realize Mrs. Fisherman had her sights on him as husband material for her daughter? It was going to be interesting to see how he handled the woman.

Mrs. Fisherman apparently caught the look that passed between her and Chase because her eyes narrowed on Claire. "It occurs to me, Lady Derebourne, now the new marquess is in residence, it is highly improper for you to be living here without a chaperone. Have you made arrangements for where you will go? You must know you cannot stay at Hillcrest Abbey, my dear."

"The marchioness is still in mourning, madam. This is still her home for the time being."

"It will not do, Lady Derebourne, to live here without a chaperone. It will inconvenience my household, but my daughter and I will come and stay with you. It is the least we can do to protect your reputation."

The foolish woman apparently chose to ignore the warning in his voice.

"That won't be necessary. My mother, Lady Kensington, will be arriving soon to act as Lady Derebourne's chaperone," he said.

She would? Had he only said that to placate Mrs. Fisherman, or had he made arrangements and not told her? Claire was grateful he had protected her from Mrs. Fisherman's scheming—and even more so, relieved to know she had a home for at least another month. But, then what?

"How kind of your mother," Mrs. Fisherman said, the disappointment clear on her face.

Chase stood. "If you will excuse me, I need to check on the boys. It was my pleasure, Mrs. Fisherman, Miss Fisherman."

He bowed and strode out of the room. Claire smiled sweetly at Mrs. Fisherman.

Chapter Seven

"Did you do anything special this afternoon, Claire?" Chase smothered a grin at her startled expression.

"Ah. Well, I, ah…yes. I took a leisurely ride to the cliffs, my lord, and enjoyed a bit of time by the sea."

"Did you, now? Was the view worth the ride? Please, Claire, stop lording me."

Pink stained her cheeks. "Yes, Chase, the view was remarkable."

Chase almost snorted. He'd trapped her in a brilliant chess move and smugly waited for her to admit defeat. She'd found an escape, however, and he couldn't resist the one question that would throw her off balance. Someday—at just the right moment—he'd admit he had seen her. That she thought the view remarkable shouldn't please him so much.

He had sent the boys to bed earlier and now he was alone with her, which he'd sworn not to allow. The woman responsible for scrambling his wits chewed on her bottom lip as she studied the board.

He wished she wouldn't do that.

"Are you going to make a move in the near future, or do I have time for a snooze?"

She grinned, her eyes sparkling with excitement. "Checkmate."

"Well, aren't you the clever one? I was certain I

had the game. Well done, Claire."

Pure pleasure lit her face. "Thank you."

Had compliments been rare in her life? "Who taught you to play chess?" Her smile faded and he regretted the question.

"My father. Chess was the only game he considered worthy of one's time. Mama could never grasp it. Papa taught me to play so he would have an opponent."

"You were obviously a good student."

She toyed with the Queen, spinning the piece on the board. "The first time I won a game, I was so proud of myself. I thought Papa would be pleased, but he wasn't. He said arrogance in a woman was not a virtue, and I needed to curb my bluestocking ways if I ever wanted a husband. He never played a game with me again."

The last was said in a whisper of hurt. Chase had the insane urge to gather her in his arms and comfort her for her father's stupidity. "I'm sorry, Claire."

"Why? You had nothing to do with it."

"No, I didn't, but every child should have loving and supportive parents, and it doesn't sound as if you were that fortunate." He pretended not to notice the tears she blinked away.

"No, I don't suppose I was. I think it's why you and your sons fascinate me. I find myself envying the way the three of you tease and laugh together. Other than being pleased that he had his heir in the nursery, Thomas had no interest in Andrew. I don't think that would have changed much as Andrew grew older. I thought that was the way it was supposed to be. Until you and the twins."

75

She was breaking his heart. Had no one in her life seen how beautiful and intelligent she was? Had Derebourne not realized her worth? Apparently not. *You were ten times a fool*, he told the dead Derebourne.

"Can I ask you a question, Chase?"

Was she going to ask for another kiss? Did he want her to? "Yes, although I may choose not to answer."

"Fair enough. My father taught me curiosity was not attractive in a woman so I have tried not to be curious about your sons, but I am failing miserably. My question is this. Bensey said he used to call you my lord. I realize they were born on the wrong side of the blanket, and I think it is very honorable of you to openly claim them, but why would you make the twins call you my lord?"

There was a flash of disappointment that she hadn't asked for another kiss. He didn't mind explaining how he had come to have the twins, but he would have to tell her about the night Teresa died for her to understand how it all came about. But he couldn't sit here where the bright candles would allow her to see his face when he spoke of his wife.

He picked up his brandy glass and stood. "I'll answer your question, but it's a long story and this room is getting warm. I could use some fresh air. Bring your wine and come with me to the courtyard, and I will tell you how Harry and Bensey came into my life."

They settled on a bench near the bubbling fountain, and Chase angled his body to face her. Clouds obscured the moonlight putting them in the shadows, which meant she couldn't see him clearly. Raw pain still showed in his eyes when he spoke of Teresa and he didn't want Claire's pity. He took a deep drink of his brandy and shifted his gaze to the fountain.

"The night my wife and child died, I walked out of my house and wandered the streets of London. I remember being in several taverns and trying to drown my sorrow in cheap drink. Somehow I ended up on a bench in Hyde Park. I was having a nice snooze when I felt something moving around in my pocket. Turned out to be Harry's grimy little hand trying to steal my watch. Without quite knowing how it happened, I now find myself the father of twins."

At her soft chuckle, he sighed in relief. If he'd told this story to any of his female acquaintances in London, they would have been horrified he'd brought two boys from the streets into his home. "I'm in the process of trying to legally have their last names recorded as Warren, though it is going to be a difficult thing to accomplish."

She touched his arm. "They're fortunate to have you."

"The twins were a grubby pair of street urchins who happened to give me a reason to get up in the mornings. I may not have sired them, but they are my sons and devil take anyone who says otherwise."

Claire fell in love.

For as long as she lived, she would remember the moment it happened. No one in her life had cherished her or protected her the way this man did his sons. His love for them was fierce and lasting, and she selfishly wanted it for herself.

The sorrow and pain in his voice said he still loved his wife. There would be no room for her in his heart. All in the same day, she'd fallen in love and had her heart broken. Blinking back her tears, she vowed he'd never know.

Forcing lightness into her voice, she said, "Thank you for telling me. I don't think it was easy for you."

He tilted his head toward her. "It wasn't."

"You told Mrs. Fisherman your mother would be arriving soon to act as my chaperone. Does she accept Harry and Bensey as your sons?"

"She does. In the beginning, she had her reservations but it took them about five minutes to win her over."

"When will she be here?" Claire was uneasy about Lady Kensington's arrival. What if his mother didn't like her and convinced her son that Claire shouldn't be allowed to stay at Hillcrest? She needed to get the business of the horses settled before Lady Kensington arrived.

"I sent her a letter today. I'd guess that she should arrive in four or five days."

Claire drank the last of her wine and set the glass down beside her on the bench. Tomorrow, she would approach him about the horses. If he didn't immediately agree, she would have three more days to argue her cause before his mother arrived.

"Claire, about your future—"

No, she didn't want to discuss this tonight—wasn't prepared for it with her emotions so volatile. Falling in love while knowing it'd never be returned was enough turmoil for one day. Before she thought better of it, she kissed him to keep him from talking. He stilled under her assault. Sweet heavens, what was she about? Embarrassed heat burned her cheeks. She tried to pull away, but his arm snaked around her back.

"Claire," he whispered.

When his tongue slid over her lips, she moaned and opened her mouth for him. She hadn't imagined kissing to be other than a pressing of the lips, but from the moment he had shown her otherwise, she'd wanted to do it again. He explored her mouth and her tongue curled around his.

She wanted to tear her gown off, wanted to feel the searing heat of his palm on her skin. His hand trailed upwards to find the curve of her breast, and his thumb flicked lightly over her nipple. Heat pooled in her belly and even lower.

"Please," she begged. *Please show me how it feels to be a woman loved by a man like you. Remove my gown and touch me in secret places—show me what this burning inside of me means.*

Instead, he pulled away. "We have to stop. You've never known passion and it would be far too easy for me to take advantage of you. I don't want to hurt you, but I will if we allow this desire to take control."

She wanted to cry, to rant and rave. He had already broken her heart, so why couldn't she have this one time with him? "I won't let you hurt me," she lied.

"Go to bed, Claire."

Was she a child to be sent to bed each time she misbehaved? Biting down on her bottom lip to stop an angry retort, she left.

"Claire."

She didn't look back. "I know, lock my door." But she wouldn't, just in case.

Chase took a deep breath. When she had abruptly kissed him, his pledge not to allow it fled. Bloody hell. No woman had ever caused him to lose his senses as this one did. Somehow, he had to put a stop to this growing attraction between them before she thought herself in love with him. No longer capable of the emotion himself, he would end up hurting her.

He removed his coat, waistcoat and cravat. His body was on fire—just might burn to ashes where he stood. He headed for the stables and made his way to his horse's stall.

"Mischief, let's go swimming."

Mischief poked his head out, alert and interested. Chase opened the door and slipped a bridle over Mischief's head. He removed his shoes, socks and shirt, leaving them inside the stall. Fortunately, the grooms were all abed and no one was around to comment on his lack of dress. At the mounting block, he threw a leg over Mischief's bare back.

Reaching the lake—his body still throbbing with need and his lips still burning from Claire's kiss—he rode the horse into the cold water. Chase let go of the reins, held onto the long, coarse mane and let his horse go where he wished. He pushed all thoughts of Claire out of his head and settled so that he was floating over Mischief's back.

With more effort than it had taken before tonight, he brought Teresa to mind. He had loved his wife—still did—with his whole being, but her heart had belonged to another. Never again would he open himself up to that kind of hurt.

Claire was experiencing her first taste of passion. If he wasn't careful, she would begin to think she loved him. He was, after all, the first man in her life to give her a taste of what might be possible.

From what he had learned, no man in her life had truly cared for her. Not her father, for certain. Chase doubted she realized how telling her words had been. Chase knew that kind of man, one so insecure that when his daughter beat him at a game of chess he demeaned her intelligence.

And her husband? What a fool he had been. How could a man have a wife like Claire and not count his blessings every moment of every day? It would be amazing if she didn't develop a tendre for the first man to come along and treat her with kindness and respect. Unfortunately, that seemed to be him.

How could she know her heart without the experience of other men paying court to her? She couldn't. It was that simple. And he would not, could not, give his heart again only to have it handed back to him when she fell in love with someone else. He had Harry and Bensey, and the Pink Slipper filled his needs when necessary. What else did he need?

Feeling settled again and shivering from the cold water, he grabbed Mischief's reins. Once back in the stable, he donned his shirt and then rubbed the horse dry.

"Thank you, my friend. A cold dunking seems to have done the trick."

Chase patted Mischief's rump and closed the stall door behind him. Slipping back into the house, he retrieved the remainder of his clothes before returning to his room. He dropped his clothing in a wet pile on the floor and climbed into bed, falling instantly into a dreamless sleep.

The next morning, Chase awoke at dawn feeling rested and eager to start the day. Deciding not to awake Anders at this early hour, he dressed informally. Breakfast wouldn't be served until eight, so what could he do with himself until then? He considered going to his study and resuming his perusal of the ledgers, but that didn't appeal. An early morning ride did appeal to him.

Pleased with his plan, he whistled as he jogged down the stairs. Approaching the stables, he noticed a young lad in the training ring atop a magnificent chestnut colored horse. Curious, he changed direction and walked up to the fence. The lad had the horse turned away from him and Chase blinked. The lad was a lassie with a long, moonlight pale braid running down her back.

"I'll be damned," he muttered. She expertly put the horse through its paces and the truth sank in. He understood now why Gordon came to her with his questions and why she disappeared for hours into the stables' office. The lady was the brains behind Hillcrest Stables.

Stepping back, Chase slipped behind a nearby tree when she turned the horse in his direction. She wore leather breeches, knee high leather boots, a white shirt and leather vest. In her leather clothing and sitting astride the big chestnut, she was the most sensual thing he had ever seen.

She stopped the horse, laid the reins over his neck and rested her hands in her lap. "Let's see how much you remember from yesterday, Thunder," she said.

Without any signal he could discern, the horse took four steps back and stopped. He then turned in a tight circle to the left, stopped and made a full circle to the right.

"Very good," she praised.

She had to be using her legs to cue the horse, but

her signals were too subtle to see. She was magnificent, and she stole his breath away.

When Claire turned the horse away from him, Chase walked up to the fence and leaned his arms over the top. With her hands still in her lap, she had the horse doing a high stepping dance. He was seeing something special—a work of art between the woman and her mount. He wished Bensey were here with his canvas and paints.

They reached the far fence and then turned back in his direction. So intent on her horse, she was halfway across the ring before she saw him.

"I am in awe," he said when she noticed him.

Claire's knees jerked and Thunder stopped in confusion. Hastily picking up the reins, she stared at the man who had tormented her sleep. Not expecting him to adapt to country hours, since his arrival she had been coming out at dawn to work her horses.

"What are you doing here?" she stupidly said.

He hoisted up onto the fence and balanced himself on the top. "I was on my way to the stables to saddle Mischief for a ride when I saw you and Thunder." He grinned, showing his dimple. Her heart skipped a beat.

"I couldn't resist watching you. I am utterly speechless, Claire. Why didn't you tell me you are the one who made Hillcrest Stables what it is? Everyone thinks it was your husband, but it isn't, is it?"

With a press of her knee, she gave Thunder a signal to move forward, stopping a few feet from the man who held her future in his hands. Her heart pounded in dread over how this conversation might go.

"No, it isn't. Everyone thought it was Thomas because he took the credit. I didn't care as long as he didn't interfere."

"It surprises me he let you to manage the stables. From all I have heard, he didn't seem like one who would allow his wife to do so."

How much should she tell him? "In the beginning, when he found out I was spending my days in the stables, he forbade it." She shrugged. "I ignored him."

Nervous, she chewed on her bottom lip. Why were his eyes focused on her mouth?

"I don't imagine he appreciated that."

Claire glanced away and remembered that day. "It was the only time he hit me," she admitted.

"The bastard."

Absurdly pleased with his anger on her behalf, she smiled. "Yes, on that day he was. But not always. He was kind to me, but I only saw him at dinner and when—" She stopped, horrified by what she had almost said.

"When he came to your bed," Chase finished for her, his voice achingly gentle. "And always in the dark."

"How do you know?" she whispered.

"You have told me in so many different ways."

"I don't understand." How did he know such intimate things about her and Thomas?

"I know you don't, Claire. But it's no longer of any consequence. He is gone and you are here. Tell me, have you always had this ability with horses?"

She stroked Thunder's neck. "No, I had very little experience with them before I came here. I had a docile little mare at home, but Papa would only allow me to ride on our grounds, never to the village. When Thomas married me and brought me here, I was alone all day.

Out of boredom, I found my way to the stables and never left."

"I see. And the leather breeches? What did Derebourne say about them?"

"He didn't pay enough attention to me to know. But for what I do, a riding habit isn't feasible."

"The Duchess of Aubrey will want a pair if she ever sees you wearing them."

Claire was intrigued. "Does she ride astride?"

"Not in London, but always when she is at their estate."

"I think I would like to meet her."

"Heaven help Aubrey if his duchess and you ever get together. Something just occurred to me, Claire."

She grew uneasy under his scrutiny. "What would that be?"

"You don't want to give up the horses, do you?"

He saw too much. He read her so easily, yet she never knew what he was thinking. It didn't seem fair and irritated her. "This isn't a conversation I want to have now."

"When do you want to discuss it, if not now? Do you wish to make an appointment? Tell me when and I'll make myself available."

Feeling at odds with him, with her life and events she couldn't control, anger bubbled inside her. She needed to be calm and rational when she made her proposal, not angry—needed time to organize her thoughts and plan her approach.

"Yes, Chase, I would like an appointment. Would today at two be convenient for you?"

She couldn't fathom why he grinned.

Chapter Eight

His grin was ill-advised, but she had turned as bristly as a hedgehog and it amused him. "Yes, Claire, today at two will be convenient."

"Thank you. Good day, then."

Being dismissed by a lady was a novel experience. After giving her a courtly bow, Chase took his leave. He glanced back to see her attention focused on the horse. Would that he could dismiss her from his mind just as easily.

After breakfast, Chase took the twins to the lake for another swimming lesson. Although he kept an eye on the trees, there was no flash of pale hair. It was for the best, and he shouldn't be disappointed.

To the boys' regret, Claire didn't join them for luncheon. After they finished their meal, he sent the twins off to their lessons and then headed for his study. It was half past one and he had a few minutes before Claire was due for her appointment.

Going to the window, he stared out at the view. As far as he could see—and beyond—now belonged to him. The property extended to the cliffs overlooking the sea, too far for his eyes to behold. Even though he'd not wanted the responsibility of Hillcrest upon first inheriting it, he was coming to love the estate and surrounding properties.

It occurred to him the boys had never seen the sea

and decided tomorrow would be a good day for a picnic. He and Harry would ride, and Bensey could travel in the carriage with the food basket.

Would Claire like to go with them? With the twins as chaperones, he wouldn't be alone with her. She would want to ride Amira and might even wear her leather breeches. Claire in breeches astride a powerful horse was a beautiful sight to behold. Perhaps he could convince Bensey to paint her.

In fifteen minutes, she would arrive to ask for the horses. He still hadn't decided on his answer. They were his now and he couldn't deny he wanted them. Chase intended them for Harry—envisioned turning the operation over to him when he came of age.

Until then, who could manage the operation for him? He was too busy with his various estates to give it the necessary time. If Claire was responsible for the stables success, what would happen when she left?

For her own good, he would refuse her request. It might not be right or fair, but it was a man's world. No matter she understood horses better than the majority of men he knew, she simply couldn't set up shop under her own name and expect to be accepted.

His plan was a better solution. She might not appreciate his intentions at first, but would come to see it was for the best to have a husband and home of her own.

Why he wanted to growl, he had no clue.

****

Claire agonized over what to wear for her meeting with Chase. Donning the black bombazine and appearing as the grieving widow was not the image she wanted to portray. She needed to come across as confident, though she was not, knowledgeable, which she most certainly was, and capable of managing her own stables. Two out of three was a good start.

It wasn't that she lacked confidence in her abilities. Training horses was her specialty, and she had her proposal prepared along with a payment plan. Her nerves were due to her uncertainty as to the Marquess of Derebourne's response to her offer.

Finally choosing a dark blue gown of simple design, she sat at her vanity while Maggie styled her hair into its usual twist.

"Do you want the lace cap, my lady?"

"No, Maggie. I think we're done. Thank you."

After Maggie left, Claire studied her image in the mirror. The image of a governess stared back at her. This just wouldn't do. The meeting would determine her future. Appearing as meek and unsure of herself would be a mistake. This was the time to be bold and daring. She had the urge to change into her leather breeches, march into his study and announce how things were going to be.

From the way Chase had eyed her this morning, he obviously liked her breeches. Perhaps if she pranced around his study with her legs encased in leather he would be too bemused to say no. She smiled at the picture that formed in her mind. It was so tempting.

If she could make it from her chamber to the study without the servants seeing her, she would do it. It wasn't that they didn't know about her working clothes. They were aware she was the force behind Hillcrest Stables, and were used to her appearing in breeches in the early morning hours. It would be an entirely different matter to be caught wearing them for an audience with the marquess.

If only she could get from here to his study unobserved. It occurred to her she could. The abbey was full of secret passages, and one of them opened into the study. Did she dare? She glanced in the mirror again. Yes, she did.

She managed to unbutton the gown herself and then changed into her working clothes. Going to the vanity, she pulled the pins out of her hair and braided it. When she finished, she liked what she saw in the mirror. This was the real Claire, not the washed-out widow needing someone to take care of her. She was perfectly capable of taking care of herself, thank you very much.

Claire hugged the wall as she made her way to the west wing. Once, she had to duck into an unused bedroom to avoid one of the maids. Her goal was her old chamber. From there, she could enter the secret passages and make her way downstairs.

What would Chase think when she stepped into the room in her breeches? Anticipation surged inside her— or perhaps it was trepidation. She had no idea which as the man confused her.

That she loved him, she did not doubt. He was everything she would want in a man. Kind, intelligent, beautiful, and able to do funny things to her body— things Claire didn't understand. But oh, she wanted to.

She had only wanted one kiss from him, or so she'd thought. She had her kiss, not just one, but two toe-curling kisses.

Now, she wanted more. She was a widow, so who would know if he bedded her? Nor would it ever be an issue. Not long after Thomas died, she'd made up her mind to never marry again. Although, she might consider it if Chase asked. Since he wasn't going to, she would settle for one night with him.

Assuredly, he could show her how it should be between a man and a woman. If that meant she was wanton and not a proper lady, who cared? She would never live in London, would never have to worry about her reputation. Just one night with him was all she asked, and she would make it happen somehow. It would also mean more heart-throbbing kisses.

Stop thinking about kisses.

This wasn't the time to think of the things she wanted to do with the marquess. Her focus needed to be on presenting her proposal in a professional manner. Her campaign had to be successful else she'd lose everything.

Claire brushed a cobweb from her face and leaned her ear to the secret panel into the study. Not hearing anything, she took a deep breath and she pushed on the door. Chase stood with his back to her, staring out the window.

What was he thinking? She never knew, yet he seemed to read her like an open book. Her gaze roamed from his long, powerful legs encased in black boots, over his firm buttocks and up to his broad shoulders. His golden hair curled over his collar, and she wanted to touch it again.

It was difficult to concentrate on the reason for the meeting when this yearning appeared at the sight of him. He stirred something deep inside her, something new and exciting. She wanted to explore these novel feelings, to touch him here and there, wanted to trail her fingers over his skin and learn him. In an effort to suppress her thoughts, she stepped back and pressed her forehead to the cold stone wall.

Think only of the horses, Claire. They're your future, not the marquess.

Her resolve in place, she quietly entered the study. "My lord."

"There you go lording me again." He turned. "I...ah." His eyes widened and he blinked as if to clear them before his gaze raked her from head to toe.

A thrill shot through her. No man had ever looked at her with such burning intensity before him. She wanted what those eyes offered so much it was a physical hurt.

He cleared his throat. "I was going to say I didn't hear you enter, but you have robbed me of speech. It seems I'm going to have to revise my opinion that there is nothing more enticing than a woman wearing a beautiful gown. Have you just come from the stables?"

She stepped closer, and his gaze fell hungrily to her hips. Oh, this was fun. She might never wear another gown. "No, Chase, I just came from my bedroom."

"Your bedroom?"

The low, husky sound of his voice and the heat in his eyes drew her forward. "Yes, my *bedroom.*"

If he decided he wanted her here—this minute—on the floor in bright daylight, she would happily agree. It was his fault she'd turned wanton.

Now close enough to inhale his scent, she took a deep breath. He stepped back, putting distance between them. She wanted to put her hands on him and pull him against her.

He tugged at his cravat with one hand and gestured at the chair in front of his desk with the other. "Shall we?"

The man was disconcerted, and the knowledge pleased her. It was only fair. She was beginning to believe he desired her, but vigorously fought against it. Would he ever be able to put his wife to rest?

When she had become fascinated with the horses, she had watched and learned until she considered herself as qualified as any man to train them. Then she had started working with damaged horses, helping them to heal.

Could she do the same for him? The idea intrigued her, and she stored the notion away for further consideration. For now, she had her future to settle. She sat and waited for him to speak.

Chase tried to keep his eyes above Claire's neck. The leather breeches hugged her long legs and bottom, and he could see the outline of her chemise through her white linen shirt. Swallowing hard, he attempted to turn his mind to the business at hand. Unfortunately, his brain didn't seem to be working properly.

If ever there came a time when women walked around in public dressed as Claire was now, men would be in serious trouble. Their minds would be so bewitched they would never get any work done. God forbid, breeches-clad women could take over the world and men would be struck too stupid to even know it was happening. All they would be thinking about was the enticing curves so clearly visible.

Chase shook his head to clear it. Claire watched him as if she knew his thoughts. His cheeks heated and he realized with horror he was blushing—the mere idea caused him to blush harder. He cleared his throat, intending to ask her about the horses.

"Would you like to go on a picnic tomorrow?"

"Pardon?"

There, he had just proved his theory. He'd obviously been struck stupid. "A picnic. The thing where you pack a basket of food and go on an outing. A picnic. Tomorrow."

He was rambling. He was daft.

She scrunched her eyebrows together as if trying to make sense of his words. He wished her luck with that. "I thought I would take Harry and Bensey to the sea tomorrow for a picnic. I'm inviting you."

When she chewed on her bottom lip—drawing his attention to it—he silently begged her to stop.

"If you can wait to leave until I have completed my chores, I would like to go. I love the sea and even though it's close, I rarely take the time to go."

Dare he remind her she had supposedly gone there yesterday? She rattled him so it would only be fair to return the favor. "Did you not tell me you rode to the sea yesterday?"

Her cheeks turned pink.

"And that you enjoyed the view?"

The pink turned to red and Chase resisted the urge to laugh.

"I believe I said I rarely take the time to go," she said. "Yesterday was the exception."

"You should go more often if you find the view so enjoyable. Would eleven be too early to leave?"

Big blue eyes blinked. "What?"

"The picnic," he gently reminded her, happy to be back in control.

"Yes. Yes, the picnic. Eleven is good."

"Splendid. You, Harry and I will ride. We'll take

the carriage for Bensey and the food. Will you instruct the cook to prepare a basket for us?"

"Certainly."

A silence fell between them and Chase realized she was waiting for him to begin the discussion. "You have my attention, Claire."

Her facial expression changed to determination. Although he would listen to her plea, he'd come to a decision and hoped he could make her understand.

Chapter Nine

Claire pressed her hand over her pounding heart. The next few minutes would determine her life. She had practiced the words she would say, but couldn't remember them. The kindness in Chase's eyes was her undoing. Tears welled and she tried to blink them away.

"Perhaps you should start by telling me the condition of the stables before you became involved."

With a few simple words, he calmed her. Her heart eased its hammering. She could answer his question with ease and gave him a grateful smile.

"I told you how I came to be interested. When I began spending time in the stables, we had one stallion and three mares of questionable bloodlines. No breeding records were kept and the offspring were sold to local families, usually as a horse for one of their children. The stallion was Thomas' personal horse and my husband's interest didn't extend beyond having a decent mount."

Warming to her subject, she explained how she had purchased a stallion and mare of prime bloodlines, how she had invested her profits from the sale of their first colt and purchased another mare, and then another. Then came a second stallion, a third—and now there were five stallions and fifteen mares.

"I keep meticulous breeding records which had never been done before. This past year, we offered stud

95

services to gentlemen wanting to breed their mares to one of my boys, and that venture has exceeded my expectations."

When she told him what she charged for stud fees, Chase whistled. Claire froze. Bells in hell, what was she thinking? He would never sell the horses to her now, and if he did consider it, she would never be able to afford his price.

"I may have exaggerated the success of the stud service operation."

Throughout her presentation, he'd given his complete attention, but now she detected amusement in his eyes. If so, she would slap his face. Then he smiled and his dimple appeared—mesmerizing her. Her foolish heart thumped in her chest. How did he do this to her with one simple smile and one captivating dimple?

"Even if you did, I'm still impressed. If not for you then, I would not be in possession of such valuable stables as Hillcrest. It doesn't seem fair, does it?"

No. No, it didn't. Trust him to understand. How could she not love him? "It isn't fair," she said to the desk, unable to meet his eyes lest he see the yearning in hers.

"Look at me, Claire."

His hands were steepled beneath his chin as he regarded her. She longed to know his thoughts, but men and their ways were as foreign to her as elephants in Africa.

"Tell me what you want," he said.

You. I want you. But she couldn't say that to him, so she cleared her mind of wishful thinking. Chasing dreams that wouldn't come true would not put food in her mouth or a roof over her head.

"I want the horses."

"We have already established that, I believe. I would give them to you if the world were a different place. Perhaps in the future women will be able to step into a man's domain and successfully own their own businesses, but that time isn't now. For your own good, I cannot send you off on your own. You will fail."

Anger burned her blood. "I don't want you to give them to me, my lord. I'll purchase them from you. Believe me, I know this business, and I—"

He held up a hand. "Pax, Claire. I know you do. Better, I imagine, than most men. That isn't the issue here. Men will not purchase a horse from a stable owned by a woman. Imbeciles that we are, we men will not believe you capable of having the brains required for such a venture. We will shun you, scorn you and laugh among ourselves that a woman has the gall to think she can enter our world. If you show even the slightest sign of success, we will sabotage you. This isn't a game you can win."

There was a truth, which was why she had Gordon. But the disappointment that Chase thought this way almost crushed her. "I considered you a better man, my lord. Apparently, I was wrong."

He sighed. "I may not agree with how most men think, but I can't change their minds overnight. Personally, I believe you are capable of running the best stables in England, but I can name only two other men who might agree. And you lorded me again, but as you did it in misguided anger, I'll overlook it this time."

Her temper eased with his words, and she couldn't help but return his teasing smile. "Who are the other men? Perhaps I could train horses for them."

He snorted. "One, the Earl of Daventry, I would not let within a mile of you. He's a good friend and would have no problem with you training his horses. But he would take one look at you in those breeches and before you knew what he was about, would have you out of them."

"Lord Daventry is interested in purchasing one of our colts, and I've invited him for a visit. If, as you say, he would be willing to allow a woman to train his horses, perhaps I'll broach the subject with him."

Chase made a noise that sounded like a growl. "No."

Well, that was interesting. Deciding to poke at him a little, she asked, "Is he as handsome as you?"

He scowled. "I don't wish to talk about Daventry."

Her heart fluttered with happiness. Chase didn't like the thought of her with another man. That had to mean something, didn't it?

"Who is the other?" she asked, letting the subject drop for now.

"That would be my friend, Aubrey. Before they were married, his duchess started a working horse venture and was quite successful at it."

He'd mentioned the duke and duchess before. Claire wanted to meet her. "I think I would like her."

"I know you would. But, Claire, believe me when I say most men would not approve of you stepping into their world."

"Unfortunately, I know you speak the truth, which is why I hired Gordon. He's my business manager and voice in dealing with prospective buyers."

"A wise move, but do you really think your buyers will believe that puppy is the owner of your stables?

Because they won't, and they will want to know who is."

Blast, she hadn't considered that. "I don't suppose there is any way I can stay here and manage the stables for you? There's a dowager house a mile from here, and I could live there."

His eyes filled with regret. "I wish it were possible as I fear the operation will suffer without your attentions, but there is no way to keep you a secret. It was one thing when you were married to Derebourne. No one thought to question your presence. Now, however, it would be remarked upon sooner rather than later. You don't deserve the scandal that would come your way."

Despair gripped sharp claws into her heart, and she wanted to be alone. "What is to become of me?" Bells in hell. She hadn't meant to say that.

"I have some thoughts on the subject. Are you willing to listen?"

Not trusting herself to speak without her voice trembling, she nodded.

"Together, we will put a value on the horses. Including stud fees, I would estimate that to be somewhere between twenty and thirty thousand pounds. Whatever number we agree on, I'll set half that amount aside as a dowry for you. Your year of mourning will end in a few weeks, and at that time we will travel to London. I'll pay to have new gowns and fripperies made for you, and then we'll find you a husband."

He sat back with such a pleased expression on his face for his solution to ridding himself of her that if she had been a man, she would have planted him a facer.

Yes, he was being more than generous. Yes, he

was looking out for her welfare. Even so, he'd just broken her heart. Did he expect her to congratulate him for his clever idea? What would he say if she voiced what was in her head?

She stood, intending to leave. "You could marry me." The echo of her utterance bounced around a suddenly silent room.

Double bells in hell. Had she really said that aloud? By the shock on his face, apparently she had. Now that the words had escaped her mouth, she had nothing to lose and rushed on. "I would make you a good wife. I know you loved her…I think you still do, so I don't expect you to love me."

She pressed her lips together to keep more words from escaping.

With the fingers of one hand, he spun his signet ring, seemingly fascinated by the sapphire stone rotating around and around. "I'll not marry again."

"You must have loved her very much. She was a fortunate lady."

Eyes full of pain briefly met hers. "If only she thought so."

"She didn't return your love?" Claire was astonished. She would count her blessings every day of her life if this man loved her.

"Her heart belonged to another."

Claire opened her mouth to say what, she didn't know.

He held up a hand. "This conversation is over. I'll never marry again and enough said. My plan to take you to London stands."

She walked out of the room, not giving an owl's hoot if any of her servants saw her leaving the master's study dressed in breeches. At the stables, she saddled Amira and, with tears blinding her eyes, spurred the mare, letting her go where she pleased.

****

Chase moodily stared at the door as it closed behind the woman who had played havoc with his senses from the time he'd arrived at Hillcrest Abbey. What was he thinking to admit Teresa never loved him?

Because Claire had surprised him, his brain had sent words he never meant to say tumbling out his mouth. Though her idea appealed to some deep part of him, he would never trust his heart to another woman, especially Claire. She scared him.

Already, he liked her too much, and feared there would be a day when his heart would come out of hiding and offer itself to her. When she broke it, he would not recover a second time.

No, his intention to find her a husband was best for both of them, particularly him. Apparently, she didn't think much of his plan. Truth be told, when he spoke of finding her a husband something in him wanted to protest.

Yes, indeed, she terrified the bloody hell out of him.

Was she all right? She had left so abruptly. Should he apologize for being brusque? He walked out to the foyer. "Smithfield, have you seen Lady Derebourne?"

"Yes, my lord. I believe she went to the stables."

There was no Claire or Amira to be found there. Chase gave a loud whistle and went to collect his saddle. When he came out of the tack room Mischief awaited him at the hitching post.

"Can you find your lady love? Find Amira." Where

would Claire go?

Why was he looking for her? It would be best to leave well enough alone. Ignoring the wisdom of doing so, he gave the horse his lead. Mischief went down the hill to the edge of the woods where Chase found Amira tied to a tree. Leaving his horse to roam free, Chase followed the path to the lake.

Claire sat on the boulder, her arms wrapped around her knees, her head bowed. Her body shook with her sobs. Resisting the urge to go to her, he stepped behind a tree. She wouldn't want him to see her like this. She'd lost so much and all she had left was her pride. He wouldn't take that, too.

Didn't she know how much she had to offer a man? She was beautiful, interesting, intelligent and a joy to be around. She had a hidden passion that begged to be explored. No man in his right mind would tire of her company. A man would be fortunate to have her as his wife.

When she found a man she liked, she'd forget this nonsense of running her own business. By the time she welcomed a child into the world, she would look back on this time and realize he was only doing what was best for her.

Chase muttered a curse and willed away the image of a baby girl with Claire's pale hair and sea-blue eyes.

Returning to the abbey, he spent the remainder of the afternoon with Harry and Bensey. As he had on previous nights, he brought the boys with him to dinner. Mrs. Smithfield informed him that Lady Derebourne had the headache, and had requested a tray to be sent to her room. It was difficult to say who was more disappointed, him or the twins.

After seeing them to bed, he returned to his room, poured a brandy and walked out onto the balcony. The night was warm, and the moon edged toward full. He pulled off his coat, cravat and waistcoat, throwing them carelessly back into the room.

All evening, the image of her sitting alone on the rock—her body shaking as she cried—had haunted him. Were the tears for the loss of her horses? They had to be. That was probably why she had suggested they marry, so she could keep her stables.

Surely, his offer of a dowry and his plan to find her a husband would not cause her to cry. He would make sure she chose someone who would be kind to her. He knew who the rakes and dissolute lords were and wouldn't allow her to make a mistake in her choice. If he ever found out the man hurt or mistreated her, Chase would kill him, whoever he was.

A picture of a faceless man kissing her formed in his mind, and his grip on the glass constricted, shattering it.

Bloody hell. It had been a mistake to kiss her—to learn her taste, the softness of her lips. Shaking his hand, he dislodged the slivers. He walked back into the room to find Anders picking up the clothing.

"I have never known you to be so careless with your clothes, my lord. It wouldn't be a lovely widow disturbing your thoughts, now would it?"

"Anders, do you ever mind your own business? You are just like my horse, always nosing into matters that do not concern you."

Anders gave a hearty laugh. "How else is one to find things out, my lord?"

"How else, indeed. I'm taking the twins on a picnic

tomorrow. We're going down to the sea, so be sure they dress appropriately for the outing."

Would Claire still come with them? She hadn't appeared for dinner and might cry off from their outing.

"Are the twins still awake?"

"They were a few minutes ago, my lord."

"Wait here until I return."

He entered the boys' room, pleased to find them awake. "I want you both to write a letter to Lady Derebourne asking her to go with us on our picnic tomorrow. I think it would please her immensely to be invited by the two of you."

They scrambled out of their beds and went to their desks. Chase read Harry's note as he wrote it.

Dear Lady Derebourne,

It would be ever so grand if you came with us on our picnic. Father and I are riding our horses (Bensey won't ride, so he will be in the carriage) and I know Amira will be sad if she is left behind. Please say you will.

Harry

"Is my letter good, Father?"

"It's perfect, Harry."

Bensey handed him his. "Read mine."

My Lady,

Please come with us to the sea. I read in my flower book that sea campion and thrift live on the rocks at the sea in Kent. You can help me look for them. If you want to. Do you want to?

Bensey

Perhaps he wasn't playing fair, but this was for her own good. She needed cheering up, and a day with the twins would do the trick. He tousled Bensey's hair. "It is also perfect."

Chase took their letters, herded them back into bed and gave each a kiss on the forehead. God, he loved the little scamps. It occurred to him that he had never told them so.

"Good night, my boys. I love you."

Their eyes widened. "Do you really love us, Father?" Bensey asked.

"I really do. Now, go to sleep and I'll see you in the morning." He blew out the candle and turned to leave.

"Father?"

"Yes, Harry."

"We love you, too."

"We really do," Bensey added.

Tears burned his eyes. Would he have made it through the past year without his boys? He didn't think so. "Good night, my sons," he softly said.

Back in his room, he handed Anders the letters. "See that Lady Derebourne receives these. Tonight, if she is still awake. If not, first thing in the morning."

"Yes, my lord."

Chase smiled, feeling surprisingly good. He should have told the twins he loved them long before now. Children needed to know they had the love of a parent. His mother had frequently told her children she loved them. She still did.

His father was another matter. All he'd loved was women, drink and gambling. After his death, Chase swore he wouldn't bring more shame on the Kensington name.

Before his marriage to Teresa, there had been his

fair share of women. To keep from being like his father, however, he'd never set his sights on girls fresh out of the schoolroom or another man's wife. After Teresa had married Hollingsworth, he'd tried to bury his pain with any woman who looked twice at him—though still avoiding virgins and married women.

Then...

Then Aubrey had brought Teresa home from France after her husband was killed. Chase had stopped seeing other women, and set about making Teresa his. From that day until eight months after she died and he had walked through the door of the Pink Slipper, he hadn't touched another woman.

His infrequent visits to the Pink Slipper were only out of necessity when the need built up and he required release. There was no threat to his heart in those visits. No worries he would lose it again to someone like Teresa. Or Claire. She was a new threat, one he was having trouble resisting.

Claire was as different from Teresa as night from day. Teresa had been broken and what remained of her had been as fragile as a crystal glass—easily shattered if not handled with extreme care. In the end, she had shattered despite his gentle care. Thinking back on their time together, he realized he had been more of a caretaker than a husband.

He had put aside his own needs hoping that one day she would heal and be the kind of wife he wanted. Someone to stand beside him, someone he could trust with his heart. Teresa had tried—God knows she had— but she had never been able to put the past behind her.

She had never loved him and for that reason alone, he would not risk his heart again. It was only through sheer will that he'd patched the splintered pieces back together.

Claire might be the one woman who could be all the things he had once wished for, but what if he was wrong? What if there was another Harry out there somewhere waiting to claim her heart?

He should avoid her. It was the wise thing to do, yet he kept finding reasons to be in her company.

He closed his eyes and settled into a troubled sleep.

Chapter Ten

The devil lord didn't play fair. Claire clutched the letters from the twins in her fist and paced the floor of her bedroom. She had planned to send a note in the morning excusing herself from the outing.

The man she loved planned to take her to London to find her a husband? How dare he! Was she a piece of unwanted furniture to be sold to the highest bidder? When word of the wealth Chase planned to bestow on her leaked out, the fortune hunters would arrive on her doorstep in droves.

The blasted man.

If she had to have a husband, why couldn't it be him? He desired her. Even in her inexperience, she knew that much. It wasn't love, but it was more than she'd had with Thomas. Why couldn't he see how a marriage between them would benefit them both? She could give him an heir, be a mother to his boys, manage his stables and be his friend. It would be the perfect arrangement for him.

As for her, well, she would have him.

But the ghost of his wife stood between them. How could she break down his walls? Unfortunately, she had no clue how a woman went about getting a marriage proposal from the man her heart wanted. She only knew how to get a horse's attention. If only it were that simple.

As Claire sought sleep, the idea of how to make Chase want her played on her mind. Several hours later, she sat straight up in bed.

"That's it!" she exclaimed.

She would go about it in the same way she would with a frightened, damaged horse. Granted, he wasn't a horse, but he was damaged. Although his scars didn't show, they were there all the same. Until he healed, he would be too skittish to risk his heart again, and he had such a big heart.

It was there in his love for the two boys he had rescued from the streets. It was there in his love for his family, and even in his love for his silly horse. The man surrounded himself with only who and what he trusted to never betray him. Like a horse that had learned not to trust an abusive master, Chase had learned not to trust a woman.

She had worked with abused horses. Too many men thought the way to train a horse was to beat the animal into submission with the whip and harsh treatment. Too often, the results were a mean, savage beast or a quivering mass of horseflesh afraid of its own shadow. Their spirits were stolen, their pride destroyed. Through trial and error, she had developed her own unique methods for giving a horse its pride back.

She had never met a horse she couldn't help. Could she help heal this man? Too excited to return to sleep, she planned her strategy for what she decided to call The Training of a Marquess.

The first stage in working with a troubled horse was to let him see her, to let him wonder about her. Horses were curious animals.

When she worked with one of her yearlings, his

first questions was, *Who are you and what do you want from me?* If it was a damaged horse, the question would be a suspicious, *What are you going to do to hurt me?*

It was up to her to prove the horse was safe with her. The very challenge she faced with Chase. She had taken the first steps in getting him to notice her, but he needed to be more curious. He needed to wonder about her. The Training of a Marquess would start first thing in the morning with Stage One: Notice Me.

****

Chase led the twins into the stables at precisely eleven. His carriage was harnessed and his coachman stood in front of the cattle. At the hitching post, Mischief and Victory stomped impatient hooves— saddled and ready to go. Claire and Amira were the only missing invitees to this outing. Amira's stall was empty so he went to Claire's office and found Gordon.

"Have you seen Lady Derebourne?"

"Yes, my lord. She said to tell you to go on and she would catch up with you."

It irritated him that she wasn't here and ready. He returned to the front of the stables. "Let's go," he told the boys.

"Isn't Lady Derebourne coming with us?" Harry asked.

"Harry said my lady would go on our picnic. Harry said our letters would do the trick," Bensey said, close to tears.

"She said we were to go on ahead and she would catch up to us. Is the food basket in the carriage, Bensey?" Chase asked to divert the boy's attention.

Bensey peered in the carriage door. "Yes, Father."

"Good. No sneaking any cakes before we arrive at

the seashore." Bensey he would trust not to sneak a cake—Harry, never.

"I won't." Clutching his book on the plants of coastal England and his satchel, Bensey climbed into the carriage.

Chase and Harry mounted their horses and rode out ahead. Chase's mind turned to Claire. Where was she? The last time he saw her, she had been sitting on a rock crying. There was no reason to worry. If she chose not to come, so be it. It only meant he didn't have to contend with another sad woman. After Teresa, he didn't have it in him.

He rode alongside Harry, half-listening to the boy's chatter. As soon as Lady Anne arrived, he'd remove himself from Claire's presence. His mother would be able to comfort Claire and deal with her melancholy much better than he.

Deep in thought, he didn't hear the approaching horse until it was right behind him. Harry gave a delighted laugh, and Chase turned to see what amused his son.

A laughing, pale-haired sprite wearing black leather breeches raced past them. Amira's mane boasted flowers and tinkling bells, and her tail was braided with colorful ribbons.

What the deuce?

Claire—a big grin on her face—pulled up and turned her horse to face them.

Where was the despondent woman he expected? Not that he regretted her good cheer, but Chase didn't know what to make of her. She was a vision in her leather breeches and a red silk blouse, astride a horse decorated as if it had stepped out of a fairy tale. She wore her hair in a braided tail that reached her waist. Red and silver earrings dangled from her ears. The only thing that kept her from being mistaken for a gypsy was her moonlight pale hair.

She muddled his mind and stirred his blood. He didn't understand her. There was a time in his life—before Teresa—when he prided himself on knowing women better than most. Now, he was as confused as the next man.

"I say, Amira is ever so pretty, my lady," Harry said

Her bells jingling, Amira pranced as if she knew she was indeed a lovely sight to behold. Claire moved with the mare as if she and the horse were one. The festive Arabian and the intriguing woman captivated Chase. How hard was it going to be to convince Bensey to draw them?

"Thank you, Harry," the enchantress said. "Amira's quite proud of her flowers and bells."

The carriage caught up with them and Bensey leaned out the window, grinning from ear to ear.

Claire rode closer to him. "What do you think of Amira's flowers, Bensey?"

"I think she is beautiful, my lady. May I draw you and Amira?"

"Amira would be honored, as would I."

Well, that answers that. It seemed the twins were no more immune to her enchantment than he. Chase shook his head to clear it of the pixie dust she had obviously sprinkled in the air. He had to get her out of his mind. She wasn't for him, and if he kept hammering the thought into his mind, it might sink in.

"Lady Claire," he said, and cursed the huskiness in

his voice. "I'm pleased you were able to join us. The boys were worried."

Ignoring Chase, she gave the twins a big smile. "Well, I'm here now, so shall we go have our picnic?"

"Oh, yes, my lady," they said in unison.

She patted Bensey's hand. "Would you mind terribly if your father, Harry, and I raced for a while? I promise we'll wait for you to catch up before we reach the sea."

"No, my lady, but tell John Coachman that I won't mind if he goes a little faster."

Was that his son speaking? Normally, Bensey didn't want the carriage to go faster than a light trot. Apparently, the twins had also inhaled the pixie dust. As Chase gave his coachman instructions, the minx laughed and took off with Harry, the boy's laughter mingling with hers.

She glanced over her shoulder and grinned. "Good bye, my lord," she called.

Did she think to leave him behind?

Claire smiled at the sound of Mischief's hooves pounding the dirt as Chase raced after them. If the heat in his eyes when she'd reached them was any indication, her plan was working. She held Amira back so Harry could easily keep up.

Victory was a fine horse and could go faster, but she didn't want to push the boy past his abilities. He was a good rider for his age and if taught right, would develop into an excellent horseman. Perhaps Chase would let Harry spend some time with her in the training ring.

Harry pealed with excited laughter. "Father's almost here," he yelled. "Can we go faster?"

She inched Amira a little closer to him. "Can you keep a secret?"

When he nodded, she said, "We know we can beat him, but we're going to let him catch up. We don't want to hurt his feelings, do we?"

He gave her one of his impish grins. "But we won, right?"

"Yes, but that will be our secret."

When Chase reached them, the three settled into an easy gallop. Claire let the man and boy pull ahead. She wanted to know how well the marquess rode. She was pleased to see he had a good seat and a light touch with the reins.

There was nothing worse than a rider with a heavy hand. She could never love a man who mistreated a horse, one who jerked the bit in his mount's mouth or gave hard kicks to his flanks, or any number of things she'd seen them do.

Though, she mused, it might be better if he was one of those men. It would give her a reason not to love him. She didn't want to go to London and find a husband, couldn't imagine a man existed that she would want more than Chase.

He pulled alongside, his head bent low over Mischief's neck. Her silly heart wept for what could be if only...but all was not lost. She still had her plan. Her methods had never failed with a horse, but would they work with him?

Even at a fast gallop, he managed to send her a look of such awareness she feared she might slide right off the saddle. She almost did when he grinned, showing his dimple.

Claire managed to return his smile and nudged

Amira to pick up her speed. She raced past Chase and Harry, giving them a merry laugh. The sound of hooves pounding behind her thrilled her adventurous self.

She leaned over Amira's neck. "Show them what you can do, my lovely."

Amira, never one to hesitate to show herself off, lowered her head and raced the wind. When they were within a mile of the sea, Claire reined in the mare and gradually slowed her to a lope. Chase and Harry fell in beside her. They circled the horses, allowing them to cool down while waiting for the carriage.

"That was grand fun," Harry said, and then with a sly gleam in his eyes, added, "We didn't think you would catch up with us, Father, but somehow you did."

Chase glanced suspiciously at the boy, and Claire hid her smile. It seemed he knew his son well. Although Chase hadn't said much, his attention had stayed on her from the time she'd raced past him to the music of Amira's jingling bells.

That's right, notice me. She gave Amira the signal to rear up. The Arabian stood on her hind legs as her front hooves pawed the air above her head. Harry laughed with glee. Chase nudged Mischief alongside Amira.

"You're killing me, Claire," he murmured. "Be glad we have an audience, or…"

The carriage arrived, and he backed Mischief away. Or what? Bells in hell, she wanted to know what he'd started to say.

Pivoting Amira, Claire led them to a path that would allow them to take the horses with them to the beach. "We should remove their saddles so we don't risk them getting wet," she suggested.

After removing the saddles, Chase retrieved the food basket and they led the horses down to the beach with Bensey following, carrying his book and satchel. When they reached the bottom, Claire sat on a rock to pull off her boots and stockings.

"May we take our boots off, Father?" Harry asked.

Chase placed the basket behind a rock, out of the sun. "It would be a good idea to do so. You don't want to get them wet."

The twins seemed excited by the idea of being barefoot and immediately set to work on removing each other's boots. Claire breathed deeply of the salty air as her gaze took in the beauty of the sea. The waves were gentle today, and she always felt at peace when she came here.

She tried not to think that this might be the last time she would see it. The boys' laughter resolved her to enjoy herself and make a happy memory of this day.

She caught Chase staring at her feet and wanted to grin, but settled for wriggling her toes in the sand. "Aren't you going to remove your boots?" she asked.

He jerked his gaze up to her face. His eyes were a deeper blue, the same color as when he kissed her. If he were one of her horses, she'd say her plan was working. He gave a little shake of his head and then sat down next to her on the rock. His arm brushed hers, her skin prickling where they touched.

"Harry, Bensey, give me a hand here." He stretched out his legs and lifted a foot.

The boys pulled and tugged and, with much merriment, managed to remove his snug fitting boots. When he removed his stockings, she understood his fascination with her feet. Claire had never thought of feet being elegant, but his were. Her fingers itched to touch them when he wriggled his toes in the sand as she had. She glanced up to see him intently watching her. His lips twitched when she blushed.

Chase was thoroughly convinced he had lost his mind somewhere between Hillcrest and the sea. It probably happened the moment she raced past him on her fairy horse clad in leather breeches and wearing gypsy earrings. He shouldn't notice how the silk shirt hugged her curves, shouldn't be having carnal thoughts about her little pink toes—or any other part of her for that matter.

Nor should he like the way she stared at his feet with a hungry gleam in her eyes. Her blush when he caught her out had been charming. He glanced at his feet. They weren't ugly, but he didn't see what she found fascinating about them. Hers on the other hand…

Bloody hell, he had to stop thinking about her toes. His horse nuzzled his face, and he scratched Mischief's nose. "Silly horse. Feeling ignored, are you?"

"He wants to go swimming," Harry said.

"Does he now?" Chase stood, offering a hand to Claire. "Shall we take a ride on the beach before we have our picnic?"

She placed her hand in his, and something happened to him. This was where her hand belonged, in his. She looked at him with her big blue eyes, and he lost his bearings.

He wanted to make love to her, softly, leisurely and thoroughly. He wanted to peel off her clothes and spend hours exploring her body, wanted to touch his fingertips to her soft skin as she moaned his name. He wanted her more than he had ever wanted another woman, maybe even more than Teresa.

Bloody hell.

Chase dropped her hand and turned to Bensey. "Will you be all right if we ride for a few minutes? We'll stay in sight and perhaps you can begin your drawing of Amira and Lady Derebourne."

Bensey picked up his satchel and set about organizing his pencils and charcoal. Chase removed his coat, and then gave Harry a leg up on Victory.

He turned to Claire. "My lady?"

She placed her foot, warm from the sand, on his interlocked fingers and swung her leg over Amira. Chase squeezed his eyes shut. He had to stop thinking about her feet. Opening his eyes, he grabbed Mischief's reins, led him to a rock and mounted.

They headed for the water. Harry bounced around a little on Victory, but Claire was again one with her horse. When they reached the waves, Claire nudged Amira into an easy lope and Harry followed suit. Within minutes of riding along the water line, Harry rode bareback almost as well as Claire.

The horses seemed to like splashing through the waves, Mischief nickering from the fun of it. Without warning, his idiot horse took a hard left, heading for deeper water. Chase hadn't come as close to falling off since he was in short pants, learning to ride his first pony.

"Oh, no you don't." He pulled Mischief to a stop.

His fool horse stomped at the waves as if trying to catch them. Chase decided standing still and letting Mischief play was much easier on his arse than bouncing saddleless atop a galloping horse.

Down the beach, Claire and Harry seemed in deep

conversation as they rode side by side. Chase tried to imagine Teresa in leather breeches, riding bareback and barefoot while talking with a boy from the streets. He couldn't.

"Father," Harry called. "Lady Derebourne said if it is all right with you, I can come to the stables with her in the morning and she will teach me to train horses. I want to do it ever so much, so please say yes. Please."

The excitement in his son's eyes would have prevented any likelihood of saying no even if he had been so inclined. He wanted Harry to learn all he could from her and had planned to ask her to allow him to watch her training sessions.

"Yes, but you understand it means getting up at dawn."

"Oh, thank you, Father. I promise I'll get up when I'm supposed to. I want to tell Bensey."

He took off and Chase marveled at how easily he now rode Victory without a saddle.

"He's a natural," Claire said.

"I know. I was just thinking that I envied him." When she arched a brow, he shrugged. "Never thought to say I would envy a nine year old boy's ability to ride bareback, but there it is."

"Missing your saddle, are you?"

"My arse is missing my saddle, pardon my language."

She laughed and he joined her. Life was good. When was the last time he'd been carefree and happy? When had he last laughed with a woman he truly liked?

Sea birds called overhead. He watched them circle, their wings stretched wide to catch the draft. The sun warmed his face, the breeze tousled his hair, and he smiled. This was the best day he'd had in a long, long time. There would be no thinking today, no worries about tomorrow. For now, there was only this day, this woman, his sons, the sound of the sea, and the sun warm on his face.

In easy companionship, he and Claire walked their mounts along the edge of the water. He listened to her voice and liked the music of it, liked the way she looked into his eyes when she spoke. Teresa had rarely met his gaze.

"Thank you for allowing Harry to spend time with me at the stables. I think he has much potential. I've always wanted a promising student. My training is different, but it seems to work better than the way most train their horses."

"You're welcome, but you should know I was going to ask it of you. His natural abilities with horses was a surprise, especially if you consider he had never been on one before a year ago. From the first time I put him on a pony it was as if he found his passion in life. It's important the twins have a purpose as they cannot inherit from me. For Harry it's horses, for Bensey, his art."

"I hadn't thought of it that way, but you're right, it's fortunate they each have found something that will sustain them through life. I know how adrift I felt before I found my purpose."

He had never considered life from a woman's point of view. They were raised to be wives and mothers. Never had he thought it might not be enough for some. For her. How was it fair for a woman to be told she had to give up something that was a part of who she was? Not only would he make sure the husband she chose was kind and gentle, but the man would have to love horses and be willing to allow her to have a hand in training them.

If he found her a husband. Bloody hell, where had that come from? Of course, he was going to follow his plan.

"Would you would mind if the twins addressed me as Lady Claire?" she asked. "I'm friends with them now. Lady Derebourne sounds so formal and distant. They're such charming boys and I like them tremendously. Would you allow it?"

"If that is what you wish."

Her warm smile was so pleasing his dead heart flickered to life. His reaction to her smiles should concern him, and it would—tomorrow.

They returned to Bensey. Chase swung his leg over Mischief's back and slid to the ground. He turned to Claire and lifted her off Amira, lowering her down. His hands lingered on her waist longer than they should. His gaze lingered on her pink lips longer than it should.

Harry held out Bensey's sketchpad. "Look at Bensey's picture, Father."

Chase tore his gaze away. Christ. How did one rid oneself of pixie dust?

"Oh, Bensey, it's beautiful." Claire said.

And it was. Bensey had drawn them riding on the beach, Claire's red blouse, gypsy earrings, the flowers in Amira's mane and the ribbons woven into her tail the only bright colors. He had used muted blues and grays for the sea and sky, and white for Amira and the sand.

"Once again, you amaze me, son."

Bensey grinned, took the pad from Harry and flipped the page. Chase stared at it a moment before bursting into laughter. Bensey had caught him at the instant he had almost fallen off Mischief. In the picture, he was leaning at a precarious angle with one leg raised above his head. The look on his face was comical.

The other three joined him in his laughter, and a seed was planted in his mind. This is how it feels to have a true and loving family.

They settled on the rocks, sharing a lunch of cold chicken, cheeses, apples, and to the twins delight, cakes. They talked about the sea, fish and turtles, the sea birds and the best way to build sand castles. They teased each other, told riddles and laughed more than he ever remembered doing so.

While a part of him joined in the conversation and the teasing, another part marveled over how much fun he was having.

After Teresa died, there had always been guilt whenever he felt good, or laughed or forgot about her for more than a few minutes. But she had made her choice, and for the first time, he realized it was her choice to make. She had decided to never let go of her Harry instead of holding him in a special place in her heart and moving on with her life.

Chase had never resented her love for Harry, but he had deeply resented how desperately she held onto the past. Yet, wasn't that what he was doing? Seeing him now, she would not have been pleased. She would have wanted him to remarry and have the family he'd always longed for. His thoughts watered the little seed and tiny roots sprouted. He had much to think about.

"I have a splendid idea," Harry said.

Chase slapped his hand over his heart in mock horror. "Be afraid, Lady Claire. When Harry has an idea, it's time to run for the hills."

His son punched him on the arm. "This one is a very good idea, Father. We can have a sandcastle building contest. Me and Bensey against you and Lady Derebourne."

"What say you, Lady Claire? Are you any good at building sandcastles?"

"Oh, I certainly am. And, Harry, I would be honored if you and Bensey addressed me as Lady Claire."

Harry grinned. "We would like that ever so much, Lady Claire." Bensey nodded in agreement.

They teamed off and went to work on their sandcastles. Each promised not to sneak a peek at the other's until they were finished and could judge the results. True to her word, Claire was good at the thing, so Chase took his direction from her. When they finished, he thought they had a magnificent sandcastle. Until, that is, he saw the twins' creation.

"Ye gads," he said.

Claire followed his gaze. "Oh, my God."

For no good reason, they fell into a fit of laughter. "Amazing," he said when he caught his breath. Harry was no one's fool, thus his choice of a teammate. Chase had no doubt it was Bensey, the artist, who was responsible for the most awe-inspiring sandcastle ever built.

"Have you ever seen anything like it?" Claire asked.

"No, I don't believe I have. I wonder what would happen if I gave him a lump of clay."

"You should try it and see."

"Did we win, Father?" Bensey asked.

"Yes, I believe you did."

"What did we win?" Harry asked.

"You won a kiss from the sea monster." Chase held his hands high like claws. They screamed and he chased them down the beach.

Chapter Eleven

Claire sat on the sand as Chase ran after his laughing boys. It hurt, this yearning to belong to their family.

The first stage of her plan seemed to be working, giving her hope. He was aware of her, of that she was certain. One moment stood out. He had been watching the sea birds, then had lowered his head and smiled.

It was the first true smile he had given her.

The boys ran back and hid behind her. "Save us from the sea monster, Lady Claire," Harry yelled.

"Where are the little scamps?" the sea monster said. "I'm hungry and little boys are mighty tasty."

Claire pointed to the sea. "I think they went that way."

The twins giggled. "I heard that," the monster growled, making a grab for them. They shrieked and took off running.

Chase dropped down beside her. "If I had half their energy, I could rule the world."

The boys played at the water's edge, trying to keep the waves from touching their feet. "Do they remember their parents?"

"When they first came to me, they remembered bits and pieces, but even those memories are fading. They said their father died first and then later their mother became sick and died. Harry thinks his father worked on the docks. From the best I can gather, they were alone for at least a year before I found them."

Claire shuddered at the thought of such young children living on the streets. "It's hard to understand how they survived."

"Bensey wouldn't have without Harry," he said, and she knew it was true.

"Then he was fortunate to have had Harry and both are fortunate to have you." He didn't seem aware that his foot caressed hers as he spoke. Little shivers traveled up her leg from his touch. Not wanting to call notice to his action and have him stop, she kept her attention on his face.

"I'm blessed to have them." He stood and held out his hand. "We should probably head home."

She put her hand in his and he pulled her up. Surprising her, he gave her a quick kiss.

"Thank you for today, Claire." He grinned and kissed her again. "That one was for loving my boys."

Oh, my. She didn't know which she liked best, the brief kiss or his dimple when he smiled.

"Your boys are easy to love." *As are you.* There was a new lightness in his voice and eyes. She would give almost anything to know if her plan had anything to do with it.

He called to the boys and then whistled. Hearing his master's call, Mischief trotted toward them with Amira and Victory following.

Claire called for baths upon reaching home. She had sand and salt in places she didn't even want to consider and imagined it was the same for Chase and the boys. Deciding she was done with black, she chose a lavender gown to wear to dinner. Picking up a brush, she curled up on her window seat. While she dried her hair, she considered the next step in her plan.

When she worked with a damaged horse, her strategy was to stand in the middle of the ring and while staring into his eyes, she would speak softly, telling him what she was doing and why.

Invariably, the horse would stay as far away as possible, rightfully suspicious of her. He had no way of knowing she was different from the previous humans of his experience. The trick was to engage his curiosity, and when his attention focused on her, she'd retreat.

Advance and Retreat—repeat. Each time he tentatively approached her, she would retreat. It resulted in a confused horse, but his determination to learn what she was about grew.

He anticipated being hurt and she wasn't living up to his expectations. The moment his ears stopped flicking in all directions and focused on her, she had him. He was saying, *I don't know what you are doing, but you have me curious to know what it means to me.*

She would still her rope, square up and face him, maintaining eye contact. When he started showing signs of wanting to join with her, a lowering of his head and a chewing motion with his mouth, she would repeat the process of Advance and Retreat. She kept at it until she was sure he was being honest when he told her he wanted to join her herd.

She then broke eye contact, turned her back and waited for the magic to happen. He would slowly approach and nudge her shoulder. The moment his whiskers touched her neck never failed to affect her profoundly.

The whole process was to achieve one thing.

Horses were herd animals. In the wild and without a herd, they were vulnerable to predators. The need to belong to a herd was a survival instinct ingrained in them. The poor, damaged horse had no family and she would offer the gift of what he needed most. Some took longer than others depending on how deep their hurt, but in the end she had never had one reject her offer.

Claire had spent endless hours observing horses and the way they interacted with each other. Then came the magical day she witnessed a mare discipline a frisky filly and realized the horses had a language they used with each other.

She was stunned. Everything she thought she knew, she threw out the window and began again with an empty mind. She watched them, practiced what she learned—make some mistakes and corrected them—until she believed she could honestly say she understood their language and what was on their mind at any given moment.

The question played through her mind. How could she use the knowledge on Chase? He wasn't a horse she could drive around the training ring until he wanted to join her herd. Giggling, she closed her eyes and imagined him in the ring running ahead of her flickering rope, going through the steps until he was nuzzling her neck. She shivered and opened her eyes.

After spending the day with him, seeing how loving he was with the twins, hearing his easy laughter and touching his bare feet, she wanted him more than ever. But did he yearn for a family? Oh, he had the boys, but they couldn't give him what he really needed. She could if only he would see it.

So, how to go about it? She reviewed the next stage

of Advance and Retreat, considering the different ways she could adapt it to work on The Training of a Marquess.

****

Chase entered the drawing room to find Claire waiting for him. She handed him a brandy, her fingers brushing against his. Awareness prickled where she touched.

"Are Harry and Bensey joining us for dinner?" she asked.

"They couldn't keep their eyes open long enough to eat dinner and are snugly tucked into their beds."

She smiled. "A day at the sea does tend to do that. As for myself, I almost fell asleep in my bath."

His brain instantly supplied him with a picture of Claire, her skin wet and glistening, her pale hair hanging over the tub inviting him to comb his fingers through it.

Now, her hair was swept up in a casual way, allowing tendrils to coil around her neck. Without thinking, he reached up to touch one, but she turned and walked to the sofa, leaving his hand suspended in midair. He stared at it for a second wondering what had just happened. Dropping his hand back to his side, he joined her, leaving an appropriate space between them.

He had done much thinking on the ride home and later while bathing and dressing. The realization this afternoon that he had been holding onto the past—making him no different than Teresa—had shaken him. He had sworn not to remarry, not to risk his heart again to that kind of pain.

But one question plagued him. Did he want to live his life alone? He had Harry and Bensey, but they wouldn't stay boys forever. Then what? Would his solitary-self sit alone in his mansion in Mayfair waiting for their weekly visit? The idea of it didn't settle well.

Dare he offer his heart again? And if so, would it be to this woman? She fascinated him and, without doubt, stirred his blood. She liked his sons and he believed she could grow to love them.

If not her, then who? There wasn't another noble lady he could think of who would accept two street urchins even though they were clean now...usually. That would be one of his primary conditions. No, it would be his foremost condition. Love me, love my sons.

Chase took a sip of brandy, peering at her over the rim. She arched a brow, and he returned her raised brow with one of his own. She grinned. Yes, indeed, she stirred his blood.

"Did you enjoy today, Claire?"

"I did. I don't think I've ever had as much fun before. What of you, my lord, Chase?"

From what he knew of her, she hadn't had many fun days in her life. "I can honestly say the same and stop lording me."

The minx playfully tapped his hand. "As you wish."

She sipped her wine, and when she licked her lips he almost groaned. The tendril of hair curling around her ear still tempted him. His mind focused on one thing—wrapping a silky strand around his finger while he kissed her. She'd welcomed his kisses before, even asked him to do so, and he thought she wouldn't be adverse to another.

He put his arm along the back of the sofa and

danced his fingertips over the soft skin of her neck. She shivered under his touch. Unable to resist any longer, he leaned toward her intending to kiss her. She stood, leaving him hanging over empty air.

What the devil?

The confusing woman set down her wine glass and held out her hand. "Come, I believe dinner is ready."

Chase stood and offered his arm. She lightly rested her hand over the sleeve of his coat, peeked up at him and smiled.

A man could forget his name when she smiled like that. He was tempted to try and kiss her again just to see what she would do. More than curious about her behavior, he escorted her to dinner, inhaling the fresh scent of violets as he walked beside her.

All through their meal, it seemed she found reasons to touch him. A light touch to his hand, his arm as she talked, and once she smoothed back a strand of hair that had fallen over his forehead. The woman intrigued the hell out of him.

What was she up to?

She asked him about the Duchess of Aubrey and her Shire horses. He'd noticed before how well she listened. Later, he tried to remember how it came about, but he found himself telling her about his father, a surprise as Chase rarely talked of his father to anyone.

No opinions, sympathy or platitudes were offered, she just listened. He liked that about her, but he was puzzled. If he touched her, she subtly removed her hand or arm. The more she removed herself from his touch, the more he wanted to touch her. Damned strange, that.

Then came dessert. Cook served a berry pudding. After tonight, he would never look at pudding again without thinking of Claire. Who knew a woman could seduce a man with nothing but a spoon and dessert? When she closed her eyes in ecstasy, licked the spoon with her pink tongue and moaned, his blood sizzled. By the saints, he almost took her then and there on the table amidst the china. Did she have any idea her affect on him?

She finished her dessert and eyed his—which he hadn't touched. Had, in fact, forgotten about.

"Are you going to eat yours?"

He shoved it in front of her. "No, I want you to have it." Was there such a thing as pleasurable torture?

With the last drop licked from her spoon, she sighed. "That was delicious."

She was delicious, and he ached with the need she stirred in him. If they were married, he would order his cook to serve pudding every night. Odd that the thought of marriage to her didn't send him running for the hills. When she licked her lips, he pushed away from the table and stood.

"Would you like to join me for a glass of wine in the courtyard?"

She tilted her head and smiled. "Thank you for the offer, but we had a long day. I think I'll go find my bed."

The devil, but he'd be more than happy to help her find her bed. Disappointed and confused, he escorted her to the stairs. "Good night, Claire," he said and attempted to steal a kiss. She danced up the steps and once again, he was left leaning into empty air.

"Good night, Chase. Sweet dreams."

Sweet dreams, indeed. He went to bed frustrated, confused and wanting.

****

Claire rang for Maggie, and as her maid helped her undress, she recalled the expression on Chase's face when she left him. The question had been in his eyes. *What are you about? You have me curious.* It had to mean her plan was working.

"What has you smiling so, my lady?"

"I had such a wonderful day, Maggie."

"Are you sure that's what has you smiling like a cat what found the cream? I thought it might be because of a certain lord."

"Oh, he is beautiful, isn't he?"

"That he is, my lady."

Maggie wouldn't carry tales below stairs. Her maid had been her only friend from the time she arrived at the abbey and had never betrayed a confidence. Maggie handed Claire her nightdress and wished her mistress a good night. Claire climbed into bed and blew out the candle. Hugging a pillow, she reviewed every detail of the evening.

Chase had tried to kiss her twice, and when she ate her pudding, it had taken all her control not to swoon at the heat in his eyes. His gaze never left her mouth and when she moaned, he'd tugged at his cravat. There was a moment when she thought he might throw her on the table and have his way with her. The mere idea excited her.

How long should she continue this stage before moving to the next? He had told her tonight he'd received a message from his mother that she would arrive on Friday. That left only two more days before her chaperone arrived. Claire fell asleep wondering how having his mother in residence would alter her plans.

****

When Claire arrived in the breakfast room, not only was Harry awaiting her but Chase as well. They bowed and greeted her.

Her silly heart fluttered at the sight of the marquess. "Do I have two pupils today?"

"Harry is your pupil. I only wish to observe, if you don't mind."

"Not at all." She walked past him, brushing her fingers over his hand. "Come and fix a plate. Eat well, Harry, it will be a long time before lunch."

Chase prowled alongside her, piling food on his plate. She glanced at Harry's plate to see his appetite matched his father's. Harry peppered her with questions all through breakfast, wanting to know everything they would be doing this morning.

Although Chase remained quiet, his attention stayed focused on her. Except to ask him an occasional question, she ignored him. Once, he rested his hand on the table and she pressed her fingers over his when she made a comment to him. He stared hard at her hand on his, then his eyes flicked up to meet hers, bewilderment shimmering in their depths.

In the same way it happened with her horses, she knew exactly what he was thinking. *I don't yet know what you're doing, but you have me curious to know how it is going to play out.*

Perhaps men were as simple to understand as horses.

Stifling a smile, Claire stood. "Come along, Harry, it's time to go to work." She walked out of the room with Harry, leaving Chase to follow.

****

Chase leaned on the fence. Claire had one of her yearlings in the ring and in less than an hour had a saddle on the colt's back. He wouldn't have believed it if he hadn't seen it with his own eyes. Before she brought the colt out, she had carefully explained to Harry what she was going to do and why. She'd then boldly stated she would have the youngster saddled and ridden within an hour. He and Harry had shared a look of disbelief.

"Then you've been training him before today?" Chase asked.

"No, this will be his first time in the ring."

He almost snorted in skepticism. But from the time she brought the colt in, Chase had been riveted in place—almost forgetting to appreciate the sight of her in black leather breeches. Not quite, however, as Claire now lay over the saddle on the colt's back, her marvelous bottom high in the air. He was becoming rather fond of her breeches. She looked spectacular.

As she slowly rose, she swung a leg over the saddle and then trotted the colt around the ring. Chase checked the time on his pocket watch. Fifty minutes.

"Bloody amazing," he muttered.

Harry came to the fence, his eyes shining with excitement. "Did you see, Father?"

"I did and if I hadn't seen it with my own eyes, I wouldn't have believed it."

"I know, and it was the best thing ever. Lady Claire is going to teach me how to do it. Isn't she splendid?"

"She most certainly is."

He smiled at his besotted son. It was a safe bet the twins wouldn't think much of his plan to find her a husband. He was no longer sure himself.

Claire stopped the colt in front of Harry. He reached up and scratched the horse under his chin. "What is his name, Lady Claire?"

"I don't know. He has yet to tell me."

Harry's eyes went wide. "He's going to tell you his name?"

She grinned. "They always do."

Harry stared at the colt as if waiting for him to speak.

Chase chuckled. "I think she means that if you observe him long enough, his name will come to you."

Claire winked at him, the first woman in his one and thirty years to do so. She dismounted and placed her hand on Harry's shoulder.

"Your father's right. For example, you remember Honey, the little filly I introduced you to this morning?"

Harry nodded.

"Well, her name is Honey because she is the sweetest horse I've ever met." Claire held her hand under the colt's mouth and he snuffled her palm. "Tell me, Harry, what you have observed about this one?"

Without hesitating, Harry listed all the things he had noticed. "And he prances," he added lastly.

Claire studied at the colt thoughtfully. "You're right, he does. Very good. So, if you were to give him a name, what would it be?"

"Prancer!" Harry exclaimed.

She made a show of giving Harry's choice serious consideration. "I think you almost have it, but not quite." She tapped a finger over her lips. "Let's see. Prancer, Ancer, Lancer—"

"I know! I know!" Harry cried, jumping up and down. "It's Dancer. His name is Dancer."

136

Claire clapped her hands in delight and borrowing Harry's favorite word, said, "Splendid. See, I told you he would give you his name."

Harry's face lit up in bliss and Chase's heart did a funny dance. He wryly wondered just how large her supply of pixie dust was. His son looked at her with calf eyes and he feared he just might be, also.

"Would you like to ride him, Harry?" she asked.

"Oh yes, please."

"Are you sure it's safe?" Chase asked.

"Yes, Dancer's calm for his age." She gave Harry a leg up and handed him the reins. "Only at a walk, and remember, use a gentle hand."

She stepped back to the fence and they watched Harry walk the colt around the ring. "He has a light but firm hand. I'm going to enjoy teaching him." She reached up and smoothed a lock of his hair. "Thank you for allowing it."

Chase almost purred. What was she doing to him? "Claire?"

There was a question in there somewhere, but damned if he knew what it was. He took a deep breath and inhaled her scent—horse and leather mixed in with violets. The essence of Claire. One side of her mouth curved up in a secretive smile before she walked to the center of the ring, turning her back to him.

Had she just dismissed him? Again? What the devil was the meaning of that smile? Chase wanted to climb over the fence and demand answers. She was ignoring him, all her attention on Harry and the colt.

He wanted her attention on him, wanted to bury his face in her neck and inhale her fascinating scent. He wanted...well, there were a lot of things he wanted to do to her. The woman confused the hell out of him. Disgruntled, he left to go spend time with Bensey.

Claire smiled when Chase strode away. His eyes had smoldered when she'd smoothed his hair. When he had taken a deep breath, she somehow knew he was taking in her scent. It had taken all of her resolve to walk away from him. She sensed it would soon be time to move to the next stage of her plan.

"You can bring Dancer up to a trot, if you wish, Harry."

Harry grinned happily as he and Dancer trotted around the ring. Keeping an eye on them, she considered the next steps of her strategy, the Ignore Him stage.

During the Advance and Retreat stage, she would get the horse used to her touch and then back off, keeping his curiosity focused on her. When he showed true interest in her, she would turn her back and ignore him. She had yet to meet a horse that liked to be snubbed.

Had Chase reached the point of true interest? Her instincts said he had and she always trusted her intuition with the horses, so she would trust her feelings now. The Ignore Him stage would begin as soon as his mother arrived.

Ignoring Chase was going to be a difficult thing to do.

Chapter Twelve

Harry monopolized the luncheon conversation with a passionate recounting of his morning to Bensey. Every sentence began with, "Lady Claire said," or "Lady Claire did this, or that." To Bensey's credit, he listened attentively.

Chase leaned toward Claire. "I do believe you have an ardent admirer, Claire," he murmured.

She brushed her hand over his and sighed. "I've always wondered how it felt to be admired."

His skin rippled under her touch. "And how does it feel?"

"Wonderful." Such a blissful smile lit her face that his mind immediately set about conceiving ways to make her happy just to see her smile like that again.

"Lady Claire said the colt would tell me his name, Bensey, and he did. He told me his name was Dancer. Isn't that the most splendid thing ever?"

Bensey gave a sad little shake of his head. "Horses can't talk, Harry. Even I know that."

Bensey's comment sent Harry off on a detailed explanation of how the colt had told him his name. Chase turned his mind to Claire's comment. It bothered him that she had never had anyone in her life to admire her. When her father should have admired her skills at chess, he had, instead, demeaned her. Her husband hadn't appreciated her talent with the horses even though she had made a name for Hillcrest Stables to the benefit of his pockets.

This beautiful, talented and loving woman had so much to offer, and he didn't understand how the two most important men in her life hadn't been her biggest admirers. It didn't make sense to him when even a nine-year-old boy could see her worth. He felt a surge of anger on her behalf. Someone should show her how special she was. An idea sprouted in his mind.

"Would you like to go with me to the conservatory this afternoon, Lady Claire?" Bensey shyly asked.

"I would be delighted to. Shall I meet you there at four and we can sit and admire the flowers while we have tea?"

His son smiled in sweet pleasure. Love me, love my sons, Chase thought for no good reason.

An approaching carriage sounded from outside. Claire went to the window. "Oh dear, it's the Fisherman's carriage."

The twins exchanged a look of panic and fled with a quick, "Excuse us," tossed over their shoulders. Chase longed to join them.

"I must go and change into a black gown or Mrs. Fisherman will be scandalized."

He clenched his teeth. "Heaven forbid." Claire only had two weeks left of official mourning. As far as he was concerned, her lavender gown was perfectly appropriate.

"You don't know her, Chase. If she sees me in anything but black she'll tell everyone, making it sound as if I'm a horrible woman who doesn't mourn her husband."

No, he did know Mrs. Fisherman's kind—didn't

mean he had to like it. "Go and change. I'll manage until your return."

She gave him a grateful smile before she, too, fled. Chase chose an apple from the plate of fruit, pared it and sliced it into neat wedges while he waited. Smithfield entered with a card on his silver tray.

"My lord," he said, holding out the tray. "Mrs. Fisherman is asking for you. Mr. Fisherman and Miss Fisherman have accompanied her." Smithfield opened his mouth and then snapped it closed.

"Go on, you obviously have something more to say."

"Mrs. Fisherman did not inquire after my lady," Smithfield sniffed.

"Then your lady is more fortunate than I," Chase said, amused to see the butler's lips twitch. "Show Mrs. Fisherman and family to the drawing room. I'll attend them after I finish my apple."

"Yes, my lord."

Chase removed his pocket watch and placed it on the table. Slowly nibbling on the apple, he managed to waste seven minutes. He'd been aiming for ten. Heaving a great sigh, he stood and left to face the dragon.

"Mrs. Fisherman, Miss Fisherman," he said upon entering the drawing room.

The family stood, and the Fisherman ladies curtseyed. "Lord Derebourne, it is a pleasure to see you again. Allow me to introduce my husband, Mr. Fisherman."

Mr. Fisherman bowed. "My lord."

"A pleasure, Mr. Fisherman. Ladies, please have a seat."

Mrs. Fisherman immediately took control of the conversation. "As I am sure you know, Mr. Fisherman is the vicar, and it is his duty to welcome you. He hopes to see you at services on Sunday. It is important for the villagers to see their lord uphold his Christian duty."

"Now, Miranda—" Mr. Fisherman began.

"I am sure, my lord, you appreciate how important your support means to the village," she said, talking over her husband. Mr. Fisherman gave Chase a sympathetic smile as she continued on. "Not to speak ill of the dear departed, but the previous Lord Derebourne was lax in his duty to the village. Why, I was telling my dear Rhonda, I'm sure things will improve now that you are in residence. Do you not agree, my lord?"

Chase thought Mrs. Fisherman was sure of many things and that Mr. Fisherman must be a saint. Much to his relief, Claire stepped into the room before he had to respond. He happened to see Mrs. Fisherman's lips thin when Claire entered. He and Mr. Fisherman stood.

"Ah, there you are Lady Derebourne. I wasn't sure if you were aware we had guests," Chase said.

She wore her black gown and white lace cap. He didn't know which he hated most. Pleasantries were exchanged and Claire took a seat next to Miss Fisherman.

Mrs. Fisherman again took control of the conversation. "Lord Derebourne was just agreeing to attend services Sunday morning, my lady, and we were discussing how important his support is to the village. It was sadly regrettable, my dear, that your dear departed husband did not take more of an interest. I have always wondered how, as his wife, you didn't have more influence with him."

She waved a dismissive hand at Claire. "But it is of no matter now, as the new marquess will certainly prove to be up to the task."

The woman's cheek astounded him. Never mind he hadn't agreed to attend services, but to insult Claire in her own home was beyond the pale. He glanced at Mr. Fisherman to see his reaction and, by God, if the vicar wasn't asleep. Well, now Chase knew how the man tolerated his wife.

Claire gave Mrs. Fisherman a tight smile. "I'm sure you're right, Mrs. Fisherman." She turned a smile on Miss Fisherman. "It's nice to see you Rhonda. You look lovely. Blue is a good color for you."

The girl blushed, but there was pleasure on her face at the compliment. Chase smiled at the girl attempting to hide behind Claire's back. "Lady Derebourne is right, Miss Fisherman, blue is a lovely color for you." The color was nice, although all the bows and flounces were unfortunate.

Her pink blush turned a deep red and she peeked over Claire's shoulder. "Thank you, my lord."

"The dress was delivered yesterday, my lord. I told my dear Rhonda I was certain you would like it. Did I not say so, Rhonda?"

"Yes, Mother," Miss Fisherman said so softly Chase strained to hear her.

"Wait until you see the gown we had made for the assembly, my lord."

Chase didn't at all like the sly gleam in Mrs. Fisherman's eyes.

"Rhonda's dance card fills quickly, Lord Derebourne, so you will want to claim a dance without delay upon your arrival."

Miss Fisherman disappeared behind Claire. If there was a potion for invisibility, Chase was certain Miss Fisherman would gratefully drink it. He seriously doubted her dance card filled all that quickly, but he felt sorry for her.

"Then I shall claim a dance now. Would the first dance be acceptable to you, Miss Fisherman?"

"Yes, my lord," she whispered.

Mrs. Fisherman set back with such a satisfied expression that Chase wanted to shake her for her insensitivity to her daughter's feelings. It was obvious he intimidated the girl. Thankfully, she didn't seem to want any part of her mother's matchmaking attempts.

Just how much longer was this visit going to last? In the drawing rooms of London, the Fisherman's would have far surpassed the time of a polite fifteen minute call. The good vicar still napped, oblivious to his daughter's discomfort.

"It doesn't appear as if your mother has arrived to act as chaperone for Lady Derebourne, my lord."

Startled out of his contemplation, Chase met Mrs. Fisherman's calculating eyes. "My pardon?"

"My lord, it isn't seemly for Lady Derebourne to reside here in the abbey alone with you. I would once again offer myself as chaperone. Of course, my Rhonda shall remain as well. We have our valises in our carriage and can stay immediately as I am sure you do not wish to risk Lady Derebourne's reputation."

Chase counted to ten. "No need, Mrs. Fisherman. My mother arrives tonight, so as you see, it isn't necessary to disrupt your household."

A flash of irritation crossed her face before she turned to Claire. "It is a shame, my lady, that you will

144

not be able to attend the assembly as you are still in mourning."

Chase blinked. Oh, no, no, no. Perhaps it would be inappropriate for her to dance, but be damned if he would attend the assembly without Claire. Deciding it was best not to gainsay the woman now, he stayed quiet.

If only his mother were here. Mrs. Fisherman would be child's play for Lady Anne. Chase scanned the room. The vicar still slept, Miss Fisherman hid herself behind Claire, and Mrs. Fisherman prattled on about who knew what.

Enough was enough.

"I beg your forgiveness, but I have an appointment with my steward and must take my leave. Mrs. Fisherman, Miss Fisherman, it has been a pleasure."

"Surely, my lord, your steward can wait a few minutes," Mrs. Fisherman protested.

"Surely, madam, he cannot. Good day."

The rat. Claire narrowed her eyes at Chase's retreating back. She'd had to bite her cheek to keep from grinning at his curt response to Mrs. Fisherman. Not that she blamed him, but manners prevented her from doing as she wished and following him out.

It meant suffering through another twenty minutes of questions concerning Lord Derebourne before Mrs. Fisherman woke her husband and the family took their leave. What did his lordship like to eat, what was his favorite color, how long had Lord Derebourne been a widower followed by an interrogation about the twins.

Claire kept her answers as vague as possible, saying only that she didn't know the man very well as they had not had much contact since his arrival.

She thought it best not to mention the two searing kisses they had shared or that they had seen each other's toes. The satisfied gleam in the woman's eyes when Claire admitted she didn't know the marquess very well grated. What right did Mrs. Fisherman have to try and put a claim on Chase?

Claire wanted to shout at the woman to give over, that there was a better chance of falling through a fairy ring than Chase marrying Rhonda. Her heart went out to the girl, and she wished there was some way she could help Rhonda and Bobby. When the back of the Fisherman's carriage finally disappeared from sight, she went inside to find the traitorous rat that had jumped ship and abandoned her to the clutches of a determined Mrs. Fisherman.

"You may enter," a cautious voice responded when she knocked on the door, and then she was certain she heard a muttered, "As long as you are not Mrs. Fisherman."

If only she had the gift of mimicry. It would serve him right if she could impersonate Mrs. Fisherman's voice. She opened the door and entered, preparing to tell him how she felt about his abandonment. Before she could speak, he gave her a boyish grin and her eyes fixated on his dimple.

"You are here to chastise me for leaving you alone with the dragon and rightly so. I'm sorry, Claire, but I just couldn't take any more. It makes me angry every time she's rude to you. I had to leave before I spoke my mind."

Warmth spread through her. No one had ever cared enough to get angry on her behalf. All right then, maybe he wasn't a rat. And she really did like his dimple.

"Apology accepted." Grinning, she added, "She really is awful, isn't she?"

He shuddered. "Indeed. Have a seat and visit with me for a few minutes."

Since she wasn't at the Ignore Him stage, she accepted his offer. "I feel sorry for Rhonda."

"As do I. She's the shyest girl I've ever met, but she seems nice enough."

Claire nodded. "She is very sweet. You do know Mrs. Fisherman is determined to have you for her daughter."

Another shudder. "Not in this lifetime. It doesn't appear to me Miss Fisherman agrees with her mother, or is that only wishful thinking on my part?"

"No, you're right. You scare Rhonda nearly to death. She's in love with Bobby, the blacksmith's son. He's as shy as she, but he finally found the courage to ask Mr. Fisherman for her hand and was denied. It's too bad, really, as they suit each other very well."

"Why don't they elope to Gretna Green then? That's what I would do if I were them."

Claire hadn't considered such a thing. In their world it would be a scandal, but for Bobby and Rhonda, it was the perfect solution. "Mrs. Fisherman would be furious, but I don't think the vicar would be terribly upset. I think he only denied Bobby because of Mrs. Fisherman."

Claire chewed on her bottom lip as she considered the merits of dropping a few hints to Rhonda and Bobby.

"Don't do that," he said gruffly.

She looked at him in puzzlement. "Do what?"

"That thing you do with your lips."

"It bothers you?" Well, this was interesting. Unfortunate for him she had this new knowledge.

"You might say that."

She suppressed a smile and chewed on her bottom lip.

"Claire."

The growl of his voice sent heat to places she hadn't given much thought to before. She'd never known a man's voice—the right man's voice—could make her want things she had never thought to want.

Giving him a reprieve for now, she asked, "You told Mrs. Fisherman your mother was arriving tonight. Is she?"

"No, tomorrow as I said. I only told the dragon that to keep her from moving in."

"Will she like me, do you think? Your mother that is."

"I assure you, she will. Lady Anne has little patience with the Mrs. Fisherman's of the world and will, believe me, extinguish the dragon's flame. You she'll like, so stop worrying about my mother."

Of course, she would worry about his mother. It might mean the end of her plan if Lady Anne didn't like her. "I hope you're right. I had best go have a room made ready for her before I meet Bensey for tea."

"Claire," he said when she reached the door.

"Yes?"

"Take that ugly cap off. Burn it and change your gown."

She walked back to him, leaned down and gave the arrogant lord a quick kiss. "Thank you for everything."

****

What the bloody hell did Claire mean by everything? Chase sincerely wanted to know so he could continue doing whatever everything was. This new need to see her happy concerned him. Did it mean he was developing feelings for her?

With Teresa, it had been love at first sight—for him, anyway. That hadn't turned out so well. If there was something developing between him and Claire besides lust, then he wanted to take it slow until he was certain he could trust her.

She wouldn't intentionally hurt him, but then neither had Teresa wanted to. He was only now reaching the point where he could think of his wife without feeling profound grief or deep anger. The urge to pack up the boys and race back to London warred with wanting to put a claim on Claire.

She might believe she felt something for him, but he was the first man in her life to give her attention and treat her with respect. Therein was his problem. She had been practically a child when she married and had never had a Season. How could she know her true feelings without having the experience of having other men dance and flirt with her? She'd never been courted, never admired.

Well, he admired her and desired her, that much was certain. Could he come to love her? Probably. If he offered for her, what would happen the first time he took her to Town?

What if she found her true love? The pain of loving a woman who loved another was something he never wanted to experience again. If Claire was developing a tendre for him, how could he know for certain it wasn't only a passing infatuation?

There was only one solution. He would take her to London when her mourning ended and would court her while giving her the opportunity to experience the attentions of other men. Not only did he need to be sure of her, but she must know beyond doubt she wanted him for a husband.

The fact that he'd like to pummel those faceless men into the ground was telling, he supposed. Fortunately for him, he had the advantage of several weeks to begin his campaign. And begin it he would, starting tonight. His lips curved into a smile as he headed upstairs to find his sons.

They had a party to plan.

The twins bounced with excitement over the surprise for Lady Claire. Chase sent Bensey off to the conservatory at four with his promise not to reveal their secret. "I'll come down in thirty minutes, and you will excuse yourself so you can complete your project. No hints to Lady Claire, mind you."

"I won't, Father," Bensey said and left.

Chase sent Mr. Edwards off with instructions for the housekeeper and the cook. Anders left to talk to Claire's maid. Chase sat next to Harry and they went to work on their part of the plan.

****

"Have you ever been to Kew Gardens?" Claire asked Bensey, amused when he launched into the history of the gardens. He proved to be quite entertaining and she was enjoying their time together. He paused long enough to take a drink of his lemonade before continuing his story of how Fredrick, the Prince of Wales, had begun to design the gardens in 1730.

He trailed off and gave her a shy smile. "Father

says I sometimes get carried away, Lady Claire. I don't mean to, but I like talking to you."

"Thank you, Bensey. I like talking to you, too. It's perfectly all right if you get carried away when we are together. I didn't know the story of Kew Gardens and find it fascinating."

She couldn't imagine a sweeter boy. Although the servants couldn't tell them apart, Claire had no trouble knowing which was which. Bensey had a soft sweetness to him, and Harry had a worldly edge that was missing in Bensey.

"I forgot to answer your question, Lady Claire. I have never been to Kew Gardens, but I have a book about them and it has pictures."

"That's good, but it isn't the same as seeing the gardens for yourself. You'll have to get your father to take you sometime."

"I'm to take him where?"

The deep masculine voice teased her senses and gave her heart a reason to beat faster. Chase came to stand in front of her, smiling down at her. *It's only a dimple*, she told her silly, thumping heart.

"Lady Claire said you should take me to Kew Gardens, Father."

"Did she now? Would you like that?"

"Oh yes, I would like it very much."

"Then we'll have to go someday. Perhaps Lady Claire would also like to see the gardens."

Bensey turned hopeful eyes her way. "Would you, Lady Claire? I could tell you all about the gardens. Lady Claire said she doesn't mind if I get carried away, Father."

Claire glanced at Chase to see laughter in his eyes.

Did mothers and fathers share these intimate moments when their children amused them? Never having witnessed her parents doing so, she wouldn't know.

She turned back to Bensey. "I would love to see the gardens with you."

He jumped up in excitement. "When? When can we go?"

Chase rested his hand on Bensey's head. "I don't know, son. We'll talk about it later."

"When later?"

"I don't know that either, but soon, all right? There are things you need to do. Are you finished with your visit?"

When he gave Bensey a meaningful look, Claire wondered what message had just passed between them.

"Yes, Father."

"Then thank Lady Claire for inviting you to tea."

Bensey dutifully thanked her and was gone before she could respond. Chase took the seat Bensey vacated. "There will be no peace until I take him to Kew Gardens. Each time he starts in on it, I'm going to send him to you as the blame for it rests squarely on your shoulders," he said in an accusatory voice, then ruined the reprimand by waggling his eyebrows and grinning.

Playing along with the game, she sighed. "You are a hard man, my lord."

His eyes gleamed with devilish glee. "Oh, Claire, if you only knew how hard I am."

She sensed there was an insinuation in his words, but had no idea what. At her puzzled expression, he burst into laughter.

"I don't understand what's so funny," she said, which caused him to laugh harder. His mirth was contagious and she joined him. She just wished she knew why.

"Ah, Claire, such innocence. It really is quite appealing. Perhaps I'll explain it to you some time, but not today. Did you enjoy your visit with Bensey?"

"I did, very much so. Your sons are wonderful. I never knew children could be so interesting."

"Harry and Bensey are not your typical children, and I think they are more interesting than most their age. But then, I'm their father and I'm supposed to think so. It pleases me that you like them."

Actually, she loved them—wanted to claim them as hers. "I like them very much. It's amazing how they look exactly alike, yet are so different from each other."

"Thank God," he said with feeling. "Can you imagine two of either one, especially Harry?"

Recalling she was in the Advance and Retreat stage of her plan, she slid her hand over his. "Heavens, no, but they are perfect as they are."

His gaze followed the movement of her hand before lifting and colliding with hers. Time stilled as they stared into each other's eyes. There was such heat in his that it was a wonder she didn't burn to ashes where she sat. Warmth pooled in her stomach, and then to lower parts—her most private parts—making her ache. Her gaze fell on his mouth, lingering there.

"Claire," he whispered.

She chewed on her bottom lip in indecision. Advance or Retreat?

"I warned you not to do that."

What was she doing? He stole her ability to think about anything but surrendering to him. It was time to retreat until she could find her mind again. A mistake now and her campaign would be lost. She gave herself a mental shake and stood. He rose, blocking her escape route.

"Are you leaving?"

She nodded, afraid if she spoke she'd beg him to kiss her, maybe nuzzle her neck.

"Not before I do this."

"Do what?" Her voice sounded raspy, not hers at all. Perhaps she was getting sick.

He trailed the back of his hand down her cheek. "This."

His mouth touched hers, and she slid her eyes closed as she swayed toward him. This wasn't their first kiss, but it wasn't the same as before. There was an intensity from him that was new. He settled his hand on the curve of her hip, the heat from his palm seeping into her skin. Claire grabbed onto his waist to keep from sinking into a boneless heap at his feet.

A low hum sounded in his throat and he pressed his tongue between her lips seeking entrance. She craved his taste—wanted it more than anything—but the small amount of brain still working screamed at her to retreat.

"No." She put her hands on his chest and pushed away.

"My apologies, I thought you were agreeable" he said and stepped aside.

Because there was hurt in his eyes, she offered an explanation. "I was…I am, but it occurs to me this isn't the time or place." She smiled and added, "It was a very nice kiss, and I'm not sorry so no apologies are necessary. Thank you, my lord."

As she walked away, she made a little wager with herself that he would have something to say by the time she reached the doorway.

"Claire."

She stopped and put her hand on the door, but didn't turn. "Yes?"

"Stop lording me."

"As you wish, my lord." She grinned and left before he could reply.

Returning to her room, Claire found Maggie waiting for her, a warm bath at the ready. "What is this?"

Maggie rolled her eyes. "A bath, my lady. Surely, you have seen one before."

Claire rolled her eyes right back. "You well know what I mean."

Maggie handed her a piece of paper and Claire unfolded the note.

Lady Claire,

Stop questioning Maggie. Follow her instructions and prepare for a special evening.

Chase, Bensey and Harry

She read the note again. If it had only been signed by Chase, she might have melted into a puddle. Bensey and Harry had also signed their names, so this wasn't the beginning of a seduction by their father, but something else entirely. Intrigued, she put the note on her vanity.

"Do with me what you will, Maggie."

Maggie nodded. "I thought you might agree, my lady. Turn around and let me unbutton your gown so we can get you into this bath. It's violet scented by order of Lord Derebourne."

Claire glanced at her maid. "He knows my scent?"

"His lordship was very specific, so yes, I imagine

he does."

As Maggie unbuttoned her gown, Claire considered how much attention he had paid to her without her realizing it. She stepped into the bathwater and all she could think about was him. Her lips still tingled from his kiss. What would it feel like to lie with him, to feel him inside her?

Would it be the same feeling of duty as it had with Thomas? She'd never regretted the nights Thomas came to her because it resulted in Andrew. But it had never been pleasurable and had sometimes hurt. The intriguing thought that it would somehow be different with Chase teased her mind. The warm water relaxed her and she closed her eyes. Her mind drifted to Chase and the three kisses he had given her. She wanted more.

After her bath, Maggie performed a miracle with Claire's long straight hair, twisting and curling it into a soft, pleasing style with curls flowing down her back. When Maggie held up a pale blue silk gown, one Claire hadn't worn in almost a year, she shook her head.

"No, Maggie, I cannot wear that. It would cause too much talk among the servants."

"Lord Derebourne had a word with Smithfield and told him to tell all of us that anyone who dared to have a wrong word to say about you would be dismissed immediately. Besides, my lady, you have always been kind, and there is not a one of us who would want to see you hurt, so there is nothing to worry about. Now, hold up your arms."

Claire's eyes stung. To have someone care enough to protect her shouldn't make her want to cry. Maggie slipped the gown over her head, careful not to disturb her hair. She had worn black for so long that it was hard to reconcile the woman in the mirror with the image of the grieving widow of the past year.

"Perfect," Maggie said from behind her. Her maid picked up a bottle of Claire's violet scent. "Mustn't forget this." She dabbed some behind Claire's ears and on her wrists.

Claire fastened a pair of blue sapphire earrings on her ears and decided to forgo the matching necklace. She liked the simplicity of the gown without any adornments other than the earrings.

"I'm ready," she said.

Maggie glanced at the clock on the mantel. "You have ten more minutes before you can go down. Lord Derebourne said you were to arrive at precisely six."

Claire's excitement grew. What were the Warren men up to? The ten minutes seemed like an hour, but at three minutes to six, Maggie told her to go as it would take at least that much time to walk to the conservatory.

Claire resisted the urge to run down the stairs in her eagerness to experience the first surprise of her life.

Chapter Thirteen

The twins awaited her outside the conservatory wearing identical smiles on their faces. Claire grinned at the sight of the adorable boys dressed as little men.

She curtseyed. "Good evening."

The boys sketched a most proper bow. "Good evening, my lady," Bensey said. "We have planned a special evening for you because you are our special friend." He turned to Harry. "It's your turn now."

"I know that, Bensey."

Claire stifled a laugh. What would Harry say?

"You look ever so lovely, Lady Claire," Harry said. Bensey vigorously nodded. "Bensey and I would be honored to escort you inside." Each held out an arm.

"I'm delighted to have two such handsome gentlemen as my escorts."

There would come a day when young ladies would near swoon to have those smiles turned their way. She yearned to be around to witness it. Although it was dusk and light still came through the conservatory glass, candles had been placed along the walkway forming a path to their destination. Her heart beat a rapid tattoo as they led her past fruit trees and blooming flowers, their sweet scents filling the air. Escorting her around a corner, the twins led her into a fantasy land.

She stopped. "Oh, my."

"Do you like it?" Bensey asked.

"It's beautiful," she said. And so was the man standing in the center of it all.

He made a courtly bow. "Welcome, my lady."

Claire stepped forward, stopped a few feet from him and curtseyed. "I am honored, my lord."

She pivoted in a slow circle taking it all in. An area had been cleared and decorated. Walls of lush trees and large bushes gave the space an intimate feel. To her left, a sitting area complete with sofa, chairs and a low table had been formed. An exquisite orchid and candles of various heights decorated the table.

To her right, a dinner service as formal as any she had seen—with linens, china and crystal goblets—were set out. The centerpiece was another beautiful orchid surrounded by candles. Behind the dining table, a long sideboard held platters of food.

On a two foot high platform set back in the trees, the twin's tutor, Mr. Edwards, sat with a violin across his lap. He inclined his head in acknowledgment, picked up the instrument and began to play. Completing her circle, Claire faced the marquess. The night was beautiful, he was beautiful and no one before him had created an evening just for her. Words escaped her.

His warm smile said he understood. The boys came to stand beside him—the three Warren men her heart wanted to claim for itself.

Chase held out his hand. "Come, my lady."

She placed her hand in his. He led her to the sofa, settling down next to her. Bensey and Harry took seats across from them. Smithfield stepped through the wall of trees bearing a tray. He poured champagne for her and Chase, gave the boys glasses of punch, then disappeared back into the foliage.

Chase lifted a chin toward the twins. "I believe Bensey and Harry have something they want to say." The boys stood and lifted their glasses. Bensey began to speak, but Harry nudged him. "I'm supposed to go first this time." Bensey snapped his mouth closed. Harry cleared his throat. "To Lady Claire, a splendid lady who talks to horses. I'm ever so glad to have you as my friend."

Bensey stepped forward and gave her the shy smile she adored. "To Lady Claire, who doesn't mind when I get carried away. I like having you as my friend."

Claire walked around the table, gathered both boys in her arms and hugged them. Bensey stiffened under her touch and she dropped her arms. "I'm honored by your gift of friendship." She didn't know what they planned for the remainder of the evening, but if the night ended now, she would still consider it one of the most special times of her life.

"My turn." Chase said. "This evening is dedicated to an extraordinary lady whom my sons and I admire greatly. May you always be our friend."

The tears she had been fighting welled up and one rolled down her face. Chase grinned, handing her his handkerchief. "I came prepared."

As the violin played softly in the background, she wiped her eyes, touched beyond imagining.

"Are you sad, Lady Claire?" Bensey asked.

Laughter bubbled up. "Heavens no, Bensey, these are happy tears. May I say a few words?" Three heads nodded. "To the Warren men. It is an honor to count you as my dearest friends." She clicked glasses with each and took a sip of her champagne. "Thank you for tonight. I'll never forget it."

The next few minutes were spent chatting while they finished their drinks. Harry kept sneaking looks at the food. Claire glanced at Chase to see if he noticed. He smiled and gave her a little nod. The gesture made her feel like a part of their family. If it ever came true, she would love them fiercely and forever.

"Shall we have our dinner?" Chase asked.

The boys stood so fast she almost laughed.

"I take that as a yes," he said.

He offered his arm, and Claire placed her hand over his as he led her to the table. A deep yearning overtook her. This was where she belonged, by this man's side.

Once seated, Smithfield emerged from the trees and served them. The dinner consisted of cold foods: a selection of sliced cold meats, bread, cheeses, boiled eggs, pickled relish and fruits. Music played in the background and the conversation flowed easily among them as they talked of things that interested the twins. Dessert was slices of cake and berry pudding. "Enjoy your pudding," he murmured

Claire blushed, remembering the show she had put on for him. If the boys weren't present, she would have been tempted to do it again just to see the heat in his eyes.

Tomorrow she would ignore him, but tonight was for her and she was going to be selfish. She would take his attentions, his heated looks, his burning touches on her skin, and when next alone in her cold bed she would wrap the memories of this magical evening around her and snuggle into their warmth.

The last piece of cake disappeared into Harry's mouth, and Smithfield appeared to remove their plates.

He refilled their champagne glasses before vanishing back into the shrubbery. "Can we give it to her now, Father?" Bensey asked.

"I think now is a good time," Chase said.

Bensey and Harry jumped up and held out their hands. They led her back to the sitting area where a covered easel stood. It had not been there earlier, and like everything else this evening its appearance seemed magical.

The boys moved to stand on each side of the easel. Chase stood off to the side and nodded to the twins. Claire sat on the sofa and clasped her hands in an attempt to contain her excitement. Harry held up a piece of paper and clearing his throat, began to read.

> *A poem to Lady Claire*
> *She has the prettiest hair*
> *And big blue eyes*
> *That tell no lies*
> *And her smile*
> *Hides no guile*
> *And that is why*
> *Father, Bensey and I*
> *Think*
> *She is a splendid lady to have as our special friend*

Harry finished the poem with a big grin. "Father helped a little, but I mostly wrote it myself. Do you like it, my lady?"

Claire blinked against the burning in her eyes. "Oh yes, Harry. It's a marvelous poem."

He handed her the paper. "Do you want to keep it?"

Claire took the poem and held it against her heart.

"I'll treasure it always." And she would. It was her first poem from a gentleman. "Lady Claire, I have a present for you, too," Bensey said.

"I hope you have painted me a picture."

He pulled the cover off the easel. At the sight of the picture, she gave a delighted laugh. He had painted her and Amira in caricature. Claire was wearing her leather breeches and having a conversation with her mare. He'd somehow made it look as if Amira was speaking to her. Claire's head was inclined as if listening intently to the mare. Underneath the painting, the caption read, *A Conversation with Amira.*

"Bensey, it is marvelously clever." She kissed each boy on the cheek and smiled to herself when wide grins appeared on their faces. "My poem and my painting are the best gifts ever. Thank you, both. A thousand times, thank you."

Her heart ached to call these boys her sons. She wanted to stand beside their father and watch with him as the twins grew into young men. She wanted to cry with them when they were sad and laugh with them in happiness

"Father has something he would like to ask you now, Lady Claire," Harry said. "Ask her, Father. You promised you would show us how it is done."

How what was done? Chase stepped forward and sketched a bow. It was entirely possible her heart was going to pound itself out of her body and land at his feet.

"May I have this dance, my lady?"

Yes. Oh, Yes. She hadn't known what to expect, but it wasn't this. "It would be my pleasure, my lord." She placed her hand in his.

Sandra Owens

The evening had grown dark and candles flickered among the foliage, the perfume of flowers and rich earth scented the air. The beginning notes of a waltz lifted from the violin and he slid his hand down her spine to her lower back. Goose bumps rose on her arms. Magic claimed the night, enchanting her and the lonely, empty place inside her was all but forgotten.

Chase twirled her around the floor while his mind and heart argued. His mind had only one thought. Mine. His heart wanted to believe it, but feared the what ifs. What if it was only a passing infatuation on her part? What if her true love came along—her own Harry—and stole her from him? What if he put his heart in her hands and she dropped it?

He was only now beginning to look forward to each new day and he knew, just knew this woman had the power to destroy him for good. Throughout the evening she had charmed his sons. She would be a good mother to them, might one day love them as he did.

But he had to be sure of her, would not risk her hurting the boys. He would keep to his plan and take her to London. It would be a test and though it might be unfair to not explain his reasoning, he believed it was the only way he could be sure of her.

"I feel like I am in a fairy tale tonight," she said. "You and the twins have made this a night I'll never forget."

A glow of happiness surrounded her. Her blue eyes sparkled and her cheeks were rose tinted. The angry, pale woman who had greeted him on arrival was nowhere in sight. He liked this woman.

Chase twirled her around and brought them close to the boys. Bensey had his sketchpad out, his hand

164

busy drawing. Harry intently watched he and Claire dance, most likely memorizing the steps. The boy was going to be dangerous to the ladies when he came of age, Chase thought with fatherly pride.

"If this is a fairy tale, then you are the princess," he said. "I and my two fellow knights will slay your dragons and rescue you from the evil witch." She gave him her courtesan's laugh and he felt it down to his toes.

"Oh, Sir Knight, such chivalry must be rewarded. Pray tell, what is your desire?"

My desire is to dance you into my bed and to spend hours, perhaps days, loving you.

"Would you gift me with a kiss, Princess?" He pulled her closer and put his mouth next to her ear. "After my fellow knights are abed and we have the night to ourselves." A shiver passed through her and he forced himself not to claim his kiss right then.

"A simple kiss, Sir Knight? Not gold or jewels?"

"A simple kiss implies a peck on the lips, Princess. Is that what you want?"

Her eyes darkened. "No," she whispered.

Chase was in danger of forgetting his manners, throwing her over his shoulder and carrying her off to bed. He glanced at Mr. Edwards and nodded. The music trailed off and he led her into one last twirl.

"I think it's time to send my wee knights to bed." He tugged at the front of his coat in an effort to hide his erection. "Go see what Bensey is drawing, and I'll retrieve our champagne."

He needed a moment to regain his control. Bless Smithfield, he had left the champagne bottle out. Chase filled a glass and downed it, then refilled two glasses.

Behind him, Claire exclaimed over Bensey's drawing and then he heard her promise Harry she would dance with him the next time they had a party.

"Would you like me to get the boys to bed?" Mr. Edwards asked from beside him.

God, yes. "Please." Claire gave the boys a good night kiss on their foreheads. His sons approached him and he knelt, placing a hand on each of their shoulders.

"Did you enjoy tonight?"

"Oh yes, ever so much" they said in unison.

Chase marveled at how often the twins said the same thing at the exact same moment. "Good. I'm positive we made Lady Claire happy tonight, but it's time you were in bed." He gave each a kiss on the cheek and told them he loved them.

Mr. Edwards led them away and he turned to Claire. She stood in the middle of the room, hands clasped in front of her, her features soft in the candlelight. Her lips curved in a shy smile.

Picking up the glasses of champagne, he prowled toward her. He promised himself he wouldn't bed her tonight, but he was about to come damn close. As long as he kept his breeches on, she would be safe. There would be no regrets between them if his courtship didn't go as he hoped.

At the point the tips of his shoes disappeared under the hem of her gown, he stopped and handed her a glass of champagne. He clicked his glass to hers. "To a beautiful woman. Thank you, Claire, for your care of my sons." Why the wistful smile?

"How could I not? They are lovely boys."

Taking her hand, he led her to the sofa, sat next to her and angled his body toward her. He placed his arm along the back and his fingers found a strand of silky hair.

"I like to think Andrew would have grown to be as interesting as the twins."

The reason for her melancholy smile? Talking about her son wasn't how he expected the evening to go, but she had never talked about him before. Perhaps she needed to.

"Did he look like you?"

She gave a little humorless laugh. "He had my eyes, but otherwise, he was the very image of Thomas. I'm so afraid one day I'll forget what he looked like."

Chase took the champagne out of her hands and set both glasses on the table, noticing the picture Bensey had drawn of the two of them waltzing. Her face was alight with joy and his expression—well, he looked as if he were about to devour her. His son saw too much.

"Come here." He pulled her into his arms. "Tell me about Andrew."

Tears pooled in her eyes, and she buried her face in his chest. "There isn't much to tell. I only had him for two wonderful weeks and then he was gone. He had a fever and Thomas wouldn't let me comfort him."

She stopped talking and he waited for her to continue. He rested his chin on her head. When she remained quiet, he asked, "Was Thomas afraid you would become sick?"

She made a guttural sound. "If that was the reason, I might be able to forgive him. No, I was only allowed one hour a day with Andrew. Thomas feared if I spent more time with him, I would turn his heir into a Mama's boy. Two weeks—one hour a day. Fourteen hours to remember my son by."

"My God, Claire." He pulled her onto his lap, wrapped his arms around her and held her tight. What a damn fool Derebourne had been.

"Now you see why I'm afraid I'll forget. My memories of him are so few and precious, and even now, it's hard to picture my baby's face. I used to sneak into his nursery in the early morning hours and watch him sleep.

"I didn't dare pick him up. If he woke up and cried, his nurse would have reported me to Thomas. I would put my finger on his hand and his tiny fingers would wrap around mine and hold tight. I would imagine he knew it was me...that it made him feel protected to know I was there. But it didn't work. I couldn't keep him safe."

The tears she had been holding back came and she sobbed into his chest. His eyes burned and he squeezed them shut. He'd lost his child, too, and didn't know which was worse—to never have held him or to have been given two short weeks to love him. There was nothing he could say to make it better, so he just held her while she cried.

She quieted and he tilted his head. Her eyes were closed and he wondered if she had fallen asleep. But no, she slid her hand up to his neck. "Kiss me, Chase. Make me feel. Please."

He understood and couldn't have refused her if his life depended on it. The kiss began as an offer of comfort, soft and gentle. She wasn't having it and need slammed through him when she slipped her hand under his waistcoat.

He just had to remember to keep his breeches on.

Chapter Fourteen

Claire needed his touch, needed to know she wasn't only a figment of her imagination. She existed, she lived and breathed. The worst thing possible had happened to her, and somehow she'd survived. Now, life just might offer her a chance at happiness after all.

His lips brushed over hers, warm and teasing. Pulling his shirt out of his breeches, she slid her hand under the crisp linen. His belly was hard and hot and she wanted her hands everywhere at once. Wanted to memorize his planes and angles so she could say to herself, I know him. Trailing her fingers up his side, she counted each rib, felt the indentation between the bones. She moved her hand to his chest to feel the beat of his heart against her palm.

His mouth teased hers with feathery kisses and little nips. He appeared to be in no hurry, didn't seem to have the same aching need as she. She wanted his breath harsh and hot on her skin, to know he desired her as much as she did him.

She wanted…she didn't know what. This need inside her was new and unexplored, but he could show her. There had to be more than a quick lift of her gown accompanied by a few grunts on the man's part, leaving her messy and sometimes sore.

She skimmed her fingers over a nipple and suppressed a satisfied smile when he hissed against her lips. In an instant, his kiss turned demanding and his tongue invaded her mouth.

Yes, this is what she wanted. She'd never dreamed a man's tongue—his tongue—in her mouth could build a fire in the deepest parts of her, could make her tremble with want. He moved a hand to the side of her face, the other finding its way to the curve of a breast.

Tonight, she'd purposely not worn a corset, thus the only barrier between his palm and her skin was her silk gown and chemise. Thin as it was, it was too much. She wanted skin to skin. His erection pressed against her bottom and every single inch of her body throbbed with want.

This had never happened before.

Because of Thomas, she had believed having a man inside her was a thing to be endured. The duty of a wife to her husband. When Thomas had come to her bed, her mind turned to the next day's training session, planning which horse she would work with. After Andrew was born, she had gratefully been relieved of her wifely duties.

When they thought her asleep, she overheard the doctor tell Thomas that it would be three months before she could have marital relations again. Immensely pleased by that information, she had fallen into a restful sleep. She now understood it had only required this man to see how foolishly naïve she had been.

The hand cradling her face moved to the buttons on the back of her gown. When he had them undone, he slid the gown and chemise off her shoulder. Freeing a breast, he cupped it in his hand. When he flicked his thumb over her nipple, the pleasure was so intense she gave a startled jolt.

"Easy," he said with a soft chuckle. He picked her up as if she weighed no more than a newborn kitten and turned her so she straddled him. "Ah, perfect." His lips found the tip of her breast, sucking a nipple into his mouth while his hand skimmed over her back in a lover's caress.

Oh, God. Oh, God. There must be strings attached to her breast and running through her body. With his mouth, he pulled on the strings sending tremulous vibrations on a journey through her bloodstream. How ignorant she had been believing this should be done shamefully in the dark.

She was an adventuress exploring exotic new lands. Closing her eyes, she let him take her to a new world of sensual bliss.

With his mouth still latched to her breast, he tugged the other sleeve off her shoulder, and she slipped her arms out of her gown. She almost cried out in protest when he pulled away. But no, his mouth moved to her other breast, and all was well.

"Don't want it to feel neglected," he murmured.

Claire gave a breathless little laugh. "No, we can't have that."

Apparently, there were strings attached to this one, too. The ache in her private place intensified to an unbearable need and she rubbed against his erection. The friction of his trousers, the feel of his hardness scraped against her. A pressure built inside until she burned as hot as molten lava. Moaning, she pressed her face into his neck and rubbed harder against him.

"Claire." He let go of her breast, pulled her face to his and put his mouth on hers.

Just that. Claire. But it was the way he said it, like

hers was a sacred name, one to be whispered in reverence. She wanted to say to him, *I love you*, but he wasn't ready to hear it so she held the words in her heart.

Oh, dear God. She was so close to something new and breathtaking. Something wondrous.

Chase squeezed his eyes closed and fought for control. The world as he knew it reeled on its axis. This woman was burrowing her way under his skin whether he wanted her to or not. She was so incredibly responsive and sensual. Christ, the things he could teach her if she belonged to him. He wanted to wrap her heat around him and never let go. A long suppressed yearning to love and be loved by someone special made itself known.

When she rubbed against his erection he knew he could have her, could remove his breeches and sink into her slick wetness. And he wanted to, badly. He slid his hand under her skirt and cradled her bottom. She stilled.

"No, don't stop," he rasped against her mouth.

"All right," she said, and blessedly began to move. He slid a finger into her sheath. She was tight, dripping and hot. What would it feel like to bury himself deep inside her? She wouldn't stop him.

No regrets, he reminded himself. He had made many promises in his life and had kept them all. He would keep this one. His breeches would stay buttoned.

Chase sucked her tongue into his mouth as his fingers mimicked the movements his cock ached to make. She moaned long and deep telling him she was close to release. She gasped for air and he pulled away from her mouth, wanting to watch her reach her first ever climax, wanted to see on her face what he had brought her to. Her eyes turned vague and she rubbed herself over his cock, hard and fast.

"Oh, God," she said and he happily fell off the cliff with her. It was one of the most incredible climaxes he had ever experienced. And he had kept his promise and kept his clothes on. His laugh startled him. Never before had he exploded in his trousers—hadn't been this green when he was a green boy. She had no idea the affect she had on him. That was probably a good thing.

Still breathing hard, she pushed away from his shoulder, hurt in her eyes. "Why are you laughing?"

He couldn't tell her the truth. She would never understand. "Why do most people laugh?" he asked instead.

Her expression turned wary. "Because something's funny?"

"Or because they are happy." He trailed a finger across her soft lips.

"Oh," she said and smiled.

Her smile went straight to his gut. It crossed his mind to say to hell with London and claim her here and now. But he had to be sure for his sake and for the twins. She already had the power to hurt him and that scared the hell out of him.

"Does this mean we don't have to go to London?"

He put his hand behind her neck and pulled her to him for a last kiss, then gently pushed her away.

"We need to talk. Move over and I'll refill our glasses."

The light faded from her eyes. She scooted away and pulled her dress up, covering her beautiful breasts. Wordlessly, she turned her back to him and he buttoned her gown. She sat back on the sofa, putting space between them.

Her hair was mussed, her lips swollen from their kisses and her gown wrinkled. She looked like a woman who had been thoroughly ravished. He hadn't thoroughly ravished her, but bloody hell, he wanted to. He hardened to life at the thought. The devil, he couldn't be ready to go again so soon. His cock begged to differ.

She watched him like a skittish animal unsure of what was about to happen, and Chase regretted the caution he saw in her eyes. He didn't want to wound her, he only needed to be sure he wasn't a passing infatuation. How to explain it to her?

Standing, he picked up their glasses, went to the table and poured more champagne. He was going to have to tell her about Teresa and their marriage. His wife was the last person he wanted to talk about after what he'd just shared with Claire, but it was necessary.

He sighed and returned to the sofa. Handing her the champagne, he wondered how to begin. He walked a fine line by not telling her why he had to go through with his plan. But she needed to understand his motivations without knowing he wanted her for his wife. Shying away from talk of Teresa, he decided to address the issue of London.

"Claire, going to London is something you need to do for yourself. You have lived a sheltered life, too sheltered, and I don't think you can possibly know your own mind until you have experienced a Season in town."

Her eyes flashed angry sparks and she opened her mouth to speak. He held up his hand. "Please, allow me to finish and then I'll listen to everything you have to say." She nodded, but the anger stayed in her eyes.

"Your father shielded you from life, allowing you no friends and no way to learn about yourself. You went from the overbearing protection of him to a husband when you were more of a child than a woman.

"Even after four years of marriage, you have no life experiences to build your foundation on. Imagine a table laden down with all sorts of enticing foods. How can you truly know which treat to choose when you've never been allowed a taste of anything but the bread?" He winced. Did that even make sense?

"I want you," she whispered and coward that he was, he pretended not to hear her.

Staring at the flicker of the candle's flame, he returned to the past. "I loved my wife, Claire. The moment I set eyes on her, I said to myself, she is the one."

Claire flinched at his soft words, shamed by her jealousy of a dead woman. Knowing he had more to say, she remained quiet.

Sometimes with a damaged horse she would patiently wait for him to put his past abuse up against the safe haven she offered. He would tentatively take one step toward her and stop. *I'm wanting to trust you, but I've trusted before and look where it got me.* It was his decision and she could do nothing more than wait for him to take a leap of faith.

So, she waited for Chase to take the leap and trust her with his hurts.

He glanced at her, then turned back to stare at the candle. Sometimes the horse couldn't look at her either before he faced the past and put it behind him. Chase had no idea how much patience she had. She guessed a full three minutes passed before he began to speak again.

"Teresa was a year older than me and the sister of my closest friend. If you know anything of a gentleman's code of honor then you know one doesn't covet his friend's sister, especially when that friend is a future duke. So I kept my love for her hidden, but it was here."

He put his fist to his heart and glared at her. She wanted to smile, but didn't. How amusing it was that men and male horses apparently had the same need for bluster. In her experience, a mare was always able to see the bright side of things faster than her male counterparts. That said much about females in general.

"Do you know what it means when someone refers to a man as a rogue?"

She nodded.

"Well, when she fell in love with Lord Hollingsworth and married him, I lived up to the definition. In an effort to forget her, I bedded every unmarried, experienced woman who looked twice at me. It is to my shame that I can't remember many of their faces or names."

Chase stared at her as if daring her to be offended. He had been hurt deeply, and even then, he had held to a code of honor. She didn't think he realized he'd just told her he hadn't touched married women or innocents. When she made no comment, he sighed.

"Then something terrible happened. She and Lord Hollingsworth were set upon by cutthroats as they were leaving France. Her beloved Harry was killed, and unspeakable things were done to her. She lost the baby she was carrying. I never wished for something like that to happen, but it did and there she was, back in my life again."

Claire no longer felt jealous of his wife, only sadness for the woman who had lost so much and couldn't heal.

"Eventually we married. I knew she didn't love me the way I loved her. But she liked me and I was her friend. I thought..." His voice trembled. "I thought the day would come when she would. Love me, that is. It didn't."

His last two words were said so softly, she almost didn't hear them. She wanted to wrap her arms around him and comfort him the way he had her, but he needed to finish his story. The best thing she could do for him was to stay quiet and listen.

"We were going to have a baby, but then she died and took our child with her. The last word on her lips was Harry." He closed his eyes and a single tear rolled down his cheek.

With his last sentence, he gave her the reason for his pain. Now she could comfort him. She crawled onto his lap and laid her head on his chest. His arms came around her and held her so tight she almost couldn't breathe. She didn't care. He rested his chin on her head and she thought about what he had said. Like her, he'd lost a child. At least, she had held her baby in her arms. Her heart wept for him.

"After Teresa...after she died, I made a decision to never marry again. I swore I would never be that vulnerable again."

She understood him now. His choice of the word vulnerable had been telling. It had been awful his wife had died, but that wasn't the root of his pain. No, he feared risking his heart and not having his love returned. Like her horses, he was going to have to believe she was his safe haven, to believe he could trust her with his heart.

"Do you understand, Claire?"

She did, better than he realized. But he didn't need to know that. Not yet. She lifted her head and smiled. "I think so. Thank you for telling me. But know this. I want you in my life and in my bed. Forever and a day."

Let him stew over that. She brushed her lips over his and before he could respond, she stood. "Good night, Chase." She picked up Bensey's drawing and left.

Forever and a day. If only he could believe her. This had been a strange night. Chase was drained, depleted in mind, body and soul. He hadn't wanted to become sentimental when speaking of Teresa. He had meant to talk in a voice devoid of emotion as if he'd been reading a text on the latest farm implements.

But she was just too good of a listener. She hadn't offered her opinion, hadn't tried to tell him his decision to not marry again was ridiculous. Smart lady that she was, she was leaving it up to him to come to that conclusion on his own.

Forever and a day. The words held an enchantment that promised an ending of happily ever after. After tonight, he was surer of his feelings for her. It wasn't love yet, but he believed he was headed in that direction. It wasn't love at first sight like it had been with Teresa, but he was damned glad.

He liked Claire and she fascinated him. For a certainty, there was desire on both their parts. If he were to marry again, he wanted a wife who desired him as much as he did her. No more cold nights sleeping alone while the woman he loved sent him back to his chamber after the rare nights she allowed him into her bed. As for Claire, any concerns he might have had there had been put to rest tonight.

Then there were his sons. He believed her care for them was true and not something she was doing to impress him. He didn't doubt she could grow to love them—a requirement he wouldn't compromise on.

The one thing holding him back, the reason he would proceed with caution, was his fear that she wasn't experienced enough to truly know he was the only one for her. It was the question he had to know the answer to.

So, nothing had changed. He would still take her to London and give her a Season, would introduce her to the best looking men, the richest men, and men with high ranking titles. If none turned her head then his heart would trust her.

She had put the words in his mind, and now he would accept nothing less from her than forever and a day.

Chapter Fifteen

After returning to her chamber, Claire donned her nightdress and curled up with Bensey's drawing on the window seat. Bensey had a true artist's eye and saw so much.

She studied her face first, seeing the happiness that shone from her eyes. It was the face of a woman in love. Bensey had seen it even if he was too young to understand, but had Chase?

She didn't think he had and she hoped she was right. It was too soon for him to know she loved him. It was all right for him to think she wanted him, that she desired him. But he didn't believe she had enough experience to know what she wanted and wouldn't trust her love for him. He could give her a Season in London this year and the next and the next. It wouldn't make any difference; she would still love him. Her heart knew what it wanted.

Holding the drawing up to the light, she studied the expression on Chase's face. He stared down at her as if he wanted to swallow her whole. Yes, there was lust, but something more. She thought it might be longing, but maybe that was only wishful thinking. He'd claimed to have taken many women to his bed and she was sure most of them, if not all, were more experienced than she.

Why had he held back tonight? He must have

known she would not have stopped him. He had given her a taste of pleasures she never knew existed and she wanted more. She wanted all of him. Should she continue on with her plan?

After careful consideration, she decided since she had come this far she should see the thing through to the end. But she would delay ignoring him for one day. It seemed wrong to start punishing him the day after he had trusted her with his hurts. Besides, his mother arrived tomorrow and it would be best she not act like a shrew toward Lady Anne's son on the lady's first day at Hillcrest.

Deciding she should go to bed and get some sleep, she stood and took the drawing to her bedside table, wanting Chase's image close to her while she slept. It made her feel like he was watching over her, keeping her safe.

****

Turning onto his back, Chase peered at the window. The gray light of dawn showed through the edges of the curtains. His sleep had not been restful. Dreams—half remembered now—had plagued him throughout the night. In one, he had been dancing with Teresa. He had twirled her around and when she faced him again she had turned into Claire. Disconcerting, that.

In another, he vaguely recalled something about riding Mischief up the steps and into White's. Why he would dream he rode the horse into his club, he hadn't a clue. There was one dream he wished he didn't remember. In it, he was attempting to draw a picture of a baby.

He turned over on his belly, pulled the pillow over

his head and tried to go back to sleep. *One hour of dreamless sleep, please*, he begged his muddled mind. Just as he dozed off, his bed shook. The pillow lifted from his head, and he opened one eye to see Harry ogling him.

"Are you awake, Father?"

"No." He pulled the pillow from Harry's grasp, covered his face and tried to ignore the sound of the boy's breathing. When it became obvious his son wasn't going away, he lifted the edge of the pillow and peered at his son.

Harry grinned. "Are you awake now?"

Chase sighed. "Why are you here, in my room, in the middle of the night?"

Harry scrunched his eyebrows together. "But it isn't the middle of the night."

"Close enough. What do you want, Harry?"

"It's time to meet Lady Claire for breakfast, and then I'm to have my lesson. Do you want to come with us?"

"No, I want to sleep. You go and have fun. Good bye."

"Why don't you want to come? I thought you liked Lady Claire."

Pray save him from enthusiastic children appearing at his bedside at dawn. "I do like her, but right now I like sleep more. You may have Lady Claire all to yourself this morning." He gave a limp wave with his hand. "Away with you now."

"Splendid," Harry exclaimed and took off.

Chase let the pillow fall back over his face and tried to return to sleep. Twenty minutes later, he realized that whatever chance he had of dozing off had disappeared with Harry's appearance at his bedside. The elusive extra hour of sleep was regrettable. He could have used it after his unsettled night. The blame for that rested on one particular woman.

I thought you liked Lady Claire, the boy had said. Chase snorted. "If you only knew, Harry."

Sitting up, he ran his hands through his hair and yawned. Well, if he was to be awake this early, it was only fair Anders join him. He stood and stretched, then padded to the bell pull, tugging on it more times than were necessary. After slipping on his dressing gown, he made himself comfortable in a wing chair and waited.

The door slammed open and Anders stumbled into the room wearing breeches under his nightshirt and slippers on his feet. His hair stuck out in all directions looking as if he'd been caught in a whirlwind.

"My lord! What is the emergency?"

Chase let his eyes drift from his valet's head down to his slippered feet, then back up to his disheveled hair. If only Bensey were here to capture this moment on paper. He could blackmail Anders for the remainder of his life with such a picture. In all the years he had known Anders, he'd never seen the man not dressed to the nines.

Chase raised a brow. "Who are you and what have you done with my valet?"

"What? Ah...I mean, pardon, my lord?"

The confusion on Anders' face was priceless. Chase gave a dramatic sigh. "I detest repeating myself. I said, who are you and what have you done with my valet?"

Anders looked behind him, then back at Chase and frowned. "It is me, Anders. Are you not feeling quite the thing this morning, my lord?"

Well, he hadn't been, but who knew having fun with one's valet could cheer one up so marvelously. He might have to do it more often.

"If you truly are Anders, then I daresay it is you who isn't feeling quite the thing."

"What I feel is that I'm in the middle of a play and have forgotten my lines," Anders grumbled.

The devil, but this was entertaining. "It's not a play, it's a farce and you have the lead role."

"And my next line is, my lord?"

"Oh ho. You are vastly amusing this morning. Have you looked in a mirror lately?"

Anders gave him a suspicious stare before going to the mirror. "Aargh!"

Chase burst into laughter. "Aargh, indeed."

"My lord, I must return to my room immediately."

"I'll be patiently awaiting your return, Anders," Chase called to the man's back.

Anders returned twenty minutes later, perfectly dressed and coiffed. Once perfectly dressed and coiffed himself, Chase headed for Bensey's room. While Anders shaved him, the dream in which he had been drawing a baby played through his mind and an idea began to form. He just wasn't sure it was a good one or if Bensey could do it. Over breakfast with his artistic son, he would get Bensey's opinion on the idea.

"I could if I knew what a baby looked like," Bensey said with confidence.

"There's a portrait of Lady Claire and Lord Derebourne I think would help. Lady Claire told me her son had her eyes, but favored his father. Let me find out if there's a baby in the village and if I can arrange for us to pay a visit. Are you sure you want to try this?"

Bensey nodded. "I want to do it for Lady Claire. I like her and I don't want her to be sad."

Chase squeezed his shoulder. "You're a good boy, son."

The child who didn't like to be touched stepped forward and pressed himself against his father's chest. Chase hugged him and inhaled his boy scent. If anyone had told him a year ago he would see a day when he considered himself blessed, he would have called them a liar.

"Did I remember to tell you that your grandmamma will arrive this afternoon?"

Bensey stepped away. "Yes, Father. May Harry and I sit outside on the steps and watch for her carriage?"

Chase chuckled. "I'm not sure you'll be able to get Harry to sit still while you watch the road, but you are welcome to try. I was thinking we might go down to the lake and have another swimming lesson after your brother finishes with Lady Claire. Would you like that?"

"Oh, yes."

"Good. I'm going down and watch Harry learn how to train a horse. Do you want to come with me?"

"I promised to meet Anders in the conservatory after breakfast. We're going to graft some fruit trees."

He enjoyed a breakfast with Bensey and then left him to go see Harry and the woman who had disturbed his sleep.

Chase leaned on the rail and observed Claire with Harry. She had a calm patience with him, and to Harry's credit, he paid rapt attention to her. As usual for her training sessions, she wore her leather breeches. He was becoming quite fond of them.

And he quite liked the way she wore her hair in a long braid down her back when she worked—could imagine holding onto it while she rode him. Growing hard at the mere idea, he turned his mind to the arrival of his mother in an attempt to rein in his lust.

It was going to be interesting to see his mother's reaction to Claire. Lady Anne could size up a person in the blink of an eye, and he had never known her to be wrong. Chase thought his mother would be intrigued by Claire and would like her. He sincerely hoped she would not take an instant dislike to the woman he hoped to marry.

It was doubtful he or Claire would be able to hide their attraction from her. His mother had the eyes of a hawk and the instincts of a fox. If anything, he was certain Lady Anne would welcome Claire with open arms as soon as she realized her son had an interest in the lady.

Her grandest wish was to see him happily married and filling his nursery with grandbabies for her to spoil. He was going to do his best to accommodate her, but could only hope she didn't meddle too much in his courtship.

Claire had her back to him and he let his gaze linger on her bottom. He hoped she wouldn't stop wearing the breeches after his mother arrived. Lady Anne would probably want a pair if she saw them, and he chuckled at the image of his mother marching around clad in a pair.

Claire glanced over her shoulder and arched a questioning brow. He shrugged and she returned her attention to Harry and the horse. It occurred to him that he needed to sure she understood she was not to change her routine just because his mother was here. He wanted her to continue spending time with Harry until they left for London, and that meant she needed to continue wearing her breeches.

Claire's skin prickled. Even though she had her back to the fence, she had known the moment Chase arrived. Where he was concerned, it seemed her senses were sharply honed. He chuckled and she glanced over, catching him staring at her bottom.

Why was he chuckling? Did he think her bottom funny? Her concentration was broken and it was his fault. She wasn't going to be able to focus on Harry and the horse until she knew the meaning of that chuckle.

"It's time to make Thor circle the ring, Harry. You know what to do so I'm going to step away and let you take it from here."

Harry nodded, his concentration obviously still intact, but then it wasn't his bottom his father had chuckled over. Harry had a natural instinct with the horses and if she was fortunate to have enough time with him, he would surpass her abilities.

Her dream was to have a whole class of little boys to train, and then she would send them out into the world to teach others. Perhaps then the day would come when men stopped abusing their mounts. She backed up to the rail until she stood next to Chase.

"Good morn, Claire," he said, his voice low and intimate.

She might be willing to crawl over hot coals to hear that voice rumbling in her ear every morning for the rest of her life. "Good morn to you, Chase. What has you so amused?"

"Pardon?"

"You were eyeing my bottom and chuckling."

His grin was pure wickedness. "A fine bottom it is. You do understand this is not a proper conversation for us to have? Talking about your bottom, that is, even though your bottom begs to be admired and poetic words written of its tantalizing allure. You must promise me, however, you will not discuss your bottom with anyone other than me."

Mercy. She wanted to drag him off somewhere private and have him do those wonderful things to her again. She truly was a wanton.

"You are a wicked man, my lord."

He put his mouth next to her ear. "Having held those silken globes in the palms of my hands, I find I am feeling a bit possessive of the thing. Your bottom, that is."

"You really shouldn't say such things, my lord." Even if she did like it, and when had the day grown so hot?

"Tell me you wouldn't like to slip away right now, *my lady,* for a repeat of last night."

Of course, she would, but did he want her enough to put the ghost of his wife to rest forever? No, he wasn't ready, and at this point with a damaged horse, it was time to retreat so his desire for what he couldn't have grew.

Claire stepped to the side creating a space between them. "No, I don't believe I would."

"Liar." The corners of his eyes crinkled in amusement.

Was she so obvious?

"I was chuckling because I was trying to imagine my mother wearing leather breeches," he continued as if he had not made her dizzy with all his words coming between her question and his answer.

Mention of his mother cleared the fuzziness from her head. "Why ever would you think such a thing?"

"I have no idea. That's not true, actually, I do. I was thinking that when Mama sees yours, she will want a pair for herself."

Claire gasped in horror. "No. Absolutely not. She will not see me dressed as I am now. You will not even hint of it to her."

"Will I not? Be sensible, Claire. You train horses and you cannot do so wearing a gown."

"Then I won't work while she's here."

"Yes, you will. This is what you do, what you love. And what of the horses? It would not be good for them to go on holiday, now would it? Then there's Harry. These mornings working with you are important to him. I know Lady Anne, and I daresay she is going to find you fascinating. As I said, if anything, she will want a pair."

Claire couldn't imagine wearing breeches in front of Lady Anne. But, bells in hell, he was right. It was one thing for her to step away from the training, but the horses were another matter altogether. There was Harry to think of, also. She couldn't bring herself to disappoint him.

She glanced at the boy standing in the middle of the ring. He had Thor circling him at an easy lope. One of Thor's ears angled toward Harry, paying attention to the boy's commands. Harry showed no indecision or hesitation in working the horse.

Claire had worked with Thor for several weeks, and he'd proven to be a calm, intelligent yearling and showed great promise. He had confidence in himself, but was open to learning new things. She had rightly thought he would be the perfect horse for Harry to practice his skills on.

"Now, Harry," she called, "let him stop and do what I showed you. I think your father will be impressed." She tapped Chase on the hand. "Watch this."

Harry let Thor come to a stop and then squared off facing the horse. Harry and Thor engaged in a staring contest for a few minutes before Thor's head lowered.

In a soft voice, she gave Chase a commentary. "Being a youngster, Thor is full of himself and needs to test his boundaries. By squaring up and facing Thor, Harry is showing him that he is the leader. Thor tried to challenge Harry by staring him down. When Harry didn't back down, Thor decided to save his challenge of the leader for another day. See how his head is lowering?"

When Chase nodded, she continued. "He's showing his desire to join with Harry. Horses are herd animals and their survival in the wild depends on belonging to a herd. When his chin is lowered almost to the ground and his tongue is hanging out of his mouth, his acquiescence to Harry's leadership is complete."

As if on cue, Thor's chin brushed the ground and his tongue hung out of the side of his mouth. "Now Harry will let his eyes roam down Thor's body to his flanks and then he'll turn his back to Thor. That's when the magic happens."

It never ceased to thrill her, this moment when the

horse joined with her. Now, Harry would experience it for the first time. It would delight him as it did her. Her heart filled with pride, as if he were her son in truth.

The awareness almost staggered her. She loved this man, yes, but she also loved the twins. She wanted to tell him of this grand new insight, but it was still too soon. His chin had yet to touch the ground and his tongue wasn't dragging the ground. To keep from giggling, she bit down on her bottom lip.

"I have told you, Claire, not to do that. Have you forgotten what happened the last time you didn't heed my warning?"

What was he talking about? She glanced at him to see he stared at her mouth, and she remembered how he had given her a passionate kiss the last time he caught her doing it.

"I remember," she whispered.

He tapped a finger against her lips. "Good, because you now owe me a kiss."

When? "Do I?" She licked her lips, and the blue of his eyes darkened. This flirting business wasn't so difficult, after all.

"Oh yes, Claire, you do."

With only a heated look he had her blood pulsing, wanting more of what he'd shown her last night. Merciful heavens, he was dangerous to her sanity.

"Watch Harry," she said to divert his attention so she could recover her wits.

Chase swallowed a grin. "Yes, ma'am." Thor took a few a tentative steps toward Harry. He stopped a moment before moving again. When he walked to Harry's back and nuzzled his neck, Chase was certain Harry's grin touched both his ears.

Amazed, he shook his head. "I have seen you do it and now Harry, yet, I'm still having trouble believing my eyes."

"It is remarkable, isn't it? Harry's exceeded my expectations."

"Well, I'm going to steal him away. I want to take him and Bensey to the lake for a swimming lesson before luncheon. I would invite you along, but we swim in our drawers, and I fear the sight would be too much for your delicate eyes…or would it, I wonder."

He winked at her and walked away. Her eyes had widened in alarm and Chase smiled to himself. One day he would get her to admit to spying on them. Sadly, with his mother due to arrive in a few hours, Claire wouldn't sneak down to watch them today.

After an hour of swimming, followed by luncheon, the boys went out to wait for their grandmother's carriage. Chase went searching for Claire. She owed him a kiss and he wanted to collect on it before his mother arrived. He found her in the hallway outside the drawing room, talking to Mrs. Smithfield.

He stopped a few feet away and shook his head. This wouldn't do at all. She wore one of her black gowns and a white lace cap. After the housekeeper left, he approached her.

"Why are you dressed in black, Claire?" Chase plucked the cap from her head. "I recall telling your maid to burn this." She made a grab for the cap and he held it out of her reach, backing into the drawing room.

"Give it to me, Chase."

"No."

When she passed the doorway, he spun and closed the door. Her eyes danced with excitement, and that was all he needed to know.

"What are you doing? I can't be alone with you while the door's closed. And give me my cap."

He dangled the thing in the air. "Come and get it."

She narrowed her eyes and he answered with a raised brow. When she took two steps forward, stopped and held out her hand, he shook his head.

"Give it to me."

"If you want it, you'll have to take it from me." He waved the offensive cap at her. One more step and she would be within his reach. He waited. Having no idea of the danger she was in, she took two more steps. He dropped the cap, grabbed her around the waist, spun her and pressed her against the door

"Oomph."

"Oomph to you." He kissed her.

He hadn't slept well because of her, hadn't been able to think of anything but her all day, and he punished her for it with his kiss. She tried to resist him, but when he pressed his body against hers, she sighed into his mouth and wrapped her arms around his neck. Christ in heaven, he loved kissing her, loved the taste of her. His control was in danger of slipping. If he didn't stop, he would take her up against the door.

Chase rested his forehead against hers. "There, I've collected the kiss you owed me."

"Will you give me my cap now?"

"No. I'm going to instruct your maid to burn all your white caps. You are never to wear one again. And go change out of that horrid gown." If he was being high-handed, he didn't care. He detested seeing her in the black mourning gowns and god-awful caps.

"I am still in official mourning, Chase. I don't want

to scandalize your mother."

"Remind me sometime to tell you about my mother's response when my father was killed. But for now, you're going to have to trust me. Wear one of your lavender gowns if you must, but I never want to see you in black again." He stole one more kiss. "Go change." He kissed her nose. "Please," he added belatedly and stepped away.

"Do all rogues kiss as good as you?" she asked and left without waiting for an answer.

Chase scowled. He honestly couldn't answer, having never kissed another rogue before, but felt an irrational jealously at the thought of her kissing any man besides him, rogue or otherwise.

Harry poked his head inside the front door. "A carriage is coming," he yelled.

Chapter Sixteen

Claire willed her heart to slow down. She wanted to make a good impression when she met Lady Anne, but feared Chase's mother was going to think she wasn't good enough for her son.

Although glad he'd convinced her—ordered more like—to change out of the black gown, she wasn't entirely sure it was the right thing to do. Well, she couldn't stand in the hall all day debating with herself. The twin's excited voices filtered through the door as they told their Grandmamma they were learning to swim. Claire took a deep breath and stepped inside.

"And we get to swim in our drawers!" Harry exclaimed just as she entered the room.

The image of seeing Chase in his drawers sent heat upward to her cheeks. Bells in hell. All the room's occupants turned their eyes to her. Oh God, did they know what she was thinking? She froze and turned to Chase in panic. His eyes were alight with unholy glee, and she had the urge to pound him into the ground.

"Ah, Harry, we don't mention our drawers when ladies are present," the devil lord said.

He did not look at Harry when he said it. No, he stared straight at her and mentioned his drawers. She didn't think her face could get hotter, but she could feel it doing just that.

Lady Anne was attempting—with little success—to

keep a straight face. Claire relaxed a little. She forced her feet to move forward, grateful when the twins came and took her hands.

"Grandmamma, this is Lady Claire. She's our new friend," Bensey said.

"She talks to horses and she's teaching me to do it," Harry added.

"Claire, I would like to introduce you to my Mama, Lady Anne," Chase said.

Claire curtseyed. Lady Anne was the tiniest woman she had ever met and how in heavens had she produced such a big, strapping son?

She reminded Claire of a lovely china doll with golden hair and blue eyes. She would have known Lady Anne was related to Chase, but would have guessed an older sister.

"It is a pleasure to meet you, Lady Kensington. I apologize for any inconvenience I have caused by taking you away from your home. I do thank you."

"A pretty speech, but unnecessary, my dear. When I received my son's letter requesting my presence, I frightened my maid, Lorrie, half out of her wits when I shrieked in a most unladylike fashion, 'By the saints, Lorrie, pack my trunks' and then performed a little jig.

"My reaction to Kensington's letter was due in no small amount to a bout of ennui that could only be cured by seeing my son and grandsons. So no apologies, please, as it is I who should be thanking you, Lady Derebourne, for being the reason Kensington…I suppose I need to learn to call him Derebourne…invited me to Hillcrest. How exciting to learn my charge talks to horses and is going to teach Harry how to do this marvelous thing. Why, imagine their surprise when I tell my friends. Who would have ever thought such a thing possible? However do you do it?"

Claire found herself taking extra breaths on Lady Kensington's behalf. Wherever did such a small woman store away so many words? Her nerves eased on seeing the amused smile on Chase's face.

"It is simple, really, Lady Kensington. I could teach you if you wish."

"Oh, my heavens, no. I have no desire to know what my mount thinks of me. I have never been able to achieve even the status of adequate horsewoman, and if a horse is having amusing thoughts of my incompetence, I so do not want to know. It is my size, you see.

"The few times I have allowed someone to talk me into climbing atop a horse, it was an embarrassment for both me and the wretched animal. There is not enough of me to weigh me down, you see. I bounce atop a horse like a feather in the wind. God invented carriages so that Bensey and I would have a dignified way to get from one place to another without being the entertainment of a snickering beast. I would, however, love to watch you teach Harry how to talk to a horse, if you don't mind. What a clever skill for Harry to have. Please, my dear, my father was a duke, so call me Lady Anne."

They were still standing. Chase and the boys seemed used to Lady Anne's rambling speech. It might take her time to become accustomed to it, but Claire was captivated by the woman's charm even though the mere idea of conversing with a duke's daughter and the mother of an earl and a marquess was beyond her wildest imagination. She curtseyed again Was there more she should do when meeting such a noble woman?

"Come and have a seat next to me, Lady Derebourne. We shall have a nice chat and become acquainted. I just know we're going to be good friends, you and I." She sat on the sofa and patted the space next to her. Claire obediently took a seat.

"Harry, Bensey, I believe Mr. Edwards is awaiting you. After your lessons, please dress for dinner and you can spend time with your Grandmamma then," Chase said.

After they left, Chase settled in a chair close to Claire and she wished he had taken the one near his mother. She was too aware of him and feared she might give herself away.

"Now then, have my son and grandsons been behaving themselves?"

Claire nodded, and opened her mouth to speak, but Lady Kensington continued on. "It must have been difficult for you when Kensington…blast, I'll never remember to call him Derebourne. How could I when he's been Kensington for so long? What was I saying? Oh, yes. When my son arrived towing along two small boys, it must have overwhelmed you. I know if I were in your place, I would have resented a stranger coming in and taking over my home. It's obvious the twins like you and that you like them. A friend of the boys is a friend of mine.

"You have such pretty hair, my dear. It's almost silver. Very unusual, but striking." She gave Chase what Claire thought to be a calculating look. "Kensington wrote—" She stopped and sighed. "It's going to take me forever to imprint Derebourne on my mind. To address him as Derebourne feels like I am speaking of someone else. How should I address you, Kensington?"

"Whichever you prefer, Mama."

"Why, I prefer Kensington, of course. When I say Kensington, I know I am speaking of my son, but, silly me, when I say Derebourne, I am not sure who I am speaking of." She tapped Claire on the hand. "Do you mind, my dear, if I continue to call him Kensington? I know the Derebourne title is an old one and highly respected, but to me, my son is a Kensington. Of course, when among other company, I'll have to somehow remember to refer to him as Derebourne."

Claire thought she might dance on the rooftop at midnight if this endearing lady asked it of her. "Then you must continue to think of him as Kensington."

Lady Kensington bestowed a brilliant smile on her. "When I read Kensington's letter, I knew I was going to like you."

What had Chase said about her?

"Now, where was I?" Lady Kensington said. "Oh, yes. In his letter to me, he said you will be going to London in a few weeks. I see you are in half mourning, but if you are anything like me, you cannot wait to give your black and lavender gowns to charity. We are going to have such fun ordering you an entirely new wardrobe.

"I have two daughters, but they are not out yet, so I will be able to practice on you and then maybe I'll get it right with them. It's only fair I warn you, do not allow me to choose your gowns. For that, you must rely on Kensington. If he says a gown will look lovely on you, you should believe him." She patted Claire's hand again. "You mustn't worry, my dear, you are going to be a smashing success. The gentlemen are going to overwhelm you with their attentions."

Claire found herself taking extra breaths again as she tried to keep up with Lady Kensington's various changes of subjects. She darted a glance at Chase to see his reaction to the last comment. He wasn't smiling, but she wanted to. Lady Kensington might prove to be an ally in her campaign to win his heart.

"Do you think so, my lady?"

Lady Kensington nodded. "I am certain of it. Don't you agree, Kensington?"

She smiled at her son with such innocence that Claire realized his mother knew exactly what she was doing. Hadn't Chase said she had the eyes of a hawk and the instincts of a fox? Did it mean Lady Kensington approved of a match between her and Chase? Yet, how could she? They had only just met.

"If you are certain of it, Mama, then it must be so. How was your journey? I trust you didn't have any problems?"

"You are changing the subject, Kensington. But that reminds me. I met the most interesting family at the coaching inn when we stopped for luncheon."

As she regaled them with her story, Claire's mind drifted. Had he been jealous at the thought of gentlemen paying attention to her? He still hadn't changed his mind about taking her to London. The closer the time came to go, the more she looked forward to it.

She had never been to Town and wanted to experience the balls and musicals—wanted to go to the theater, the opera and the museum. But she wanted to do it on Chase's arm. Whether she got what she wished for would depend on the success of her plan. What would Lady Anne think of The Training of a Marquess?

****

Chase asked himself if he was an idiot for insisting on taking Claire to London and giving her a Season. He was used to his mother's long-winded stories and had learned to listen with half an ear while his mind contemplated other things. And the only other thing on his mind lately was Lady Claire. What if some man did catch her interest?

He'd never understood his father fighting a duel over a woman, but for the first time, he could appreciate why a man might do such a foolhardy thing. Of course, his dissolute father hadn't fought the duel because he had any particular feelings for the woman. He'd only had the misfortunate to have been caught by the woman's husband and a challenge had ensued.

Even though he'd sworn to never go down that road, if any man hurt Claire, he would challenge the man without hesitation. He would just have to not let it come to that. As he would be with her and able to watch over her, he'd be able to step in at the slightest hint of trouble.

If she met someone she wanted to marry and the bloody man was worthy of her, then Chase would give her his blessing and step out of her life. He gave a little grunt of satisfaction. Taking her to London was the right thing to do.

"Are either of you listening to me?" Lady Anne asked. "And good heavens, Kensington, you sound like you're growling. Don't you feel well? Perhaps you should go have a lie down. I know a little nap always helps me when I'm not feeling quite the thing. I had a nice snooze in the carriage and now feel refreshed and quite clearheaded. Off with you, now," she said, waving her hand at him. "It will give Lady Derebourne and I time to become better acquainted."

Chase blinked in confusion. "Off with me?"

Lady Anne tsked. "The poor creatures can be so dense at times. Go away, Kensington, and leave us ladies alone to have a nice chat."

He had serious misgivings about leaving his mother alone with Claire. She hadn't been here an hour, and already she was meddling. There had been no expectation he'd be able to hide his interest in Claire, but had hoped it would take his mother longer than a few minutes to see it.

Apparently not.

He stood. "You're free to tell her to mind her own business, Claire. In fact, I wish you would." He walked over to his mother and gave her a kiss on the cheek. "Behave yourself, Mama. I'll have Mrs. Smithfield send in a pot of tea," he said and left, closing the door behind him.

Apprehension stirred up Claire's nerves again. Why did his mother want to speak to her alone?

"Now then, my dear." Lady Anne patted her hand. "How serious is this thing between you and my son?"

It was the shortest speech Lady Kensington had made since Claire had entered the room. She wished desperately for her to go on talking in her usual fashion, but Lady Kensington kept her mouth closed.

"I'm not sure what you mean," Claire hedged.

"Don't be silly, my dear, of course you do. I haven't seen my son interested in a woman since his wife passed. I want him to be happy, and I think you may be the woman to make it so. He watches you and you sneak looks at him. If you tell me you care for him, then you can count on me to support you. Do you care for him, Lady Derebourne?"

"I care for him," she admitted. A heavy weight lifted and she met Lady Kensington's astute gaze. "I love him, but he thinks I don't know my own mind."

"Why is that?"

Claire had never talked to anyone other than Chase about her father and her marriage, but she knew Lady Kensington wouldn't be satisfied until she had the whole story.

There was a knock on the door and Mrs. Smithfield entered with the teacart, giving Claire time to collect her thoughts. After Claire served her, Lady Kensington set back on the sofa and sipped her tea. Her dainty little feet didn't touch the floor and Claire's affection grew for this talkative, diminutive woman.

"I guess I should start at the beginning," Claire said.

"That usually is the best place to start. Though I can talk your ears off...my children have been known to call me Chatty Attie, but that's neither here nor there. I can manage to keep my mouth closed long enough to listen. Tell me your story, my dear."

Claire told her new friend about her father, her husband and her son. She spoke of her sheltered life and how the horses had given her purpose. She told the mother of the man she loved why the stubborn man insisted on taking her to London. And though she hadn't meant to, she told Lady Kensington about the plan she called The Training of a Marquess.

The thing that amazed Claire the most—aside from

confiding in someone she had just met—was that while she talked, Lady Kensington had not uttered a word. It was probably the reason she said so much. If she'd been interrupted, Claire thought she probably would have been more guarded in what she said.

"The Training of a Marquess." Lady Kensington clapped her hands. "I absolutely love it. You must follow through and begin your strategy to ignore him. He will hate it and will follow you around like a neglected puppy trying to get your attention. This is so exciting. I couldn't be more pleased that I'm here to see this play out. My son needs a good shake up. He doesn't speak of Teresa, so I'm encouraged he talked to you of her. Did he tell you what happened?"

"Yes, and it's an appalling and heartbreaking story. He also told me she never stopped loving Lord Hollingsworth. I know Cha—Lord Derebourne grieved her death, but I don't think it's why he vowed never to marry again."

Lady Kensington took a handkerchief from her sleeve and wiped her eyes. "He never told me of his vow, but I feared that might have been the way he was thinking."

"He told me of his great love for her, but that she never saw him as more than her dear friend. I think if she had returned his feelings, then her loss would have been devastating, but he would have eventually recovered and been open to finding love again. Because she didn't, he fears trusting his heart to another woman and not having his loved returned. He said he wouldn't survive it a second time. I can understand his need for self-preservation."

"No, Teresa never loved him. She tried, I know she

did, but her heart only ever belonged to Hollingsworth. No one could have stopped Kensington from marrying her, but she wasn't healthy for him. He changed after they married, became completely focused on her, on making her happy to the extent that he lost something of himself. Their life revolved around her and there didn't seem to be any thought from either of them as to his needs.

"Don't think I didn't like her, I did. She was like a sweet, damaged child that one felt compelled to cherish and protect. I only wish it wasn't my son who took on her troubles. Have you told him you love him?"

"No, he isn't ready to believe it. He thinks I must have a Season and the experience of being courted by other gentlemen before I can be sure of my feelings."

"He isn't altogether wrong, Claire. May I call you Claire? I feel we have shared many confidences today and that we are friends."

"Please, I would be honored. I have never had a female friend before and have always wanted one."

Lady Anne took Claire's hand. "Well, now you do have a woman friend. As I was saying, he's right in that you should experience a Season. Mind you, I'm not saying you don't know your own heart. There's no harm in taking some time to have a little fun and proving to Kensington and yourself that there's no other man for you than him. Because, Claire, friend or not, I will do serious harm to the next woman who dares to hurt my son."

Claire didn't doubt Lady Anne one bit, but an image of the tiny lady trying to pummel her into the ground made her want to smile. Of course, there were many ways Lady Anne could do harm other than physical. Claire could only respect Lady Anne for wanting to protect her son. She was saved from having to respond by a knock on the door.

Chase entered and sat in the chair closest to Claire. "The two of you have been closed up in here for well over two hours. I trust by now you know all there is to know of the other. You look none the worse for wear, which must mean you are now bosom friends. What have you been talking about all this time?"

"Why you, of course," Lady Anne said and Claire choked in surprise at Lady Anne's candor.

"I was afraid of that." Chase grinned. "Are you all right, Claire? Do you want some water?"

Claire shook her head. "No, thank you, Cha…Kens… Lord Derebourne." Bells in hell, she'd never get his name right now.

"Do not stand on ceremony because of me, Claire. Call him Chase and be done with it."

"Yes, Lady Anne," Claire meekly replied.

Claire waited for Chase to ask for details of their conversation, but he began to tell Lady Anne of the twin's activities. Claire excused herself, giving mother and son time alone together.

Chase turned from watching Claire leave to see a smirk on his mother's face. "Why are you making faces at me, Mama?"

"If you believed I wouldn't notice there's something between the two of you, son, then you aren't as intelligent as I thought. I am not blind, you know. She watches you, you watch her. Several times, I thought I could leave the room and neither of you would have noticed. Not that you will ask for it, but I approve wholeheartedly. I like her enormously.

"How a father could marry his daughter off so young and to a man almost three times her age, I'll never understand. Of course, I never understood half the things your father did, so what do I know about men? Not enough to fill a teacup, I wager. But that's neither here nor there.

"If she can make you happy, if she can give me back the cheerful son I miss ever so much, then in my eyes, she is an angel sent straight from heaven. Come to think of it, she's exactly what I would imagine an angel to look like with her big blue eyes and silvery hair. Have you ever wondered what angels look like, Kensington?"

"Not until Claire," he answered honestly.

****

A deep sense of contentment settled over Claire as she listened to the lively dinner conversation going on around her. With Thomas, dinner had been a quiet affair, the only sounds the clinking of silverware on china. Even in his presence she had been lonely.

He never asked her how she was, about her day or about anything. If she tried to start a conversation, he would stop eating and set down his fork and knife. He would listen politely, give her an answer if required, and then resume eating.

Mrs. Smithfield had told her once that his mother taught him it was vulgar to continue eating while a lady spoke. It made Claire nervous to interrupt his dinner, so she had stopped trying to talk to him and her loneliness grew.

But Thomas' mother had been wrong. This is how it should be. The Warrens teased and debated, they spoke of things important, and things not so important.

The affection they had for one another was there to see, and she badly wanted to belong to them.

Chase touched her arm, her skin tingling from the contact. "You are being too quiet, Claire. What are you thinking?"

Conversation stopped as they all turned their attention to at her. Did they care about her thoughts? No one ever had before this man came into her life. It was a new, exhilarating feeling and she found she wanted to be honest with them.

"I was thinking how much I'm enjoying your conversations. Neither Derebourne or my father encouraged talk at the dinner table, you see, and now I'm wondering why." She lowered her gaze to her empty plate. So immersed in their discourse, she hadn't realized she'd cleaned it. Claire gave a self-conscious laugh. "Even the food tastes better when there's lively dinner conversation."

Chase gave her arm a gentle squeeze and then removed his hand. She wanted to pull it back, wanted to keep the touch of him on her skin. She glanced at Lady Anne and saw fondness in her eyes, a look Claire had never seen from her own mother.

After dinner, they retired to the drawing room and spent time with the twins before Chase sent them to bed. Claire and Lady Anne were engaged in a spirited debate over their favorite books when Bensey crept into the room and went to Chase, whispering in his father's ear.

Chase's eyes grew wide. "Are you bamming me?"

Bensey shook his head. "No, Father."

Chase stood and bowed. "Continue on with your visit, my ladies. I must see to Harry."

"Is he all right, Kensington?" Lady Anne asked. "Do you need our assistance?"

Chase and Bensey burst into laughter. "Ah...no Mama, that won't be necessary." They left the room, the sound of their mirth trailing behind them.

"Are you as curious as I?" Lady Anne asked.

"I am. At least we know Harry isn't hurt or they wouldn't be laughing."

"True. I'm tempted to follow them to see what is afoot. However, as a mother of two boys, I can say with experience that sometimes ignorance is bliss. I remember one time when Kensington and Robert were small and decided they wanted to be Highlanders.

"I had read them a story the night before about a young Scottish boy setting out alone to prove he was a man. I should have known better. They decided it would be great fun to follow the boy's example, so they packed a food basket, strapped on their toy swords and set off to conquer the world. Kensington was nine and Robert, six.

"By the time we found them the following day, they had managed to travel three miles from home. They lost their clothes...we never did get to the bottom of that story, had gotten into a patch of nettles and had a rash from head to toe. They had apparently finished off their supply of food shortly after setting off on their adventure and were hungry.

"Somehow, they did manage to hold on to their toy swords. You must picture it, Claire. Two filthy, naked boys with red skin holding on for dear life to their little swords. I didn't know whether to beat them to death or hug them to death."

"So, you hugged them," Claire said, grinning. This

was a story of Chase as a little boy she would treasure.

"So, I did. It was weeks before I could bear to let them out of my sight again. And just when I thought they had learned their lesson, they would invent new ways to torture their poor mother. The two kept me on my toes, they did," she said fondly.

Would there ever come a day when she would have her own little boy stories to tell? Claire tried not to think of Andrew and the adventures he would never have. She was grateful when Chase returned and diverted her thoughts. He had a lopsided smile on his face, and she could picture him as a little boy up to no good with the same silly grin.

"Well, Kensington? We are near expired with curiosity, Claire and I. Do tell what trouble Harry got up to."

Chase turned and closed the door. Crossing the room, he took his preferred chair near Claire. His mother was going to love this story. "First, I must have your promise you will not even hint to Harry that I have told you. Not only would he never forgive me, but he wouldn't be able to look you in the face again. Perhaps when he is forty we will be able to drag the story out and have a good laugh with him."

Both women gave him their solemn promise. "I'm not sure how to tell you. It would be much easier to speak of it if you were men." He stared off trying to think of words he could use that would not offend them.

Lady Anne frowned. "Good lord, Kensington, just say it. Pretend you're talking to Aubrey, if you must, but get on with it."

"Very well, it's like this. My pardon, but there's no other way to say this. Apparently, Harry has always wanted to go in a bottle." They gave him blank looks. He sighed. They were going to make him say it. "Urinate," he said, though if he had truly been telling Aubrey, his word would have been cruder.

Their mouths opened in perfect little O's at this announcement and both moved closer to the edge of their seat. Chase shrugged. "It's perfectly understandable. Well, perhaps not to a woman, but to any man. Why not want to try such a thing when you are a nine-year-old boy? Anyway, he found an empty bottle and—" He struggled not to laugh as he wondered if their eyes could grow any wider.

"And?" his mother said.

"And, he got stuck."

Their expressions, so alike a moment ago, veered in two different directions. His mother understood immediately and her lips quivered in an effort to keep a straight face. Claire showed nothing but puzzlement.

"His little boy part got stuck, Claire."

He counted to five before understanding crossed her face. She clapped a hand over her mouth, but couldn't stop a noise that sounded half snort, half giggle.

His mother lost her battle for control then and fell into a fit of laughter. Claire reached over and pulled a small pillow up, burying her face in it. Her shoulders shook and Chase would wager his entire fortune she wasn't crying.

"However did you...you know?" his mother asked between gasps.

"You'd be amazed at the many uses for duck grease."

That did it. His mother and, hopefully, future wife

fell into each other's arms in the grandest fit of hilarity he had ever witnessed.

Poor Harry, to be the brunt of such feminine amusement.

Chapter Seventeen

Claire couldn't stop thinking about the laughter. She had never had any in her life, not as a young girl living with her parents, and not as a wife. She hadn't known she should wish for it, but now she did. Laughter felt good, it made her happy.

She turned over, fluffed her pillow and tried to go to sleep. But she couldn't stop thinking about the family who laughed so easily. She added Lady Anne to her list of Warrens she coveted. If she was fortunate enough to meet Chase's brother and sisters, she would probably want them, too.

What a greedy girl she was becoming.

She huffed an exasperated breath. It was no use, she was wide-awake. Maybe a glass of wine would help. Barefoot, Claire made her way to the dining room and poured a wine into a goblet, then walked out to the courtyard. Chase sat on the wall where she'd seen him the first night. No need to try and fool herself. She'd hoped he would be here.

He lifted his brandy and saluted her. Her heart thumped hard in her chest as she approached, stopping a few inches from his knees.

"Hello, Claire," he said, his voice soft and intimate. "Have you come for another kiss?"

Yes, that and more. "I couldn't sleep." She lifted her glass. "I thought a little wine might help."

He wore the same clothing as before—a shirt and breeches. She glanced at his bare feet, almost dropped to her knees so she could slide her hands over them. Would they be firm and leathery or soft like hers?

"Claire?"

She jerked her gaze up. "Yes?"

"Are you going to answer my question?"

What question? A small half smile appeared on his face, just enough to reveal his dimple. The butterflies living in her belly went into a frenzy, and she swayed toward him. He took the glass from her, setting it on the wall next to his brandy. Taking her hands, he placed them on his knees. It was so wickedly intimate to be resting her palms on his legs.

"Have you forgotten my question?" he asked, a hint of amusement in his voice.

"Yes."

"I asked if you have come for another kiss."

"Yes," she whispered.

He spread his legs apart. "Come here then."

Thank you, she wanted to say, but it seemed silly to say such a thing. She stepped forward, entering into the embrace of his body. Heat enveloped her as muscled arms wrapped around her. She laid her head on his chest and closed her eyes, listening to his heart pound. It pleased her to know it beat rapidly because of her.

His hands moved over her back as she snuggled further into him. He curled her hair around his hand, gently pulled her face away from his chest and stared down at her with eyes the blue of an agitated ocean, dark and stormy.

"Claire," he murmured and lowered his head.

His mouth moved over hers in a playful tease. Her

214

tongue slipped out and licked his bottom lip, wanting to taste him. He growled and the teasing turned into a kiss so deeply carnal that her legs lost their ability to support her. His arm tightened around her back, the only thing holding her up.

He broke the kiss and eased off the wall, picked her up and carried her to a lounge partially hidden by several tall potted plants. She wrapped her arms around him, burying her face in this neck. The scent of bergamot, milled soap and the male musk that was him drugged her senses. No words had been spoken between them since he had whispered her name, but none seemed needed to name this want growing inside her. Did he feel it, too?

For tonight, he would belong to her.

He would still take her to London, but it no longer mattered. He was hers and she was going to keep him. If it took weeks of gentlemen dancing attendance to prove to him she was his—always and forever—then so be it. If that was what he needed to trust in her love, then she wouldn't deny him.

Still holding her, he lowered himself onto the lounge, arranging her to his satisfaction. When he was done, she sat between his legs with her back against his chest. She leaned forward and peered over her shoulder. "I will offer you a trade. I'll remove my dressing gown if you will remove your shirt."

Before she could twice blink, his shirt was gone, tossed away to land across one of the potted plants. She smiled her approval and bent her head to unbutton her dressing gown.

"No, allow me."

His arms came around her and he expertly

unbuttoned her dressing gown. If he did nothing but sit behind her all night so she felt his warm breath on her neck as he held her, she would be happy. The way he nestled his head against hers so their cheeks touched made it easy to pretend he loved her.

Maybe the day would come when he did, but if not, she would cherish the memory of being with him.

"Sit up."

The rumble of his voice in her ear sent shivers down her back. Claire moved away to give him room to slide the gown down her arms, lifting her bottom so he could pull it down her legs. He tossed it away, and it landed half over his shirt. She whimsically imagined the garments were pleased with the arrangement.

His fingers caressed her neck as he pulled her hair aside. Lowering his head until his lips brushed her ear, he asked, "Did you wear this silk nightdress for me?"

"No, I always wear silk to bed. I like the way it feels on my skin."

Another growl, this one vibrating through her. Heat pooled in her secret place, proof of her desire she now knew. His mouth explored her neck causing her to whisper his name in a plea.

"Hush. Close your eyes, love, and just feel."

Love. It was the first time he had called her love. The word settled over her, seducing her as finely as his heated kisses and caressing hands. Obeying, she closed her eyes, giving herself over to him.

Chase inwardly cringed. He hadn't meant to call her love. He had only told one woman he loved her, but had called the women he'd been intimate with, luv. Claire deserved better. She wasn't a dalliance, not a woman he used only to satisfy his needs.

Yet, he'd called her love. Not luv. The difference was important to both of them, though she didn't realize it.

Christ in heaven, her skin was incredibly soft and as silky as the nightdress she wore. Following his own instructions to her, he closed his eyes, giving himself over to the feel of her in his arms. He nibbled his way down her neck to her shoulder, inhaling her violet scent as he explored her body.

Pulling the ribbon undone on the front of the nightdress, he slipped his hand inside and cupped a breast. A very perfect breast—more than enough to fill his hand. Her nipple peaked when he flicked his thumb over it, and he couldn't help his smile when she trembled. He slipped his other hand below the silk so that he held a breast in each hand. Tonight, he wasn't going to stop until he claimed her. That should worry him.

Sleep had been elusive because of her so he'd come down to the courtyard. Would she appear? If she didn't, then he wouldn't touch her until they went to London and he had the answer to his question. Or so he told himself. But he'd known in his heart she would walk through the door. When she did, he would break his promise and make love to her.

He would still give her a Season because if he didn't—if he didn't prove to his heart he could trust her—he would always hold a part of himself back and that was unacceptable. He was a man who when he loved, he loved with all that he was. When he offered his heart again, he would settle for nothing less than forever and a day from her as well as himself.

"Do you want me?" He slid his hand over the silk

of her dressing gown, down to her belly. "Do you want me, Claire?"

She nodded.

"Say it."

"I want you, Chase. I do."

There was nothing else he needed to hear. "Come here then." She snuggled her back against him as if there was nowhere else she belonged.

"Now what?"

"Well, that's up to you, but what I'd like is to get this gown off you."

"How remarkable."

"Hmmm?" He nibbled on her ear. "Why's that?"

She inclined her head, giving him better access to her neck. "Because we both want the same thing."

Chase gathered the material in his hand and pulled up. She lifted her bottom and he slipped the gown over her head, dropping it on the floor.

He angled his head around hers and feasted on the sight of her beautiful body. "My God, you're beautiful."

She twisted in his arms and squatted on her knees facing him. "You, too," she said, reaching for the buttons on his trousers.

He lowered his arms and let her have at him. She fumbled with the buttons and his male pride growled its approval that she was inexperienced at the thing. When she finally managed the last button, she pulled his breeches over his hips and down his legs.

For some reason, his feet seemed to fascinate her. Her hands explored his toes, the bottoms of his feet and the tops. They had never been made love to before and quite liked it. Her touch sent little shivers up his legs.

While she played, his eyes devoured her body.

She was taller than most women, her arms and legs firm from working with the horses. Her hips flared out before curving into a small waist. Her belly was flat and her breasts, as he had discovered, were perfect. Her pale hair fell down her back to her waist.

Everything about her called to something primitive inside him. He wanted nothing more than to cover her body with his and bury himself deep inside her. But she was enjoying her explorations, so he mustered his control, allowing her to have her fun.

She peered up at him and grinned. "I had wondered what they felt like. Now I know."

"And now that you have explored every inch of them, what do you think?"

"Oh, they are fine feet and I like them very much."

She turned her attentions to his legs, but her eyes focused on his erection. His cock jerked as her hands came near it.

"May I touch it?"

"I wouldn't dream of stopping you."

"I've always wondered what a man looked like."

She reached out with one finger and poked it. His laugh died in his throat when she wrapped her hand around him. It was apparent she wasn't sure what to do with him now that she had him in hand, but he didn't give a damn. Her tentative, inexperienced touches were driving him wild. Christ in heaven, what would it do to him when she gained experience? He might expire from the pleasure, but he would die a happy man.

"Enough," he said. "Come up here."

She crawled up his body. "I haven't finished learning you," she protested and then licked his nipple.

Chase almost came out of his skin. "Claire." He pulled her up so she was lying atop his body and kissed her. Her breasts pressed against him, and he trailed his hands down to her bottom. He slid a finger inside her and she was wet, oh so wet. She moaned into his mouth. The taste of her, the feel of her, the little mewling sounds she made were too much and his control flew away on the wind. Flipping her over, he covered her body with his.

"Now. I have to have you now."

In answer, she grabbed his head, pushing her tongue into his mouth, their tongues meeting in a fierce duel. Chase wrapped his hand around his throbbing cock and guided it to the entrance of her sheath. She was tight and he forced himself to go slow, to be gentle. He pushed a little deeper and stopped to let her get used to him. Christ in heaven, she felt good.

Claire knew he was afraid of hurting her, but it didn't hurt, not the way it had with Thomas. She wrapped her legs around his bottom and pressed down. "Please."

He groaned and slid fully inside her, then stilled. Burying his face in her neck, he sucked on her skin sending ripples of pleasure through her. She turned her head to the side, giving him better access. When he pulled back, she tightened her legs to keep him from leaving.

His soft chuckle sent hot puffs of breaths over the damp skin where his mouth had been. He pushed back into her and then began a rhythm she recognized, yet didn't. Thomas had done this, but it had been accompanied by grunts on his part and pain on hers. With Chase, it was so good. As he moved inside her, a pressure built. All thoughts of Thomas evaporated.

Her lungs turned to bellows as she struggled for air. Now that she understood what was possible, she greedily reached for it, wanted to feel the intense pleasure again. A drop of sweat rolled down his neck and she licked it away with her tongue, tasting salt and him. A rumble sounded deep in his throat as his movements quickened. Wanting to see his face—to know if joining with her affected him as much as her, she kept her eyes open.

His jaws were rigid, his lips pressed together and his eyes were fixed on her. He made her think of a fierce warrior of medieval days come to storm the castle. She surrendered the castle without thought. "Take me," she said.

He reached between them and flicked her most secret place with his finger. *Oh, God. Oh, God. Oh, God.* Air left her lungs and her vision blurred as her body soared to the stars.

He pumped hard twice more and then pulled out of her, his seed burning its way across her belly. Before she could think why he did that, he claimed her mouth in a kiss that was feral in its savagery. She met his beast with her own.

I will always love you. Because she didn't say it aloud, she didn't have to hear him say she didn't know her mind. But she did, God, she did.

He flipped them over so she was once again sprawled atop him. With a gentleness that touched her deeply, he pushed her damp hair from her face.

"I cannot imagine why, but all my strength seems to have deserted me," he said, giving her a dimpled, lopsided grin. "You were at risk of me collapsing on you and smothering you."

"Hmmm." She felt boneless. Wherever his strength had gone, hers had gone with it. She laid her head on his chest, closed her eyes and listened to his heartbeat slowly return to normal, falling asleep wrapped in his protective warmth.

Chase stroked Claire's back in lazy circles. She had fallen asleep. It felt right to have her in his arms. If Teresa had returned his love, this is how it could have been between them. But it had never been quite right for them. He'd tried so hard to please her, to make her happy. His best had not been enough, and he'd kept his hurt hidden. It was her loss.

His breath hitched with this new realization. He hadn't let her down, had been there for her to the end. He had offered her the moon and stars, but she hadn't been able to put her misery behind her and accept the gift of his love. The pieces of his heart that had shriveled up with her loss unfurled like a desert plant with the first rainfall. The knowledge that he could truly find happiness again staggered him.

He tightened his hold on the sleeping woman in his arms. Withdrawing before he climaxed had been near impossible, but he refused to risk getting her with child before he had a ring on her finger. He pulled a strand of hair through his fingers, bringing it to his nose and inhaling her scent.

Claire was nothing like Teresa. She wasn't needy or damaged. Even after what her father had done to her by marrying her to Derebourne, and even after the loss of her son, she had found a way to bring meaning into her life with her horses. She was strong. If he refused to marry her, but gave her a home and her horses, she would carry on with her life in a way that would bring her happiness.

Forever and a day, she'd said. He was beginning to believe her. But she could survive without him and he liked that about her. If they did marry, he could be himself. He wouldn't have to put his needs aside for her. They would love and they would fight, but they would always be there for each other. Did he love her? No, but he was getting damn close.

Should he still take her to London? Yes. The facts hadn't changed. The beast in him growled at the thought of other men coming near her, but he had set himself on this course and surely he could bear it for a few weeks.

He kissed the top of her head. "Claire."

No response, only the steady rhythm of her breathing. She slept so trustingly in his arms that he didn't want to disturb her. But the servants would be awake in a few hours and he didn't want a scandal attached to her name.

"Claire, wake up."

She mumbled something incoherent and snuggled into him. He glanced over to where her nightdress was draped over a bush. Reaching over, he snagged it with his hand. He struggled to get it over her head and through her arms, chuckling when he thought that he was an expert on removing a lady's clothing, but not so much at putting them back on.

She was so deeply asleep that it was like trying to dress a cloth doll, but he finally managed to get her nightdress on. He stood with her in his arms and lowered her onto the lounge. After quickly dressing, he picked up their glasses. Draining what was left of his brandy, he went to the kitchen and rinsed them out and returned them to the side table in the dining room.

Back in the courtyard, he looked around to be certain he hadn't missed anything, He picked up her dressing gown, and then her. Carrying her up the stairs, he realized he didn't know where her room was located.

"Claire," he hissed.

More mumbling. He grinned. Did she always sleep this deeply or had he done this to her? His manly self wanted to take the credit for reducing her to the equivalent of a sack of flour in his arms. Now what? There was only one person he trusted to be discreet and who would likely know where her room was. Chase walked down the hall and stopped in front of Anders' door. He used his foot to knock.

In less than a minute, the door opened just wide enough for Anders to poke his head out. "My lord?"

"Where is her chamber?"

"In the east wing, my lord. Is Lady Derebourne sick?"

"More like exhausted. I'm a strong man, but I can only hold her for so long. Please lead the way to her room."

"But, my lord, I am not dressed."

Chase rolled his eyes. "The only person who is going to see you in your nightshirt is me and I promise not to talk, even under threat of torture. Now, lead on."

His arms were tiring as he followed Anders to the end of the hall and into another wing that had the feel of being deserted. "Anders, who else has rooms in this wing?"

"No one, my lord, only Lady Derebourne."

Chase's jaw clenched. Why the bloody hell was

she living in a wing by herself? If something happened, if she became sick, there would be no one near to help her. Anders stopped in front of one of the doors and opened it.

"You may return to bed."

"Yes, my lord."

Chase entered her chamber, thankful the open window let in enough moonlight to see the bed.

"Don't leave," she murmured when he lowered her.

He leaned down and kissed her on the lips. "Hush, love. Go to sleep."

She sighed and turned on her side. The temptation to climb into bed with her was great. He would pull her up against him and hold her until the morning so she wouldn't be alone. With a muttered curse, he left while he still could. Tomorrow he would find out why she was here, so far away from everyone else. Then he would tell her to move into the west wing with the rest of them.

Though anxious to change her room to his liking, it would have to wait until he returned from his little trip. In the morning, he was taking Bensey to see a baby. Mrs. Smithfield had told him of a boy only one month old, and Chase had asked her to send the family a message that the marquess and his mother would pay a short visit.

He'd told Lady Anne his idea to have Bensey attempt to draw a portrait of Claire's son. Once he explained why he wanted to do such a thing, she gave her full support. He asked her to come along because he thought the family would think it strange if only he and Bensey arrived asking to look at a baby. Lady Anne had arranged for a basket to take as a gift for the new mother so the family would think that was the reason for the visit.

Chase fell asleep within minutes of his head hitting the pillow and, unlike the last few nights, slept soundly through the remaining hours to morning.

Chapter Eighteen

Claire leaned against the rail. In the corral, Harry expertly flicked a rope behind Victory's legs. He had asked if he could work with his own horse this morning.

"I would like you to tell me if I am doing everything right, Lady Claire. I love Victory and want him to be the best horse ever."

The boy's eagerness to learn thrilled her. To a degree, it validated her methods to see they also worked for Harry. The carriage moved past, stopping in front of the house. Chase, Lady Anne and Bensey, carrying his satchel, walked out the front door. A footman followed carrying a large basket.

Chase assisted his mother inside and Bensey climbed in behind her. Chase raised his hand in acknowledgement and entered the carriage. The footman placed the basket on the floor and closed the door. Claire frowned as they descended the hill and disappeared from view.

Where were they going? Why hadn't he come and told her, or at the very least, said a polite good morning? It wouldn't have taken more than a few minutes of his time.

After last night, shouldn't she be able to expect at least a smile? Had she made a mistake? What if she had given him what he wanted and he had now lost interest?

He admitted he had been a rogue. Wasn't it the goal of a rake to make a conquest and then move on?

If she had lost him because she allowed her desire to overtake her good sense, then that made her a fool. The man had a problem with trust, and perhaps she had walked into his arms too easily. What if her wanton behavior had caused him to think she could be as easily swayed by another man?

But there would never be another man for her—her fate was sealed the moment he claimed her. Being with him had been beyond anything her imagination could have conceived. She didn't know what to do other than continue on with the plan and pray she could win his heart.

"Lady Claire! Look at what I have taught Victory to do."

Claire was aware Harry worked secretly with Victory in the afternoons after his lessons. Gordon told her the boy and his horse spent hours together, sometimes in training, sometimes just having fun.

"Well done. You have a magic touch with him."

Harry grinned in obvious pleasure. They spent a few minutes discussing their plans for tomorrow's training session before she left to go to her office. An hour later, she closed the breeding log, stood and stretched. The carriage hadn't returned. Where were they? She'd asked Gordon, but he didn't know.

She returned to her room where Maggie had a bath waiting. When she came downstairs, Chase and Lady Anne were enjoying a cup of tea in the drawing room. Claire had to bite down on her lip to keep from asking where they had gone. Should she start her strategy of ignoring him now? She wasn't sure of anything anymore.

Chase stood and bowed. "Claire, we were hoping you would join us."

She was chewing on her lip again. Hadn't he warned her what would happen when she did that? Well, now the lady owed him another kiss.

Why was she doing so, however? She only did it when she was nervous or something was on her mind. Was she uneasy because of last night? Did she regret what happened between them? There were things that needed to be said between them, but with his mother in the room, their talk would have to wait.

Claire sailed past him without a glance, her attention on his mother. He frowned.

"Lady Anne, it is a pleasure to see you this morning."

"And you, Claire. Come have a seat next to me and tell me how your morning went. I watched out the window as you gave Harry his lesson on how to talk to a horse.

"I didn't see the horse speak, but then I was more interested in your manner of dress. I have never thought to see a lady in breeches, but cannot imagine why we don't wear them. I would think they must be considerably more comfortable than the gowns and other unmentionables we're expected to wear.

"Oh, I wish I were young and tall like you, my dear, because I would have a pair made for myself. Imagine all the things I could do that cannot be done in a gown."

"Such as what, Mama?" Chase asked, curious to see where the question would take her. With his mother, it was always an interesting journey.

"Well, for starters I could climb a tree, jump a fence or explore a cave. I'm sure if you give me time, I'll be able to come up with dozens of other things. Consider, if you will, how restricted you would feel wearing a gown. Don't stare at me as if I have bats in my attic, Kensington. Men have been known to wear skirts. Why, look at the Scots with their kilts. Have you ever seen a man wearing a kilt, Claire?"

Chase had been amusing himself by watching the different expressions cross Claire's face as his mother carried on. What wasn't amusing was that she had not once glanced his way. Had she purposely not done so or was it only that she was concentrating on keeping up with Lady Anne?

"No, I don't believe I have," Claire answered.

"Oh, that's a shame, my dear. It is quite a sight to see," Lady Anne said with a dreamy smile.

Thankfully, before she could give Claire a detailed description of a man wearing a kilt, which he was certain she was about to do, Smithfield announced luncheon was served.

Chase stood, offered an arm to each of his ladies and led them to the dining room. By the time luncheon was over he was as irritated as a poked bear. Claire ignored him unless he asked her a direct question, only giving him the briefest of answers before turning her attention back to Lady Anne.

What the bloody hell was going on in her mind? After last night, she should be giving him intimate smiles and secretive looks. Instead, it appeared as if she had forgotten he existed. He had half a mind to drag her away to someplace private and find out what she was about. But first, he would kiss her senseless and show her that she couldn't ignore him.

"Why the devil is your chamber in the east wing, Claire?"

"Your language, Kensington," Lady Anne chided.

Claire looked at him as if he had lost his mind and perhaps he had. He hadn't meant to address the subject now and in front of his mother, but, deuce take it, he was beginning to think he was the one with bats in his attic.

He inclined his head at the footman. After the man left, he turned to his mother. "She's in the east wing by herself, Mama. What if she gets sick and needs help? That is too far away for anyone to hear her if she calls out."

Lady Anne frowned. "Why is that, Claire? Aren't there enough rooms in the west wing with the rest of us?"

She gave his mother a little shrug. "When the devil lord arrived, I didn't think it appropriate to remain in the room attached to his, or in the same wing of the house, for that matter."

Chase suppressed a smile and raised a brow. "The devil lord?"

Her cheeks turned a pretty pink. "Well, it's how I thought of you when you arrived."

"And now?"

"Now what?"

"Don't be obtuse, my dear. You understand me."

She shrugged. "I've not decided. And don't give me another raised brow. You shouldn't have asked the question if you didn't want to hear the answer."

"Well, let me know when you decide. In the meantime, you will relocate yourself to your old room."

"It's not appropriate for me to be in the room attached to yours, and you know it."

"Keep the door locked if it will make you feel better, but I don't want you sleeping in a wing by yourself."

"No."

The fire in her eyes was magnificent. To hell with only stealing a kiss, he wanted to drag her up to his chamber and have this out with her in his bed. Yes, indeed, if they married, they would have some grand fights followed by hours of making passionate love. He grew hard at the thought and shifted in an attempt to get more comfortable.

"No? I am the master of this house and you will obey me."

Although he was baiting her, he couldn't resist. He wanted her attention on him—wanted to keep the fire in her eyes. No question, the woman stirred his blood.

"She's right, Kensington. Claire cannot be in the room attached to yours, but I'm sure there is another suitable chamber in our wing she can move into."

"Fine, it's settled then. Go and choose a room to your liking, Claire. Have your maid move your things immediately."

She stood and gave him a curtsey that managed to be insulting. "Yes, my lord and master. Right away, master." She stomped out of the room.

Chase gave her retreating back a wide grin.

"Well, that was interesting," Lady Anne said.

"Wasn't it though?" he answered, still grinning.

Claire danced up the stairs with a light heart. The arrogant, scowling devil lord was worried about her safety. The thought warmed her down to her toes. A satisfied smile crossed her face. What a fine performance she had given.

"I am master of this house and you will obey me," she mimicked as she entered her room.

"Pardon, my lady?" Maggie asked. Clothing fresh from the laundry was spread over the bed.

"Oh, nothing, Maggie. No need to put those away. I'm moving back to the west wing."

"Back into your chamber?"

"No, I think the garden room will do."

The room had a nice view overlooking the gardens and was one of her favorites. Though she'd never admit it to Chase, she was happy to be moving back to the west wing. It had been difficult to sleep in this wing knowing she was alone. Every creak and groan of the floors or walls had seemed like a warning that danger was approaching.

A knock on the door made her heart skip a beat. Had he come to make sure she was moving her things? Maggie opened the door and spoke to a footman. "You are wanted in the drawing room, my lady. You have visitors," Maggie said.

"Did he say who?"

"It's Mrs. Fisherman and her daughter. Lord Derebourne requested your presence immediately."

"Bells in hell, doesn't Mrs. Fisherman have better things to do than attempting to catch Lord Derebourne for her daughter?"

"It doesn't seem so, my lady."

Claire checked her appearance in the mirror. She probably should change into a black gown, but the lavender would have to do. True to his lordship's threat, all her black gowns and white lace caps had disappeared. When asked where her mourning gowns were, her maid gave a suspiciously innocent look and replied that she couldn't really say.

"Can't say, or won't?"

"Perhaps you should be asking the master, my lady, if you really want to know. In my opinion, good riddance," Maggie had added dismissively.

Claire stifled a smile of amusement at Chase's obvious relief when she walked into the drawing room. He stood and bowed to her. "Lady Derebourne, as you can see, Mrs. Fisherman and her lovely daughter, Miss Fisherman, have come for a visit, *again*."

Mrs. Fisherman beamed at his reference to her lovely daughter, altogether missing his emphasis on the word again. "Lady Claire, such a pleasure to see you, but there is no need to interrupt your day on our account."

Had she just been dismissed in her own home? "Oh, do not concern yourself, Mrs. Fisherman. I have nothing pressing to attend to at the moment." Claire sat on the sofa next to Rhonda. "How are you today, Rhonda?"

"I am well, Lady Claire."

Rhonda took Claire's hand and held onto it. It appeared at least one Fisherman wanted her to stay.

"Has your mother not arrived, Lord Derebourne? You must know you cannot continue to allow Lady Claire to remain in your home without a chaperone."

Rhonda's hand tightened on hers. "Sorry," she mouthed.

She squeezed Rhonda's fingers and turned to see Chase's reaction to Mrs. Fisherman's comment. If looks could melt a person out of existence, Mrs.

Fisherman would be a puddle. Fortunately, Lady Anne entered the room before Chase could make a scathing response, which she feared he was about to do.

"Kensington, I didn't know we had guests. You are a naughty son for not sending for me sooner. Although, I dare say, it is possible you did and the footman is still wandering the halls looking for me. There are over one hundred rooms here, you know It may be days before we see him again. Well, never mind that, I am here now. Introduce me please."

Chase stood. She knew damn well he had sent for her as soon as Smithfield told him Mrs. Fisherman was in the drawing room. She had changed into one of her finest dresses and her hair had been styled into an elaborate sweep of curls and twists. He'd warned her about Mrs. Fisherman and her intention to capture him for her daughter. Dressed in the height of London fashion, Lady Anne had come armed for battle.

"Mrs. Fisherman, Miss Fisherman, allow me to introduce my mother, Lady Kensington."

The ladies stood and curtseyed. "Lady Kensington, it is indeed a pleasure to meet you. I'm certain Lady Derebourne is relieved you have finally arrived to act as her chaperone."

Here we go, Chase thought. Lady Anne sat in the chair facing the ladies and waved a hand regally in the air for everyone to be seated. "Why is that, Mrs. Fisherman?"

"Surely, you do not approve of her residing alone here with Lord Derebourne?"

"Oh dear, Kens—silly me, you're Derebourne now, aren't you? Well, Derebourne, what have you done with my grandsons and their tutor and your valet and all the servants?"

"Nothing Mama."

"So they are all still in residence?"

"Yes, Mama."

She turned a brilliant smile on Mrs. Fisherman. "There, you see, Derebourne and Lady Claire have not been alone and all is well."

"But, my lady, children and servants cannot adequately supervise—"

"My son is a gentleman, Mrs. Fisherman, and would never force his attentions where they are not welcome." She cocked her head at him. "Do I speak true?"

He almost snorted at her clever phrasing. "Yes, Mama."

Mrs. Fisherman's lips thinned. "Forgive me, I never meant to imply otherwise."

"Of course, you didn't, Mrs. Fisherman." Lady Anne turned her attention to Miss Fisherman.

"Now, Miss Fisherman, Lady Derebourne speaks fondly of you and tells me you are her good friend. It is wonderful to have a good friend, is it not? I had a very dear friend when I was your age, Lady Elaine Bradford. But she married an American and moved to Boston so I haven't seen her in…well goodness, it must be over twenty years. We do write and she has invited me many times to visit her, but can you imagine getting on a ship and sailing to Boston at my age?

"It is tempting, however. I may surprise my family one day by purchasing a ticket and sailing away to a foreign land, although I am not sure how civilized Boston is. My friend writes that they have balls and musicals just like here in England, so they don't sound like the savages many claim them to be. Is Boston civilized, Kensington, do you know?"

"Yes, Mama, but do not think of sailing off to parts unknown without telling me first, I beg you."

"Silly man. Of course I will tell you before I leave. Imagine if I disappeared without notice. You would have searchers spread out all over England looking for me while I was merrily sailing away on my adventure, knowing exactly where I was. What kind of mother would do such a thing to her son? Not this one, I assure you."

Miss Fisherman's eyes were as wide as an owl's, her lips twitching. Her mother, however, had a pained expression on her face. After his father had been killed, he and Lady Anne had developed this way of deflecting the gossips and diverting their attention. By the time Lady Anne finished with them, not one could remember their question or snide comment.

"Have you ever wanted to travel to another country, Miss Fisherman?" Lady Anne asked.

"My darling Rhonda is perfectly happy where she is. She understands her duty is to marry well and give her husband an heir. The man who captures her hand," Mrs. Fisherman said, settling her gaze on him, "will be fortunate, indeed, as I have trained her well. She is versed in managing a household, embroidery and the pianoforte. My daughter comes with a decent dowry, provided by her grandfather, Baron Brisco. She is sweet and biddable, which, as we ladies know, are traits men look for in a wife."

Miss Fisherman disappeared behind Claire inch by inch as her mother attempted to hand her to him on a silver platter. Claire's eyes flashed with anger. He signaled his mother to step in with some of her nonsensical drivel before he or Claire said something best left unsaid.

"Baron Brisco? Do I know him? Let me think. No, I don't believe I do. Well, it is no matter, one can't know everyone, can they? I did meet a baron once, what was his name? Yes, I have it. Baron Stanford. I wonder if Baron Brisco knows Baron Stanford, being as they are both barons. Do you remember Baron Stanford visiting us once, Derebourne? He had some business with your father, I believe."

Mrs. Fisherman's eyes glazed over. God, he loved his mother. "No, Mama, I don't remember."

"Well, it is not surprising as you were only a young boy. I think you were about the same age as Harry and Bensey when the baron called on your father. Boys that age do not pay much attention to the comings and goings of adults. Have you found that to be true with the twins, Claire?"

Claire gave a soft chuckle. "Yes, if there is a horse in front of Harry or a flower to draw in front of Bensey, I think the king could walk past them without notice."

Apparently, not knowing when to surrender to a superior foe, Mrs. Fisherman turned to Claire. "I must be wrong, Lady Derebourne, as you are wearing half mourning, but I was certain your year didn't end for another two weeks. If I'm correct, my dear, you risk giving the wrong impression by discarding your widow's weeds too soon. People will think you do not mourn your dear departed husband."

It had been a mistake for Chase to do away with her black gowns, but Mrs. Fisherman's sly intention to shame her in front of Chase and Lady Anne incensed

Claire.

"I think you look very pretty, Lady Derebourne, and I don't think the color of a gown speaks for the heart," Rhonda said.

Claire gave her a warm smile. "Thank you, my dear."

"Well said, Miss Fisherman," Lady Anne said. "Why don't you children go for a stroll in the garden? It is such a lovely day and I know sitting here, visiting with two old ladies is likely boring you to tears."

Claire stood and pulled Rhonda up with her. She and Chase had planned this with Lady Anne should the Fisherman ladies visit again. With her arm wrapped through Rhonda's, she walked her briskly out of the room before Mrs. Fisherman could object.

Once in the garden, she led Rhonda to a bench and sat, patting the space next to her. "Come sit with me, Rhonda. Lord Derebourne and I would like to talk to you."

Chase stood a few feet away, his hands behind his back. Rhonda busied herself pressing non-existent wrinkles out of her skirt. Claire took the girl's hand and stilled it. "Be at ease, my dear, we only want to talk to you about Bobby."

"Did something happen to him?" The girl's eyes flashed with concern.

Claire hurried to reassure her. "No, but we have two important questions to ask you, and I hope you will trust us enough to give an honest answer."

"I will try, Lady Derebourne."

"Good. The questions are this, do you love Bobby and does he love you?"

Rhonda clinched her hands in her lap. "Why do

you want to know?"

"Because, if the answer is yes to both, then we want to help you and Bobby."

An expression of hope flickered and then disappeared. "You can't help. Mother is determined that I wed—" She glanced nervously at Lord Derebourne.

Chase knelt in front of her. "Miss Fisherman, you are a lovely girl, but I think you know we wouldn't suit."

"I know, my lord. I have tried to tell Mother, but she won't listen. I'm supposed to—" Her face flushed bright red.

Claire picked up Rhonda's hand and clasped it in hers. Mrs. Fisherman was planning something and they needed to find out what. "I promise you can trust us to help you. What are you supposed to do, Rhonda?"

She squeezed her eyes shut. "Mother is going to arrange for me to be alone with Lord Derebourne at the assembly, and I'm to have him kiss me so she can catch him in a compromising situation." Tears fell down her cheeks. "But I know you don't want to, Lord Derebourne, and I don't know how to make you." She gave a sad little laugh. "I'm not offended, my lord, because I don't want to kiss you either."

The poor child was miserable and Claire wanted to shake Mrs. Fisherman silly. "Rhonda, do you love Bobby and does he love you?"

"Yes," she whispered. "Yes, he loves me and I love him." She swiped a hand over her eyes. Chase handed her his handkerchief. "Thank you," Rhonda said, wiping her eyes and blowing her nose.

Claire smothered a laugh at the expression on

Chase's face when Rhonda tried to give the handkerchief back to him.

"No, keep it," he said.

"It's hopeless," Rhonda said in a steadier voice. "He asked for my hand, but Mother made Papa deny him. She said Bobby isn't good enough to be my husband, but he is, Lady Derebourne. He is!"

Claire glanced at Chase and he nodded. "Then there is only one thing to do. You and Bobby are going to elope to Gretna Green."

Rhonda's eyes widened. "We are?"

"Yes, you are. Lord Derebourne and I are going to help you."

"Mother will never forgive me if I don't marry a lord."

"Dearest girl, this is your life and happiness we are talking about, not your mother's," Claire said. "She may be angry at first, but you are her daughter. Trust me, she will come around in time. Do you want to marry Bobby above all things, even above your mother's wishes?"

"Oh, yes. He is apprenticing with his father and will inherit the blacksmith business one day, but other than a small wage, I don't think he has enough money for us to travel to Gretna Green."

"You will have more than enough coin for that and to help you begin your new life when you return," Lord Derebourne said. "I plan to give you and Bobby a hundred pounds as a wedding gift."

Rhonda vigorously shook her head. "We couldn't accept money from you, my lord."

"You can and you will. It is worth that and more to extract myself from your mother's scheme. But more so, I'm doing it because I want to, because it will please me to see you and Bobby happily married. If you wish, you can thank me by naming one of your sons after me," he said in a teasing manner.

"Derebourne? That is a big name for a baby, but Bobby and I would be honored to do so."

Claire grinned at the amusement dancing in Chase's eyes.

"No, Miss Fisherman, I was thinking of my Christian name, Chastain."

"Chastain," she repeated. "Oh, that is a lovely name."

They planned their strategy for the elopement before returning a happier Rhonda to her mother. Claire pressed on her the importance of keeping the elopement secret, not giving the slightest hint of it to her parents. Chase agreed to talk to Bobby and his father to tell them of the plan so Rhonda wouldn't need to arrange a risky meeting with him prior to eloping.

"Well, how did it go?" Lady Anne asked as soon as the front door closed behind the Fisherman ladies.

"We have an elopement to plan," Claire laughingly said.

Lady Anne sighed. "Oh, I do so love weddings."

Chapter Nineteen

Chase scowled as the ladies walked arm-in-arm down the hall without so much as a by-your-leave. Was he invisible? Something odd was going on. With the exception of the time spent with Miss Fisherman, Claire treated him like a stranger.

Whatever it was, his mother was in the thick of it up to her tiny ears. If he tried to find out from her, she would talk circles around him, and the only thing he would get would be a spinning head. He would find out from Claire, grinning as he considered several ways to go about it.

"Is anything amiss, my lord?"

Chase peered at Smithfield. "You can see me then, Smithfield?"

"Yes, my lord."

"That's good to know." He waved a hand in the air. "Carry on."

Smithfield likely thought he was cracked. Chase was beginning to think so himself. The blasted woman had him so confused he wasn't sure which way was up. If he could ever catch her alone, he would punish her for it by kissing her until she didn't know which direction her head was facing. He headed upstairs to find Bensey.

Bensey smiled when Chase entered the room. "I have finished, Father. Would you like to see?"

"I would." His breath caught in his throat upon seeing the portrait. The babe had Claire's blue eyes and Derebourne's features. If Bensey got it right, Andrew had been a beautiful baby.

Chase squeezed Bensey's shoulder. "Words fail me. I think Lady Claire's going to cry when she sees this, but, Bensey, they will be happy tears."

"I don't mind happy tears."

Harry came into the room and Bensey showed him the picture. "This is what Lady Claire's baby looked like? She must miss him ever so much."

"She does, Harry," Chase said.

He sent a prayer to the heavens for the twins' continued health and wellbeing. The boys wanted to go find Lady Claire immediately and give her the portrait, but he convinced them it would be better to wait until after dinner.

Halfway through their meal, Chase fought the urge to embarrass himself in front of his family by demanding Claire tell him what the bloody hell her problem was.

She talked and laughed with his mother. She talked and laughed with the twins. She talked and laughed with everyone but him. He pushed his plate away, sat back in his chair, steepled his fingers under his chin and glared at her.

"It isn't polite to stare, Kensington," Lady Anne said.

Her eyes sparkled with mischief and he scowled at her. Yes, indeed, whatever was going on in Claire's mind, his little mother was in on it up to her glittering eyeballs.

"Earlier, I asked Smithfield if I was invisible. He

assures me I am not, at least to him. Perhaps I'm only invisible to certain people. Can you see me, Claire?"

She cocked her head. "I see you perfectly well, my lord."

My lord? "Stop lording me."

Her lips twitched before she bit down to keep from smiling. Well then, she now owed him two kisses. Rest assured, he would collect what was due him, but he puzzled over the almost smile. Was she playing some kind of game and if so, what and why?

"I see you, Father," Harry declared.

"I can, too," Bensey said.

He arched a brow at his mother, the only one left to assure him he was visible.

She rolled her eyes. "Yes, Kensington, I also see you." She stood. "Claire and I will leave you gentlemen to your port and lemonade. We'll be in the drawing room when you're ready to join us."

They left the room and a few seconds later he could swear he heard his mother giggle. He turned to the twins. "Do either of you know what's going on between those two?"

"No, Father," they answered.

"May I go upstairs and get Lady Claire's picture?" Bensey asked.

"Yes. Harry and I will wait for you here so we can go to the drawing room together."

Chase put his mind to Claire's strange behavior. She was clearly ignoring him, but why?

****

Claire managed to hold in her laughter until they reached the privacy of the drawing room. She and Lady Anne fell onto the sofa before giving into the mirth bubbling inside them.

Lady Anne gasped for breath. "He asked Smithfield if he was invisible. Can't you just see it?"

Claire wiped her eyes. "Poor man. I feel guilty doing this to him."

"Oh, dear heart, you must continue with your plan. If he's this out of sorts after only one day, just imagine after a week of it. You'll have him following you around like a lost puppy, just as I predicted."

"I don't want him tamed, you know. I like his arrogance and self-confidence. I love him just the way he is."

Lady Anne cradled her tiny hand on Claire's cheek. "I know, my dear, and I'm pleased to hear it."

Claire closed her eyes. She leaned her face into Lady Anne's palm, pretending for a moment it was her mother. Was there ever a time when her mother showed any sign of affection in her touch?

She lifted her face away from the comforting warmth of Lady Anne's palm. "I just want him to forget his foolish plan to find me a husband."

Footsteps approached in the hallway and they set about assembling serious expressions on their faces. The twins entered ahead of Chase. Bensey held a rolled canvas in his hand. As seemed to be his habit, Chase took the chair closest to her. She didn't look at him, but sensed his attention on her. Her skin prickled in response. Would he always have this effect on her?

The boys squeezed onto the sofa, Harry on the other side of Lady Anne and Bensey next to Claire. Lady Anne wrapped her arm around Harry, pulling him against her side. Claire longed to do the same with Bensey.

"There now, I have my grandson right where I want him," Lady Anne said. "Did you talk to your horse today, and of more interest, did he talk back to you? If he did, I must know what he said. Was it something like, 'Good morning, Harry, did you bring me an apple?' Ever he speaks to me, I'll just swoon right where I stand, but I'm sure you're made of sterner stock than me. Well, don't keep me in suspense, dear boy, what did Victory say?"

Harry laughed. "He said you are a funny grandmamma, and that he loves you ever so much."

"He said all that, did he? What a wonderful horse he is. You must tell him that I love him ever so much, also." She peered past Claire. "And you, sweet Bensey, what did you do today?"

Bensey twisted the canvas he held, darted a shy glance at her and then at his father. Chase gave a slight nod, and Bensey handed her the rolled up paper. "I drew this for you, Lady Claire. Father said it may make you cry happy tears, but I won't mind."

She took the canvas from Bensey and unrolled it. Of all the things she might have expected, it was never this. "Andrew," she whispered. Oh, God. Her precious baby boy forever recorded on paper.

How had Bensey known what Andrew looked like? She'd been so afraid she would forget him, but now, she never would. She traced his face with her finger and the tears came, blurring her son's features.

"Are they happy tears, Lady Claire?" Bensey asked.

She handed the portrait to Lady Anne, and then gave him a fierce hug. "Yes, they are the happiest tears ever."

At first, he was stiff in her arms. Then he tentatively leaned into her and patted her back with his beautifully talented hand. Claire let him go, not wanting to overwhelm him with her touch.

"Thank you. You don't know what this means to me. How could you possibly have known what he looked like?"

"Father said you were afraid you would forget. He took me to see a baby this morning so I would know how to draw one." His eyes shifted to the painting over the fireplace. "If I didn't get him right, I can try again."

Claire took the portrait from Lady Anne and studied her son's face. "No, you got him perfectly right. Thank you. Thank you so very much." She looked at Chase. "Thank you," she mouthed.

His lips curved in a half smile and he shrugged. She wanted to crawl onto his lap with her picture and have him wrap his arms around her while she cried for her lost son. As if he knew she needed to be alone, he asked Lady Anne if she would mind seeing the twins to their room.

Lady Anne leaned over and kissed her cheek, then stood. "Come along, you two. How would you like me to tell you a bedtime story?"

"Pray don't tell them the one about the Highlander," Chase said.

"Trust me, son, I learned my lesson on that one." She left with the boys, pulling the door closed behind her.

The room suddenly seemed too quiet. Claire didn't know what to say to him. It had been such a strange day, first wondering where he had taken off to this morning, and then by ignoring him as much as possible.

Now the beautiful drawing of her son.

"I miss him so much," she said as the tears came.

Without saying a word, Chase moved next to her and pulled her onto his lap. He gently took the canvas from her hands, setting it on the table. Wrapping his arms around her, he held her while she cried.

He removed a handkerchief from his pocket and wiped her tears. His gentleness touched her deeply and her tears turned to body racking sobs. He held her until she cried herself out. When she finally quieted, he handed her his handkerchief.

She dried her eyes and wiped her nose. "I suppose you prefer I keep it," she said with a trembling laugh. Her head was pressed against his chest and she couldn't see his face, but she heard a smile in his voice.

"Yes, please, although Anders is going to begin to think all my handkerchiefs have grown little feet and are walking off to parts unknown."

"Thank you. I know the portrait was your idea and you can't imagine what it means to me."

"I think I do." Chase had spent the past year wondering about his child. Had it been a boy or a girl? Would it have favored him or Teresa?

"Mrs. Fisherman would be appalled at your mother's idea of a chaperone's duties," she said.

He leaned his head to the side so he could see if there were tears still in her eyes. Her small smile pleased him. "What made you think of that?"

"I was just thinking that Lady Anne left us alone here, behind closed doors."

"So she did. Mama has always marched to her own music. Society has never been sure what to make of her."

"I like her tremendously."

"As do I." He put a finger under her chin and lifted her face. "Claire, why are you ignoring me?"

Her cheeks flushed, and there it was, another kiss she owed him.

"That's three," he said.

Her thumbs made circles around each other. "Three what?"

"You were biting your bottom lip. That is the third time today so three kisses you owe me. You can't say I didn't warn you." He lowered his mouth to hers.

All day, he had ached to touch her. Every time he'd caught her violet scent, every single damned time she'd brushed past him as if he wasn't there, he'd hungered for her—had bloody burned for her. He'd make sure she knew he existed.

Chase slipped his arm around her waist so she couldn't escape and deepened the kiss. Her hand stole up to the back of his neck, her lips parted and he slid his tongue into the sweetest mouth he had ever had the privilege of tasting. Once he was certain she wouldn't try to bolt, he trailed his hand down to her bottom and pulled her tighter against him. He rested his other hand against a breast, but couldn't feel her because of the bloody corset. He grunted his displeasure.

She pushed away. "No," she said, surprising him.

Her eyes, dark with desire, said she didn't mean it. "Yes." He captured her lips again.

Her resistance melted and she pressed against him, finding his mouth again. He had decided not to bed her again until he asked her to marry him and she said yes. But he was angry with her for ignoring him, and his male pride overpowered his good intentions.

Chase broke the kiss, found her neck and trailed kisses over her skin, then took her earlobe between his teeth. His mouth curved in a satisfied smile when she shuddered. He moved his lips to her ear and whispered the question she still hadn't answered.

"Why have you been ignoring me?"

She stilled, then pushed herself off his lap and backed up to the corner of the sofa. With a little shake of her head, she stood and picked up Andrew's portrait.

"I'll tell you, but not tonight," she said and turned to leave.

"Claire."

"Yes?"

"You still owe me one more kiss."

A mysterious smile appeared on her face. "Good night, Chase."

He waited until she reached the door. "And, Claire."

She peered at him over her shoulder. "Yes?"

"It would probably be a good idea to lock your door."

Her only response was another secretive smile before she left. He leaned his head back on the sofa and closed his eyes.

What the bloody hell just happened?

****

Returning to Hillcrest Abbey after his visit with Bobby and his father, Chase was pleased with how well it had gone. He had Mischief at an easy lope, enjoying the crisp spring day. The closer it came to leave for town, the more tempted he was to call the whole thing off and stay at Hillcrest. If he married Claire and never took her to London, he wouldn't have to worry about

251

Sandra Owens

losing her to another man.

"I can't hide her away forever," he told Mischief.

Mischief's ears flicked back. It was one of the things he liked about his horse. Mischief was always interested in what he had to say and never ignored him like certain other people.

"So, I'm committed to my plan."

Mischief snorted.

"You disagree then? That's easy for you to say, it's not your heart at risk." He'd always known how to relate to women, had understood what each wanted from him. Even with Teresa, he had known she was fragile—that it was his responsibility to take care of her, to protect her.

Then along came Claire and he was suddenly adrift in a big ocean with no rescue in sight. It appeared he'd forgotten everything he ever knew about women, no wiser than a boy just out of leading strings experiencing his first infatuation. It was frustrating. It was exhilarating. Chase hadn't felt so alive in a very long time.

As Hillcrest came into view, he nudged Mischief into a gallop, anxious to see Claire and tell her about his visit with Bobby. Having missed luncheon, when he entered the abbey, he asked Smithfield to have the cook send something light to his room. In his chamber, he found Anders busy folding neckcloths.

"Good, you're here. I want to clean up a bit and change my shirt."

He didn't want to see Claire while smelling like horse. Although to her, horse was probably the sweetest of scents. After eating and freshening up, he went looking for her.

The blasted woman was nowhere to be found. No one had seen her recently and she wasn't in any room of the house. Finally, a footman coming in from outside said he had seen her walking up the path to the family graveyard. Chase had not been there, so after getting directions, he set out to find her.

The path disappeared into a stand of trees, but was well marked and easy to follow. The quietness of the woods as he followed the shaded trail was peaceful. In a few minutes, he came out of the trees into a clearing. Chase stilled and took in the sight before him.

Generations of Derebourres were buried here, some of the headstones hundreds of years old. He would come back alone one day and walk among the dead, reading their names, the dates and inscriptions. But today, he was here for Claire.

She sat on a stone bench with her back to him. She was speaking, but too softly for him to hear the words. With his gaze locked on her, he walked toward her. Her head cocked slightly at his approach, but she didn't acknowledge him.

The portrait of Andrew was open on her lap, and he was glad he had thought to have Bensey paint it. She moved over, giving him room to join her on the bench.

Taking a seat next to her, he looked at Andrew's headstone. Andrew Charles Landon Tremaine, Viscount Waverly. Too many names, it seemed, for a two-week-old boy. Chase read the inscription. *My Beloved Baby, Now in the Arms of the Angels*

Sadness permeated from her. He took her hand and clasped it in his, wanting to give her comfort. But what comfort was there for a parent who had lost a child?

"I was telling Andrew about Harry and Bensey." A

tear fell on the picture, and she brushed it off. "I need to have this framed before I damage it by too much handling. Do you think Bensey would draw a smaller one I could carry on my person?"

"I'm sure he would. Why don't you ask him to paint a miniature that you can put on a chain and wear around your neck or carry in your reticule?"

"I would like that." She carefully rolled up the canvas. "Were you able to see Bobby?"

"Yes. Let's walk and I'll tell you about it."

After one last look at her son's grave, she stood. Chase offered his arm, pleased when she curled her hand around it. Resting his other hand over hers, he led her up the path. Her hand was cool and soft under his and awareness of her flooded his senses.

He wanted to lean his head down and press his mouth against the pulse in her neck, wanted to feel her lifeblood as it beat against his lips. When he had done that, he would trail kisses over her shoulders and down to the valley of her breasts. He would feel her skin heat under his touch as his hands traced the curves of her body. He would part her legs and—

"What did Bobby say?" she asked.

"What?" His mind protested the interruption of his erotic daydream.

"I asked what Bobby said. Where was your mind?"

In bed with you. "Oh, here and there." The path led them into the trees and he welcomed the shadowed coolness. "I'll tell you, but first, you promised to explain why you've been ignoring me."

Chapter Twenty

Claire stopped and removed her hand from his arm. Turning to face him, she gave a determined shake of her head. If she answered his question, he would likely stomp off in anger before he told her if Bobby was agreeable to the elopement.

"I'll tell you, but first I will hear how your visit went."

His chest heaved in a sigh of annoyance. "Very well, we will have it your way. This time."

She wanted to smile at the arrogance in his voice. He stood tall and straight in front of her, his whole being vibrating with tension. Until yesterday, whether he realized it or not, he had been sure of her. Now he wasn't and he didn't like it.

Believing her plan was working was the only thing that kept her from walking into his arms and begging him to claim her—heart, body, mind and soul.

Forever and a day.

"Is Bobby willing to elope with Rhonda?" she asked.

"Yes. It seems the idea had already occurred to him, but his father cautioned against it, fearful of the consequences. Once Mr. Smith knew the couple had the support of a marquess behind them, he gave his approval. I liked the boy and his father. They are honest, hardworking folk.

"You were right, he is a good match for Miss Fisherman. Bobby's eyes light up at the mention of her name and I feel confident he will be a good husband to her. I gave him the monies and we went over the plan. It will be happily ever after for them, it seems."

"Oh, this is exciting, and I am so happy for them. I must go tell Lady Anne at once."

"Claire."

He growled her name, a warning that she would not escape so easily. His gaze locked on her, daring her to try and leave. Shivers of anticipation flowed through her. Her heart thumped loudly, awakening her butterflies.

He took a step toward her.

She took a step back.

His lips curved in a wicked smile. "It's to be like this, then?" he murmured and began to stalk her.

She retreated until her back came up against a tree. Trapped she was, a cornered mouse to his cat. His hands rose and he pressed them against the tree, caging her between his arms.

He leaned toward her, stopping inches from her face and stared at her mouth. Her lips tingled as warm puffs of his breath wafted over them.

She pressed her palms hard against the tree—the only thing holding her up—as he feathered kisses over her eyes, her nose, her mouth.

Streaks of fire raced through her when he nibbled on her bottom lip. Pressing his body against hers, he rocked his hips showing her his arousal. If she slid down the tree, would he follow her down, lay himself over her and bring her the pleasure her body ached for?

"Why, Claire?" he asked between feathering

kisses.

The mist invading her mind cleared. She pushed against his chest, but he was as solid as the tree behind her.

"Go stand over there." She pointed toward the path. "I can't think when you're near."

Her words produced a chuckle from him. "As you wish." He stepped back two paces.

"More."

He sketched a mocking bow. "I am my lady's servant." He backed up until there was about ten feet between them. "Is this sufficient? Any more and I will need an ear trumpet to hear you."

The devil lord was too amused. She had half a mind to march past him and leave him wondering as to the why. Of course, her chances of getting by him were...well, none. His legs were spread making her think of a pirate posed in a commanding stance on the bow of this ship. A golden, angel-faced pirate. She must have smiled because he scowled, crossed his arms over his chest and glared down his nose at her.

"Sometime today, please, Claire."

God, she loved the arrogant beast. She bit her bottom lip to keep from telling him.

"Another kiss you owe me," he said smugly.

"If you would stop talking long enough for me to think, I'll answer your question. Are you still taking me to London for the purpose of finding a husband?"

All traces of amusement left his face, replaced by a look of what? Determination? Regret? Her heart pounded as she waited for his answer.

"I am." He gave a weary sigh. "I will admit that I don't want to, but I don't feel I have a choice. May I

Sandra Owens

come closer?"

"Only a little."

He stopped halfway to her. "I have explained this before, but will again. You lived an unusually sheltered life, Claire. I want you to have a chance to experience all the things a girl does at her come out. I can't be sure of you, otherwise." He appeared startled, as if he'd said more than he wished.

He pushed a hand through his hair. "I don't know. Maybe I'm set on this course more for myself than for you for reasons of my own."

For the first time, she truly understood his insistence on following through with his plan. In the days since his arrival, they had argued, laughed together, shared confidences and had loved each other with their bodies.

Because he'd been deeply hurt, he still guarded his heart. By taking her to London and putting her in the company of other men he was testing her. Stupid, but understandable considering his past.

Her horses often tested her, especially the damaged ones. *Can I trust you?* The question that mattered to them above all others. With each one, she had done whatever necessary to earn their trust. So be it. She would do the same for him.

"Very well. I'll go to London and shop for a husband." She moved to stand in front of him and raised her palm to his cheek. "But know this, Chase. There is only one man I want."

She walked past him and down the path.

Chase stood like a human statue, legs still braced apart and arms still folded across his chest. Unreasonable as it was—as he was the one insisting—

rage had consumed him when she said she would look for a husband.

Then a simple touch of her hand and her final words had calmed the beast inside him. He dismissed his doubts about what he was doing. It was a sound plan, he was sure of it.

He turned to escort her back to the abbey, but she had disappeared. Bloody hell. The woman still hadn't answered his question.

He shook his head and grinned. She muddled his mind so easily that he wasn't sure of his own name half the time. But, he vowed, he would get his answer before the day ended. Also, she still owed him two kisses. He was keeping count and it was one of the few things he was sure of.

****

Chase stood still while Anders tied his cravat. A week had passed since the day Claire had agreed to go to London—a deuced irritating week. She had evaded him at every turn. His mother had apparently appointed herself Claire's accomplice in the game of Ignoring Chase. If Claire wasn't busy working with Harry, she and his mother were joined at the hip.

When his mother bade him goodnight, Claire left with her. He had spent hours each night sitting on the wall of the courtyard waiting for her to make an appearance, but there had been no Claire.

He had been sorely tempted to go to her room after everyone was asleep. So far, he had controlled the impulse. The only thing keeping him sane was the furtive glances he caught her giving him.

"There, my lord, all finished. One of my best knots, if I do say so myself."

"You say that every time."

Anders picked up the velvet midnight-blue coat. "And each time it is true."

Chase held out his arms as Anders tugged the coat onto him and smoothed away the wrinkles. Tonight was the assembly and Chase dreaded it. He would have to drink weak lemonade and be fawned over. Claire had begged to stay home, but he refused to even consider it. If he had to submit to torture, then it was only fair she shared the pain.

At the bottom of the stairs, he waited for the ladies. Footsteps sounded above. When Claire came into view alongside his mother, he almost shouted in anger. It took effort, but he thought he managed a normal voice. "Where the devil did that black gown come from, Claire? And take that ugly cap off."

She wrapped her arm around Lady Anne's. "I told you he wouldn't like it."

"You're damn right. I don't like it." So much for controlling his anger.

"Kensington, must I always have to remind you to watch your language?"

"My pardon, Mama, but she knows how I feel about seeing her in black."

Claire reached the bottom step and stopped in front of him. "It's either this gown or I won't go. If I don't wear black, Mrs. Fisherman will make sure everyone knows I put away my widow's weeds too soon. I refuse to be the subject of gossip tonight."

She was right, devil take it, but he hated seeing her in black, supposedly mourning a man who had treated her like a piece of the furniture. The white cap, however, was another matter and he plucked it off. Her hair was styled in a neat twist low on her neck. In his opinion, entirely suitable for the occasion.

"Very well. But, Claire, after tonight, never again. The first thing we're going to do when we arrive in London is go shopping. There will be no blacks or lavenders allowed."

"Fair enough." She gave him a grateful smile.

Chase escorted his ladies to the waiting carriage. The ride into the village didn't take more than thirty minutes. He spent the time listening to Claire give Lady Anne details of the village families expected to attend the assembly while completely ignoring him.

Before the night ended, he would find out why.

She and his mother had grown close. Although he was glad of it, he was ready for Lady Anne to go home so he could have his Claire back.

His Claire.

More and more, he was feeling possessive of her. How was he going to endure seeing her in a ballroom flirting and dancing with other men? She had said he was the only man she wanted, so he would hold onto that.

The carriage stopped and his footman opened the door. Chase entered the assembly hall with Claire on one arm and his mother on the other. The villagers were arranged in a semicircle facing the door with the Fisherman family in front. Applause broke out and Chase wanted to groan—or flee. This was going to be an interminable night.

For the first hour, Mrs. Fisherman planted herself by his side, guiding him and Lady Anne to every person in attendance for introductions. Claire had managed to slip away when Mrs. Fisherman nudged her way between them. With each presentation, Mrs. Fisherman made sure to mention how Lord Derebourne had asked her darling Rhonda for the first dance. Some of the looks sent his way at this news were speculative and others seemed to be amused.

Where the devil was Claire? Her place was by him, not sitting along the wall in deep conversation with Miss Fisherman.

Claire tried to keep her attention on Rhonda, but couldn't stop her eyes from following Chase as Mrs. Fisherman introduced him to the village families. The poor man was obviously miserable. Even so, he was breathtakingly beautiful in his formal clothes. His blue coat stretched across broad shoulders, the color bringing out the gold in his hair.

Then there were the parts of him hidden by his attire that she'd seen in all their glory. The muscular legs dusted by fine golden hairs, the dark arrow of hair leading to the most fascinating part of him, and don't forget his feet.

Merciful heavens, the assembly room was very warm. She opened her fan and waved it in front of her face.

"I don't know if I am more nervous or more excited," Rhonda said from beside her.

Claire forced her mind to pay attention to Rhonda. "Everything will go as planned tonight, Rhonda. There is no need to be nervous."

"Oh, I mean that I'm anxious about having to dance with Lord Derebourne but excited about marrying Bobby. I'm not nervous about the elopement because I know I'm meant to be with him. When does Lord Derebourne plan to talk to my father?"

"As soon as the first dance is finished he will ask to do so in private. Remember, you are to wait ten minutes before you join them."

"What if Papa doesn't agree?"

"Look at Lord Derebourne. What you see is a man capable of arranging the world to his liking." She patted Rhonda's hand. "All will go as planned, I promise."

The musicians began the first strings of a country dance. "Oh heavens, here he comes," Rhonda said.

"Just relax, dear, he doesn't bite." *Well, actually he does*, Claire thought, and had to stifle a giggle.

"Miss Fisherman, my dance, I believe."

The devil lord gave Claire a wink as he bowed over Rhonda's hand. Claire waved her fan vigorously in an attempt to cool her heated face.

Rhonda placed her hand in his and Chase led her to the dance floor. Claire longed to be the one in his arms. He was a superb dancer, and although Rhonda was stiff and uncertain of her steps, Chase expertly guided her down the floor. He said something to make Rhonda laugh and the girl relaxed a little.

"I never thought we would get away from that woman." Lady Anne sat beside her. "I had to stomp on Kensington's foot once when Mrs. Fisherman hinted to someone that she expected an offer for her darling Rhonda's hand very soon, and then looked pointedly at Kensington.

"I thought he would end the game then and there. He looked at his foot and then at mine, then raised his brow at me as if to say, is that the best you can do? But the moment passed, so all is well."

They sat in companionable silence as the dancers twirled over the floor. Claire's eyes strayed to Chase.

What would Mrs. Fisherman say if Claire told her she had seen his manly part? Laughter bubbled up at the thought of how badly she wanted to say, "Yes, his manly part is magnificent. If you think wearing lavender too soon is scandalous, my dear Mrs. Fisherman, what do you think of that? Oh, and by the way, it's mine and Rhonda can't have it." She grinned, imagining Mrs. Fisherman's reaction.

"What has you so amused? You're staring at Kensington as if you know a thrilling secret."

Horrified, Claire wished the floor would open and swallow her. Did Lady Anne suspect her thoughts? Claire feared her cheeks were blushing bright red. Bells in hells, she really was a wanton, and there was no hope of ever again being a proper woman now that she understood the pleasure he could give her. Would his mother still like her if she knew Claire coveted his manly part? Claire stared hard at the seam between two wood planks of the floor, willing it to open and swallow her.

Lady Anne chuckled and patted Claire's hand. "I was young once, my dear. Whatever it is you're thinking of Kensington, I can only imagine, but being his mother, would prefer not to know. The dance is ending so you and I must now place ourselves in Mrs. Fisherman's company and keep her occupied."

"She's headed our way now," Claire said. "She has a satisfied look on her face and most certainly wants to gloat. We must keep reminding ourselves that we are doing this for Bobby and Rhonda."

"Quite right. That will be our battle cry. For Bobby and Rhonda."

"For Bobby and Rhonda," Claire repeated. When

Mrs. Fisherman arrived, Claire stood. "Take my chair, Mrs. Fisherman. I have been sitting all night and need to stand a little."

Claire stood in front of Mrs. Fisherman, blocking her view of the room. It wouldn't do for her to notice Chase leaving with Mr. Fisherman.

"Oh, did you see, Lady Kensington?" Mrs. Fisherman gave a satisfied sigh. "Lord Derebourne and my dear Rhonda made such a lovely couple on the dance floor."

Claire refrained from rolling her eyes. "For Bobby and Rhonda," she muttered as Chase escorted Mr. Fisherman out of the room.

****

Chase ushered Mr. Fisherman onto the terrace. He had mentioned to the vicar that he needed some fresh air and the man had made it easy by agreeing that he, too, would like to step out of the hot assembly room for a few minutes. Chase took his cheroot case out of his pocket, offering one to Mr. Fisherman.

The man's eyes lit up. "The wife doesn't allow me these, my lord." He hastily took one. "But I won't tell her if you won't."

"Wouldn't think of it." Chase struck his flint and lighted their cheroots. "There's not much time, so I'll get right to the point. Your wife is set on my marrying your daughter. I'm sorry to disappoint Mrs. Fisherman and possibly you, but it's not going to happen. Please don't be offended. Miss Fisherman is a lovely girl, but I would make her miserable. Also, she doesn't want to marry me."

Mr. Fisherman lifted his cheroot and stared at the glowing tip. "I have no reason to be offended, my lord.

I told the wife she was reaching too high."

"It's not that, sir. If I loved your daughter, I would marry her. Miss Fisherman loves someone else, however, and I am beginning to believe there is someone I want."

"Lady Derebourne," the vicar said.

Apparently, his surprise showed on his face because the man chuckled.

"You would be amazed what one learns when everyone thinks one is taking a snooze. The day I accompanied my wife to your home, I saw how you looked at Lady Derebourne and knew then Mrs. Fisherman was reaching for the moon. What is a man to do, I ask you, when he only wants peace in his home, but married to someone as determined as Mrs. Fisherman? Take a good snooze and hope someone else shows her the error of her thinking, eh?"

"What of your daughter's happiness? You know she's in love with the blacksmith's son?"

"Yes, and as soon as you do me the favor of dashing Mrs. Fisherman's notions, my daughter will be free to marry Bobby."

Chase was beginning to like this crafty man. "No, that won't do. Miss Fisherman is leaving tonight for Gretna Green with Bobby."

Mr. Fisherman's brows shot up. "Is she?"

"Yes, Papa, we are." Miss Fisherman and Bobby stepped out of the shadows.

Mr. Fisherman's eyes lifted to the moon his wife had been reaching for. Chase could see that a debate was going on in the man's mind.

"Yes," he finally said. "I imagine it would be for the best, daughter."

Miss Fisherman launched herself into her father's arms and gave him a hug. "Thank you, Papa. Bobby will be a good husband, you'll see."

He placed a kiss on his daughter's forehead. "I know that, child."

Bobby came forward and held out his hand to the vicar. "Thank you, sir. I promise I will always take care of her."

The two shook hands before Bobby led his bride-to-be away. Mr. Fisherman had tears in his eyes, and Chase busied himself with his cheroot. Relieved this had been easier than expected, he glanced at the vicar to see he had regained his composure.

"Let's give them an hour before we go dashing your wife's notions, Mr. Fisherman."

"Then you are going to have to stay out of sight, my lord. If Mrs. Fisherman thinks Rhonda is with you, she won't go looking her."

"Send my mother out and tell your wife Miss Fisherman is sitting on the terrace with me and Lady Kensington. Do not fail to mention that my mother is with us."

The vicar nodded, his eyes devoid of guilt. So, Mr. Fisherman wasn't aware of the compromising position in which his wife hoped to catch a marquess. Chase liked the man even better.

"Sounds like a plan, my lord. I haven't danced with Mrs. Fisherman in years, but I suppose it would help if I did so tonight. Won't hurt to keep her occupied, you see," he said with resignation.

****

Traveling back to Hillcrest, melancholy settled over Claire. Likely due to the excitement of Rhonda's elopement being over, she supposed. Tomorrow she would begin packing for her trip to London. Chase had dimmed the lamps putting his face in the shadows. Even so, she sensed his attention on her. What was he thinking? Did he really mean to go through with his idiotic plan?

A strange tension seemed to shimmer in the air between them. She wanted to crawl onto his lap and hear him whisper in her ear that he was putting an end to his mad scheme. His foot came to rest alongside hers. When he pressed against her shoe, she knew it was no accident.

"You should have seen Mrs. Fisherman's face, Claire, when Kensington told her that her daughter had eloped," Lady Anne said, breaking the silence. "She was livid with the poor vicar for allowing it to happen when Lord Derebourne had clearly taken an interest in the girl. Kensington told her there was not a chance of a marriage between him and Miss Fisherman when the girl was clearly in love with another."

"Not a chance in hell," Chase muttered.

"Your language, Kensington. Anyhow, when she finally calmed down enough to listen to reason, Kensington suggested she and the vicar put it about that the couple eloped with the blessings of both sets of parents.

"She may be an annoying woman, but she's not a stupid one. By the time we left them, she was concocting a story of love and romance. Even now, I'm sure she's busy spreading her story to those still at the assembly. It didn't hurt that Kensington promised a generous donation to the vicarage to compensate for their troubles."

"This elopement was deuced expensive."

By his grin, Claire knew he enjoyed teasing Lady Anne.

"Your language, Kensington. You should have seen Mrs. Fisherman's eyes light up when he said that. I believe they are honest people, but I would not be surprised if in a week or so, she turns up wearing a new gown and bonnet. She will feel Kensington owes her something for not seeing the brilliance of a match with her daughter."

"The devil. It would have been worth a hundred dresses to extract myself from her clutches."

Lady Anne gave a theatrical sigh. "Your language, Kensington. So, as they say, whoever they are, all's well that ends well."

"That would be Shakespeare, Mama."

"Well, he always was clever with words, if you ask me. Have you seen Romeo and Juliet on stage, Claire?"

"No, but I would love to. I have read the story."

Even though she'd just said she had read the story, Lady Anne decided Claire should hear it again. Chase had apparently slipped his shoe off as his stocking-clad foot slid up her leg. She didn't hear a word his mother said.

Chapter Twenty-One

Chase followed his mother and Claire up the steps to the house. He leaned forward and whispered in Claire's ear. "Meet me in the courtyard in one hour."

She didn't respond, so he placed his palm against her back and gave her a warning. "One hour, Claire, or I will come to your room."

Chase paced along the wall in the courtyard. There wasn't a clock to see the time, but he estimated more than an hour had passed. The woman was making him daft. He walked to the table where he had placed a bottle of wine and two glasses. Filling one of the glasses, he drained the wine in one swallow.

He had been aware of her all night at the assembly, had wanted to tuck her next to him and keep her there—hideous black gown and all. Let the bloody gossips gossip. He refilled the glass, then filled the second one. If she didn't show, he would drink it all. Could one get drunk on wine? He had never tried, but had a mind to find out. At least, that would be one question he would get the answer to.

Just as he brought one of the glasses to his lips, the back of his neck prickled. She was here. Setting the glass back on the table, he slowly turned.

Christ in heaven, she took his breath away. Her pale hair flowed straight down her back and over her shoulders. He let his gaze roam down her, taking in the white silk, then down to her bare feet. She said nothing, only stood still under his perusal.

Raw aching need went straight to his gut, but there was also anger. Anger at seeing her in the black gown, anger at being ignored for the past week, anger at the thought of the weeks to come and having to stand aside while men surrounded her, vying for her attention. He was up to his eyes in anger.

With a primitive snarl, he advanced on her, his strides long and furious. On reaching her, he pulled her against him, covered her mouth with his and unleashed the raging beast inside him.

Let him see her ignore this. The kiss was wild and demanding. A small piece of his mind tried to warn him to be gentle and not hurt her. He attempted to ease the kiss, but she wasn't having it. She dug her fingers into the back of his neck and pulled his bottom lip between her teeth.

She didn't want tender? So be it.

His hands sought her breasts, entangling in the silk gown. He ripped it, then pushed it over her shoulders and down past her hips. This seemed to excite her and she tried to tear his shirt off. When she couldn't, he did it for her. He pulled the shirt from his arms and flung it away. Never before had he lost control like this, but the woman drove him to madness. He grabbed her bottom in both hands and pulled her up. When she wrapped her legs around his waist, he grunted his approval.

He strode to the lounge. Prying her legs from his waist, he set her on the floor. "Don't move," he ordered. He tried to unbutton his breeches, but his hand fumbled with the first button.

"To the devil," he muttered and pulled, scattering

buttons over the floor. When he had his breeches off, she took a flying leap, landing in his arms and wrapping her legs around him again.

"I thought I said, don't move."

"Are you going to punish me?" she retorted and bit his shoulder.

"Severely."

He pulled her legs from his waist him and fell back onto the lounge, cushioning her body with his. The anger he'd lived with the past week seeped away with her touch. Before the night ended, he'd find out the reason she'd ignored him, but first...this. Her mouth tasted like spiced wine and honey as his tongue stroked over and around hers.

Soft hands roamed over his chest, his sides, and every place she touched burned with need for more. He could spend eternity lost in the feel of her wrapped around him.

It seemed she had other ideas. Claire pushed to her knees, bracing her hands on his chest. Her hair curtained them, making it seem as if they existed in a world of their own. He bore her scrutiny as her eyes searched his. What was she hoping to see?

"I know you're used to experienced women, but I want to please you. Will you teach me how?"

Was she serious? "Christ, Claire, all you have to do is touch me and I forget my name. Trust me, love, you please me."

"You please me, too." She traced his lips with her finger, then leaned down and licked them. Chase sucked her tongue into his mouth and gripped her hips with his hands. Their mouths melded together, each fighting for dominance.

Lust raged through him, but he forced himself to break away before he lost all control. He'd waited a bloody long week for this. If he didn't slow down, it would be over in five minutes.

Her breasts were in front of his face, tempting him. He cupped them with his hands. "You're so beautiful. These are beautiful."

A mischievous smile appeared. "I'm glad you think so. You're the only man to tell me that."

Jealousy streaked through him. "Just how many men have seen them?"

She tilted her head as if considering her answer. "Let me see. There would be...one. You."

"You mean two. You forgot your husband."

"No, he never removed my night dress."

Although the information delighted him, he couldn't help thinking Derebourne had been the biggest fool to walk the earth.

Chase gently pinched a nipple. She gave a little shudder. "Like that, do you?" At her nod, he latched onto the nipple with his mouth.

"I like that even better," she murmured, and slid back until her bottom touched his cock.

Already as hard as a steel blade, he throbbed with aching need. He slid a finger through her curls and into her sheath, testing her readiness. She was dripping wet and hot. Her moan almost undid him.

"Ride me, Claire."

"I don't understand what you mean."

"Like this." He took his cock in hand. "Slide down on me."

She peered down between them and understanding entered her eyes. Chase gritted his teeth as she wiggled her pelvis until she had him buried deep inside her. Molten desire raged through him. He'd never been with a woman as inexperienced as Claire, yet her every touch set him on fire like no other had.

"What do I do now?" she asked.

"Now you ride me." He wrapped his hands around her waist and showed her. The clever girl caught on quickly.

"Am I doing it right?"

If she did it anymore right, he'd come out of his skin. No longer capable of speech, he made a sound and hoped she understood he meant yes. His buttocks came off the cushion when her hot, wet sheath wrapped around him and squeezed.

"Do you know your name now?" she asked.

"Haven't a bloody clue."

He cupped her bouncing breasts with his hands and teased her nipples with his thumbs. She moaned, quickening her pace. He prayed she was near her release because he teetered at the edge of his endurance. Her breath quickened, and he slid one hand down her belly to her little nub, rubbing it with his finger.

"Oh, God, yes."

She threw her head back letting him see her face as she climaxed.

"Chase," she breathed as shudders rocked her.

Christ in heaven, she was beautiful in the throes of passion. He wrapped his arms around her and flipped her over.

"My turn." He pushed himself deep inside her. Vainly tried to tame the wildness consuming him, but she wrapped her legs around his buttocks and dug her fingernails into his back.

"Harder," she said.

Chase let the beast out of its cage and thrust into her. Her eyes glazed over telling him she was going to climax again. She cried out and clinched around him. He barely managed to withdraw in time. His hot seed spurted between their bellies.

"Claire," he whispered against her neck.

Claire shivered and held onto him. *I love you.* The words were on her tongue, but she bit down on her lip to hold them in. With his face buried against her neck, he didn't see she owed him another kiss. She hadn't meant to let this happen, had only come to finally answer his question.

But when he had strode toward her—anger on his face and savage heat in his eyes—all thought of resisting vanished.

She had learned something of great magnitude tonight. He was hers, he just didn't know it, yet. Her heart leapt with joy when he nuzzled her neck. The magic moment was so close she could almost touch it.

He hardened against her belly but as tempted as she was to love him again, they needed to talk.

"Move over, please," she said and pushed against his shoulders.

He rolled off her. "Sorry. I must have been crushing you. Come here." He pulled on her arm.

She scrambled off the lounge and retrieved their clothes, handing him his breeches and shirt. "I cringe to consider what whoever finds all your buttons will think."

His eyes shuttered as he used his shirt to wipe his seed from his belly. Tossing it aside, he lifted his gaze to hers and scowled. Though she regretted spoiling the mood of their incredible time together, it reassured her to know his emotions were so deeply engaged.

"What's going on here, Claire?" His voice was edged with ire.

"I came down tonight to talk to you, not to…" She didn't know what to call it.

"Fuck?"

His crudeness startled her. He was angry, confused and lashing out at the closest target. She could have told him the confusion was within, but he had to come to that conclusion on his own. Like a damaged horse, trusting her was his decision to make.

"Never again call what we just did together that word."

He stood, pushed his arms through the sleeves of his shirt and pulled on his trousers. As there were no buttons to close the packet, they rode low on his hips. With his torn shirt hanging open and his legs braced apart to keep his trousers up, she was again reminded of a golden-haired pirate—only now her pirate had a barbaric edge to him.

"Forgive me. That was uncalled for." A strand of hair fell over his forehead, and he swatted at it with his hand. "But, Claire, you are making me bloody daft."

It was a struggle not to laugh. His trousers slipped down his hips, exposing springy golden curls. Whatever words she was about to say flew away.

He grabbed at his waistband with one hand and slashed the air with the other. "Stop looking at me like that unless you want a repeat of what just happened between us."

She jerked her gaze back to his. "I do want you, but that's what I came to talk to you about. I want to answer the question you asked me last week."

"Will wonders never cease?"

He tugged on his trousers, growled in irritation and dropped down on the lounge. His manners seemed to have deserted him along with his good nature. Claire was beyond amused, but thought she should keep that to herself. She began to pace in front of him as she tried to organize her thoughts.

"The suspense is killing me, my lady. Speak now or I'm leaving for my bed."

"All right. You wanted to know why I'm ignoring you. It's because of this stupid idea of yours to find me a husband." He opened his mouth and she held up her hand. "No, don't say anything until I'm finished." He snapped his mouth closed and gave her a curt nod.

"I understand what you mean about my sheltered life and you're right, it was as you said. I've never been courted, never learned the art of flirting, have never had the freedom to choose what I wanted. Because of that, I don't doubt I would have become infatuated with the first man to come along and treat me with kindness...to show me respect. Perhaps in the beginning, with you, it was infatuation."

She stopped in front of him. "You are beautiful and humorous...you have such a big heart. How could I not be fascinated by you? The way you brought Harry and Bensey into your home, the way you tease Lady Anne, your kindness to Bobby and Rhonda, all of it endeared you to me. So yes, I agree. In the beginning, it might have been infatuation. But now...now it is love."

She fisted her hand and pounded her heart. "I know it here." As she talked, the anger faded from his face. "I know it," she said softly, "because I would die for you."

"Claire," he whispered.

"No, I'm not finished. I understand what your wife did to you. She wasn't a bad person, but she hurt you deeply. I want your trust and if I have to go to London to prove that no man matters but you, then I will. I'll do it for you. Because, until I am certain you trust me, completely with everything that you are, I won't have you. The reason I've been ignoring you sounds childish, but I was doing it in an attempt to show you how miserable you would be without me."

How would he respond? She wrapped her arms around her waist. "I'm finished. You may talk now."

His gaze shifted away, and he stared into the night. "You unman me, Claire."

She knelt and placed her hands over his. "You couldn't be unmanned if you tried. That is a compliment, not an insult. You want to trust me, I know that. It's no different when I work with a damaged horse. He wants to trust me, but he's done so before only to be harmed by it. It's a very hard thing for him to risk it a second time because he knows now how it feels to be badly hurt. But it is a choice he has to make. I can't do it for him."

He finally looked at her. "I have feelings for you."

She smiled. "I know. I wouldn't have lain with you if I doubted it. Your problem is not your feelings, but your fear of being hurt again. So, we shall go to London and you will parade a host of men before me. I will look each one over and then shake my head no. 'Bring on the next one, my lord,' I'll say.

"We will do this a hundred times, a thousand if necessary, until you turn to me in wonder and say, 'Here is my heart, Claire. I trust that it is safe with you.'

I'm going to leave you now. I have much to do tomorrow and need to get some sleep."

She leaned up and kissed him. "Good night, Chase."

He picked up her hand, turned it over and pressed his lips to her palm, then curled her fingers over. She kept her hand closed all the way to her room.

****

Chase rested his head against the cushion and stared at the stars. He considered Teresa, recalled how desperately he had loved her. It had always been a painful thing. Had he learned to equate pain with love? This feeling he had for Claire was different. It was airy and freeing.

Except when she aggravated the bloody hell out of him, he thought with a grin. But that, too, was new. In a moment of surprising clarity, it occurred to him that he felt free to get angry at her. He'd said an unforgivable thing earlier tonight, and she had not broken down in tears or turned from him in disgust. No, she had stood up and called him on it.

He'd never dared to get angry with Teresa. She had been too fragile, and he had been too desperate to win her love to risk harsh words. Somewhere in his time with her, he had begun to lose pieces of himself. Now, in what was beginning to feel like a miracle, those lost pieces were finding their way back to him.

Until he let go of Teresa, he would never be able to move forward. A part of him didn't want to. His wife had been the center of his world for so long he wasn't sure he knew how to exist without the memory of her filling his heart.

Now, here was a vibrant woman who lived and

Sandra Owens

breathed, who looked at him with love in her eyes. One who held out her hand and patiently waited for him to take it. It was time to live again. He wanted Claire's forever and a day.

The moment had come to choose. He could hold onto a woman who was now a ghost, her memory haunting him for all she couldn't give him. Even now, a year later, the regret was heavy in his heart. He was bloody tired of it.

He closed his eyes and spoke the words he never thought to say. "Farewell, Teresa. You are with your Harry, where you always longed to be and so, I am letting you go." A great weight lifted from his heart even as tears burned his eyes. A gentle breeze carrying the fragrance of roses—Teresa's scent—brushed his face, and the whisper of her voice came to him. *Be happy, Chase.*

Chase blinked his eyes open. What had just happened? Deep in his soul, he believed Teresa wanted him to know she was pleased with his decision to let her go.

A new moon—a sign of new beginnings—hung high overhead. He thought of Claire. He would still take her to London because she needed the experience of it. But he would trust her word that she would shake her head at each man he paraded before her. If the worst happened and she fell in love with one of them…well, he would survive. It would hurt, perhaps even more than losing Teresa, but he would be happy for her.

And he would survive it.

****

The following morning, Chase entered the breakfast room thinking to find Claire, but she wasn't

280

there. He turned and walked out to the hall.

"Has Lady Derebourne come down, yet, Smithfield?"

"She's gone," his mother said as she descended the stairs.

She was gone? After everything she had said last night? What the bloody hell was going on? The woman was going to put him in an early grave.

"Where the hell has she gone, Mama?"

"Your language, Kensington."

He turned to Smithfield. "Saddle my horse."

Smithfield eyes widened and he took a step back. "Me, my lord?"

"I don't care who, just get him saddled."

Lady Anne put her hands on her hips. "Good heavens, Kensington, what is wrong with you? Claire has gone to church. She wanted to make sure there was no ill talk of Bobby and Rhonda's elopement."

The air swished out of his lungs. "Right. Forget saddling my horse, Smithfield." He spun around and returned to the breakfast room.

Behind his back, Lady Anne and Smithfield looked at each other and grinned.

****

Three carriages left Hillcrest Abbey Monday morning. Claire swallowed a grin as Chase impatiently tapped the roof while glaring at his mother. He'd wanted an earlier start, but getting everyone up and ready, fed breakfast, the trunks loaded and then all of the people, it was a little after eleven. Lady Anne had been the last to make an appearance.

She, Chase and Lady Anne were in the first carriage. The twins, Mr. Edwards and Anders in the second, and Maggie—thrilled to have a carriage to herself—in the third.

Mischief and Amira were tied to the back of theirs and Victory to the back of Harry's carriage. Two outriders rode ahead of the caravan and two behind. A fifth had gone ahead to make arrangements at an inn for a private room and luncheon.

Claire had never traveled like this, with so many people, trunks, carriages and horses. She had grown up in a small village, not leaving it until Thomas brought her to Hillcrest Abbey.

"You remind me of a child at Christmas," Chase said. "Your eyes are shining, and you're bouncing around trying to see out both windows at once."

It was true. She laughed. "I can't help it. I don't want to miss anything."

He glanced out the window. "Yes, I can see why. Those are the loveliest cows I have ever laid eyes on."

She refused to let him spoil her excitement. "They are, aren't they?"

There was something different about him today. It seemed as if a great weight had been lifted from him. Even his eyes were clearer and brighter. Gone was the sorrow she had often seen in them. She had left him with much to think about the other night and wanted to believe that something she said had helped.

"Oh, and look, Claire, there's a tree and another tree. How spectacular is that?"

She swatted his knee. "Stop it, you are being silly."

He puffed up and looked down his nose at her. "The Marquess of Derebourne and Earl of Kensington silly? Never say so!"

Claire burst into laughter and clamped a hand over

her mouth. The moment the wheels began to turn, Lady Anne declared carriage rides could only be endured by sleeping, and had picked up a pillow, positioned it just so and closed her eyes. There was a hint of a smile on Lady Anne's face, however, making Claire wonder if she slept.

All traces of silliness gone, Chase darted a glance at his mother and then peered out the window for a moment before focusing on Claire.

"I want to tell you something."

She nodded, afraid to speak. Something monumental was about to be said—could feel it emanating from him.

"I said farewell to Teresa...let her go be with her Harry."

Claire stopped breathing. "Did you?"

"It was time."

He looked back out the window. She glanced at Lady Anne to see a tear roll down her cheek. No, not asleep. Claire leaned forward and placed a hand on his knee.

"Are you all right?"

"Yes. Yes, I am." He covered her hand with his. "Thank you, Claire," he said softly.

"I didn't do anything. This was your choice to make."

"I know. You told me that and more. After you left, I thought about all the things you said. Though it was my choice to make, your words helped me put everything into perspective."

If he hadn't been in the carriage with them, she felt certain she and Lady Anne would have a good cry together. Seemingly uncomfortable with the seriousness of their conversation, he went back to pointing out silly things she didn't want to miss seeing; trees, cows and fences were high on his list.

To her disappointment, they entered London after the sun had set. As Chase had wanted to drive straight through to town, he had only allowed them thirty minutes for luncheon and a few more minutes to stretch their legs. Lady Anne had pulled Claire aside to give her a fierce embrace.

"You have given me my son back, Claire, and for that, I will always love you."

Claire tried to tell her it had been Chase's decision to let go of his wife, but Lady Anne refused to hear it.

She squeezed Claire's hand. "Now let us get busy getting the two of you married. Although I already have two daughters, there is always room for one more." She had walked away leaving Claire with tears running down her cheeks.

As the carriage rolled over the cobblestoned streets of London, Claire had the urge to press her nose to the glass to better see all the finely dressed lords and ladies walking up the steps of the mansions as they attended various balls. Soon she would be one of them. The thought both thrilled and scared her senseless.

****

Chase accepted the glass of wine Madame Jacqueline offered. His mother was with Claire in a back room where Claire was being measured by an assistant.

Regrettably, Lady Anne didn't invite him to join them. She had set herself and Claire up in rooms as far away from him as possible. First thing this morning, Lady Anne had marched into his study and warned him that there would be no improprieties between him and Claire now that they were in Town.

"Whatever the two of you got up to while in Kent is one thing," she said. "But now that Claire is in London, there will be no hint of a scandal attached to her name. Do you understand me, Kensington?"

His tiny mother barely stood higher than his massive desk. Sometimes when she scolded him, he felt like a girl of twelve years was laying down the law to him.

Rising to his feet, he'd glared down at her. "I am no longer in short pants, Mama. In case you haven't noticed, I reached my majority a good number of years ago and can now make my own decisions."

She was in no way intimidated by him, not that he had expected her to be. "As long as your decisions include keeping your hands off her until you put a ring on her finger, we don't have a problem."

After his mother left, Chase made a decision. If, at the end of two weeks from today, Claire kept her word and said no to every man he paraded before her, he would claim her for his own. He chose two weeks because that was the most time he could manage to keep his hands off her.

Maybe.

"Lady Derebourne, she is in town to find a husband, *oui*?"

"Did she say that?"

Madam Jacqueline studied him a moment, then a wide smile broke out on her face. "Such a fierce scowl, my lord. So it is that way, is it? No, it was your little *mere* who said this."

He had a few things he would like to say to his

little *mere*. "Lady Derebourne will need everything, Madam Jacqueline, including several riding habits, chemises, corset, et cetera, et cetera. She likes the way silk feels on her skin, so use silk whenever possible."

Madam's eyes were positively gleaming with amusement. At least someone was amused, because he certainly wasn't and he blamed that on his little *mere's* No Touching Rule.

"We will choose styles and colors when she joins us. I want everything yesterday, so hire however many seamstresses necessary to make it happen. I want a few ball gowns, day dresses and at least one riding habit delivered in two days. The rest to be delivered by the end of the week. Under no circumstances is anything to be black or lavender."

"One ball gown, two day dresses and one riding habit in two days, my lord, with a delivery each day following of what we have finished," she countered.

"Done." He finished his wine and handed her the glass.

Claire entered the room ahead of Lady Anne and he smiled at her. "Are you ready for the fun part of this excursion?"

"And that would be what, my lord?"

He narrowed his eyes and almost told her to stop lording him. His mother gave him her most stern look—not that it was easy to do considering her wee size, but she managed it, so he let his comment pass.

"That would be choosing the styles and colors for your gowns, *my lady*." There, he had shown his displeasure without offending anyone.

"Oh no, my lord," she said, coming right back at him. "I have no idea what styles or colors to choose."

Chase grinned in pleasure. He loved how he never felt like he was walking on broken glass around her. "Then you are fortunate I'm here, because I do." He stepped back. "Come here and I'll go through these fashion plates with you."

She stood next to him as he went through the plates. "This one," he said pointing to a fabulous ball gown featuring a low cut, scooped neck, fitted waist and flowing skirt.

"It's too—"

He cut her off. "No, it isn't. There, this one. Not that one. This one." And on it went until he came to the last page. "Definitely this one," he said of the gown, which he could only describe as elegantly simple.

It had no adornments, a high neck, long sleeves, and clung to the body. The surprise was the deep V of the back of the gown that would require a specially made corset. She would be stunning in it. He almost changed his mind at the thought of other men seeing her wearing it.

Without thinking, he rested his hand on her lower back and began to caress her. "Ouch," he said and glared at his mother. "Why did you pinch me?"

She raised a brow in answer. Well, he hadn't managed to keep his hands off Claire for one day. How was he going to manage two weeks?

"Excellent choices, my lord," Madam said. "Now for the colors. Only a deep burgundy will do for the last gown. With Lady Derebourne's pale hair, the color will look magnificent on her."

Yes, it would, and he was a fool. He should be dressing her in potato sacks, but she would probably be appealing in those, too. He and Madam chose colors for the remaining ball gowns, day dresses and riding habits. His mother didn't offer any suggestions, thank the stars. She had the fashion sense of a turnip and, fortunately, knew it. He had been choosing her gowns for years. As for Claire, she seemed dazed by the whole business.

Leaving Madam Jacqueline's, he took them to the milliner, the haberdashery and various other shops. The more he loaded up his two liveried footmen with the items he chose for Claire, the quieter she became. By the time the carriage finally turned for home, he was concerned. She stared at her hands, not paying any attention to the passing scenery.

"What is bothering you, Claire?"

Her shrug had the sign of defeat. "I feel so ignorant. Left on my own, lord knows what I would have chosen. Certainly not any of the gowns or bonnets or other things you picked out."

She stared at the hands fisted in her lap. "I don't know how to do anything except train horses. I think I will make someone a poor wife. Actually, I already have. Thomas was never very pleased with me. He must not have been or he would not have shut me out of his life so thoroughly."

"Then Thomas was a fool. Tell her, Mama."

Chapter Twenty-Two

"Oh, dear," Lady Anne said.

That didn't sound good. "Tell me what?" Claire asked.

"We have almost arrived at Kensington House," Lady Anne said. "It would be best done there."

What could they possibly know about Thomas? Why was Chase looking at her with sympathy in his eyes? Whatever it was, she wasn't sure she wanted to hear it.

When they entered the house, Lady Anne ordered tea and biscuits. "Why don't we take a few minutes to refresh ourselves," she said, and headed for the stairs.

Before she could start for her own room, Chase grabbed her hand. "Go away, Stillwell," he said to his butler.

"Yes, my lord."

"Claire," Chase murmured and snaked his hand behind her neck and slowly lowered his mouth to hers. The kiss so soft and gentle that she wanted to weep. Whatever they had to tell her about Thomas no longer mattered. The only thing important to her now was this man and winning his trust.

Do your worst, Thomas, you can no longer hurt me.

She sighed and swayed toward Chase, but he lifted his head and took his lips away. A half smile and dimple appeared on his face making her heart flutter.

"Go now," he said. "I will be waiting for you in the drawing room."

Fifteen minutes later, she entered the room to find Chase, Lady Anne and tea waiting for her. She gratefully accepted the cup from Lady Anne. It had been an exhausting day of shopping, and now she was going to hear some kind of revelation concerning Thomas. Taking a sip of the hot, sweet tea, she braced herself.

Chase left his place by the mantel and sat next to her. He tipped the glass of brandy he held over her cup and poured a measured amount into her tea. Just how bad was their news that she needed to be fortified with spirits?

She took several sips of the brandy-laced tea, then set the cup down and folded her hands in her lap. Taking a deep breath, she nodded. "I'm ready."

Lady Anne cleared her throat. "I'm not certain this is a good idea, Kensington."

"She needs to know, and I think it will help her to understand she isn't the reason for Derebourne's remoteness."

"All right, then. There is no easy way to say this. Claire, dear, your husband was in love with someone else."

Speechless, she stared at Lady Anne. She felt a nudge and accepted the glass of brandy from Chase. Swallowing too much, she coughed.

"Easy, love." He took the glass from her.

Love. The word grounded her. He grounded her. She reached for his hand and he twined his fingers through hers.

"How do you know this?"

"Quite by accident, actually. Sunday morning while you were at church, I was sitting in Kensington's study while he went through his desk to decide what he needed to bring to town with him."

Chase took over the story. "I found a book of poems buried under some ledgers in the bottom drawer and handed it to Mama."

"When I opened the cover," Lady Anne continued, "I was surprised to find the pages of the book had been removed to make room for a collection of letters. They were love letters to Derebourne. I probably shouldn't have read them, but he is no longer with us and I will admit to being curious.

"He was six and twenty when she wrote the first one. She mentions his age in the letter and that he mustn't tell his father about her. Several years later, she writes to tell him that though she loves him deeply, she will not marry him. Her reason for refusing him was the scandal it would bring on his name if he married his mistress.

"He must have tried to get her to marry him throughout their time together as there are several letters where she refuses him for the same reason. The last one was dated almost five years ago. In that one, she tells him she is dying and urges him to marry and have children, that he needed an heir. It appears she died shortly before he met you."

"So many years," Claire said in wonder. It explained so much about Thomas.

"Are you upset, my dear?" Lady Anne asked.

Claire thought about it. "No, I don't think I am. Mostly, I feel sad for them. It seems as if he loved her enough not to care about a scandal and she loved him enough to protect him from one."

Chase pressed her hand. "Do you understand now that you were never to blame for the state of your marriage?"

She nodded. "It changes everything I thought I knew. I always had terrible feelings that I was a failure as a wife. I'm sad for Thomas, but I'm definitely pleased to know it wasn't anything I did wrong. Did you bring the letters with you?" she asked Lady Anne.

"No, dear, we put them back in the book and returned it to the desk. We thought you should decide what to do with them. Did you want to read them?"

"No, it's enough to hear their story from you. I think I would like to bury the letters beside his grave, and that it would be best if no one outside the three of us knows about them."

"That is an excellent idea," Lady Anne said. "Well, the two of you wore me out today. I think I'll go take a little nap before dinner." She stood and gave her son a stern look. "Leave the door open, and remember my warning, Kensington."

"What warning is that?" Claire asked after Lady Anne left.

"Just Lady Anne finally deciding to play the role of chaperone and protect you from my wicked self. Are you all right?"

"I am." She shifted to face him, though she couldn't put much space between them as he still had hold of her hand. "You knew, didn't you, that it would help me to know this about Thomas?"

He placed her hand, palm down, on his thigh, then reached up and stroked her cheek with his knuckles. "I thought so, yes."

It felt naughty having her palm resting on his muscular thigh, only inches from the part of him that so fascinated her. Would he notice if she slid her fingers a little closer?

"Claire."

His eyes shimmered with heat, and one side of his lips curved. "Your chaperone has ordered me not to touch you, but she neglected to apply the rule to you."

His dimple stole her good sense. "How remiss of her."

"Wonderfully remiss. So you may touch me, if you wish." His gaze focused on the location of her hand. "Anywhere you wish."

Her fingers needed no further invitation, and she walked them to the place she ached to caress. He pulsed and grew under her touch as she stroked over the length of him. When he hissed, it encouraged her to continue. He lifted his hand and trailed a finger over the swell of her breast above her gown.

She tsked. "Remember the No Touching Rule."

"Hang the rules," he growled and slipped a finger down the valley of her breasts.

His erection jerked under her hand and she tried to encircle him with her fingers, but his breeches prevented it. He shifted and spread his legs giving her better access.

Claire forgot everything—forgot the rules, the open door, forgot all but him. He leaned into her and took her bottom lip between his teeth. She was on fire and only he could stop the burning low in her belly.

Suddenly, he was gone. He put her hand back on her lap. She made a sound of displeasure, her body swaying toward him until voices penetrated the haze.

The twins! She scooted to the opposite end of the sofa and tried to gain control of her breathing. Chase picked up a pillow and placed it over his lap. His chest heaved as if he had run a mile.

The boys tumbled into the room, Bensey taking a seat on the sofa between them, and Harry taking a direct line to the teacart holding a plate of cakes.

"Grandmamma sent us to visit you and Lady Claire," Harry said between bites of cake. He settled in the closest chair and balanced the plate on his lap.

"Your grandmamma is an evil woman," Chase muttered.

A giggle escaped, and Claire bit down on her lip.

Chase narrowed his eyes. "Another one you owe me."

"What does she owe you?" Harry asked.

"None of your concern, young man. Are you going to share those with your brother?"

Harry looked mournfully at the plate on his lap. "Do you want some, Bensey?"

"No, you can have them. I already had some."

Harry frowned at this news. "When did you have cakes?"

"Cook gave me some when I went to the kitchen to give her the picture I drew for her."

"It isn't fair that he can draw and I can't," Harry whined.

"You have never expressed an interest in art. The only reason you are doing so now is because it might get you cakes," Chase said.

Harry shrugged and stuffed another piece into his mouth. "Can we ride in the park in the morning?"

"I knew you would want to and was planning on it."

Claire perked up at this. "Oh, I wish I had brought my riding habit. I would so like to go with you."

Chase inclined his head and studied at her. "You are about my oldest sister's size. Ask Lady Anne if Patricia left a riding habit behind."

Claire jumped up, too excited to wait until later to ask. "If Lady Anne is sleeping, may I look for myself? Which room is Patricia's? Oh, I do hope she left one here. Do you think she would mind if I borrow it?"

Chase chuckled. "Yes. The pink room at the end of the hall on my floor. And, no."

She stilled while she matched his answers to her questions, then broke out in a wide smile and—without thinking—bent and gave him a kiss before racing out of the room.

Chase returned the intent looks from his sons. Harry's hand, holding a piece of cake, was frozen halfway to his mouth. Bensey, on the other hand, smiled serenely. Harry's mouth opened then closed. He placed the cake back on the plate.

"Is there something you want to say, Harry?"

Harry's head bobbed up and down. "Are you going to marry Lady Claire?"

Well, straight to the point his son was. "Would it upset you if I did?"

Harry's head went from bobbing up and down to a vigorous negative shaking. "We would like her to be our mother above all things."

Everything the boy wanted was above all things. Chase hadn't meant to have this conversation with his sons quite yet, but here it was, landed in his lap. He glanced down and realized he was still holding the pillow. No longer needed, he set it aside.

"It's a possibility. And, Harry, the meaning of possibility is that it's not a sure thing, so you are not to repeat our conversation outside this room. That applies to you also, Bensey."

"But don't you want to marry her?" Harry asked.

"It isn't that. I want her to be sure it's what she wants."

Harry scowled. "She doesn't want to marry you?"

"She loves him," Bensey said.

Chase turned to Bensey in surprise.

"How do you know?" Harry asked. "Did she tell you so?"

"No, I see it in her eyes when she looks at him."

Ah, his son with the artist's eye. Harry beamed as if that settled everything. Now that all was well in his world again, he turned his attention back to his plate. Chase sent them off to get ready for dinner a few minutes later.

He stood and walked to the window. Carriages passed by, but he was too deep in thought to notice much about them. She had said she loved him, but somehow, hearing Bensey say it because he saw it in her eyes made it feel real.

Was he being obstinate by insisting she prove herself to him? What did he feel for her? There was desire and a great liking for her. If it was love, then it was different than it had been with his wife.

With Teresa it had been an obsession, something he never wanted to feel again. With Claire there was a kind of peace in it. On the few—too few—times he had made love to her, it had been like coming home after a long absence. Could love feel different depending on the person you loved? It was an intriguing question.

****

Wednesday morning, Claire met Chase and Harry in the breakfast room at dawn. She had been thrilled to find a riding habit in Patricia's room. It was a little snug around her chest and a bit too short, but it would do until hers arrived.

"We usually eat light before our ride, just some toast and jam to tide us over," Chase said. "Afterwards, we return for a hearty breakfast "

"That suits me," she said.

Harry grinned at her like a madman. She assumed it was because she was joining them on their ride until Chase narrowed his eyes at the boy. Harry ignored his father and continued giving her his maniacal grin. Come to think of it, he had watched her all through dinner last night.

"Have I done something to amuse you, Harry?"

"No yet," he said mysteriously.

"So you think I am going to?"

"I hope so, above all things, my lady."

"Harry," Chase said, a warning in his voice. "Let's be off." He set his cup down and stood, not giving her a chance to question Harry further.

Claire crammed the last bite of toast into her mouth and followed them out of the room. When they reached the mews, Harry took off for the stables.

"What was that all about?" she asked.

"Just Harry being Harry." He took her hand and brought it to his lips. "Good morning, Claire. I would rather be kissing your lips, but this will have to do. For now," he added softly.

Her body hummed in response to the heat in his eyes, his touch and the male scent of him. He took the hand he had kissed and wrapped it around his arm as he led her to the stables where a saddled Amira awaited her.

Claire laughed in exhilaration as she raced alongside Chase and Harry. It had been four days since she had been on a horse and had missed it, even if she did have to ride sidesaddle. Amira reached the tree they had designated as the finish line a nose ahead of Victory. Mischief finished a head behind them. Harry eyed Amira with envy.

"No, Harry, don't even ask. You cannot have her," she laughingly said.

He hung his head and affected a pitiful face. "That makes me so very sad, Lady Claire, but if you were to promise me her first colt, I think I could be happy again."

Oh, to call this precious boy her son. "Suppose I tell you I'll consider it?" It would really depend on what happened between her and his father, but she couldn't tell him that.

"Splendid!" he said, and she knew in his mind it was a done thing.

"Claire! Harry! Let's go. Now!"

His voice held an urgency Claire had never heard before. Mischief added to her apprehension when he gave an agitated snort and laid his ears flat back.

Harry glanced behind them. "Cor," he cried and took off.

"What is it?" she asked.

"Just go," Chase ordered.

As she was gathering her reins, she heard a lady's

shrill voice. "Lord Derebourne! Lord Derebourne, wait, please."

"Go!" Chase demanded and she did. Galloping away, she glanced over her shoulder to see a heavy-set woman walking briskly toward them, waving her hands wildly in the air. Who in the world was she that she frightened the wits out of Chase, Harry and even Mischief?

When they arrived back at the stables, Harry shuddered. "That was a close one."

"Too close," Chase agreed.

He slid off Mischief and came to Claire. Reaching up, he placed his hands around her waist and lifted her down. She could feel the heat of his hands through his gloves. *Wake up, butterflies*, she thought, and they did.

"Who was she?"

"Lady Montgrove," Chase said.

"The last time we were in London, she caught me and Father in the park one morning and thought I was Father's servant," Harry said. "She looked down her nose at me. When Father tried to excuse us, she grabbed Mischief's muzzle and held onto him."

Then Claire didn't like the woman either. "But who is she?"

"Someone we want to avoid at all cost," Chase said.

"Why?"

"Because she devours men and has three marriageable daughters." He leaned down and whispered in her ear. "There is only one woman I want nibbling on me."

"Oh." The butterflies went into a frenzy.

"Oh." His face lowered toward hers, her lips

tingling in anticipation.

"Are you going to kiss her, Father?" Harry asked.

They both turned to Harry, who now stood next to them staring with open interest. Claire's cheeks flamed and she knew they had turned bright red. How did this man keep making her forget herself?

"Well, I was considering it. But I think we have embarrassed my lady enough for one day." He winked at her and gave her a little shove. "Go on ahead. Harry and I will see to the horses."

Claire returned to the house in a daze. She had almost kissed Chase in front of his son. What must Harry think? But he hadn't seemed to be unhappy about it. He had looked curious, yes, but he'd also appeared pleased.

Would he and Bensey want her for a mother? They liked her as a friend, but would they be jealous of their father's attention to her? What if they asked Chase not to marry her? She hadn't considered how the twins would feel about bringing her into their little family.

How selfish not to think of them and what they would want. But there was also the possibility they would be pleased. How would they feel if Chase asked her to marry him?

****

"I didn't mean to embarrass her, Father."

Chase sighed. "I know, son, but a gentleman doesn't take notice when a lady is about to be kissed." He rested his hand on Harry's head. "You do want to be a gentleman, do you not?"

"Oh yes, above all things."

"I thought so. Now, let's get our lady's horse brushed and settled in her stall."

They had grooms that could brush the horses, but he and Harry always performed this chore themselves. It was a part of their morning ritual and gave him the opportunity to teach Harry while also spending time with him. Chase caught sight of Mischief as he unlatched Amira's gate and disappeared into her stall.

It just might be that both he and his horse were in love.

Chapter Twenty-Three

Thursday proved to be a momentous day at Angel House. The documents making Harry and Bensey a Warren arrived, followed by a delivery from Madam Jacqueline. Chase asked his family—Claire was included in his definition of family—to attend him in the drawing room. He stood with his hands behind his back as they all filed in.

"Have a seat, please." He hid his amusement when the four crowed together on the sofa as if they were in trouble and banding together.

"It has come to my attention…" He paused. Four pairs of wary eyes stared back at him. "We now officially have two new Warrens in our family."

Harry understood immediately and let out a war cry. He jumped up, dragging Bensey with him and began to dance in a circle.

"Harry and Bensey Warren," he chanted. Bensey looked at his father in question, and Chase nodded. Bensey's smile was a beautiful thing to see.

"Do you know what this is about, Claire?" Lady Anne asked.

"I'm not sure." Claire said.

Before he could explain, Harry suddenly stopped his little dance. "Does it say we are Warrens on paper, Father?"

Chase removed his hand from behind his back and

held out the document. Harry reverently took it from him. "The important part is the last paragraph." But it seemed Harry was determined to read the entire thing. Chase took a seat near Claire.

"I have officially had their names recorded as Warron. Eventually, I'll have to explain to them why it is spelled with an o and not an e."

Harry came and handed him the paper. "They spelled it wrong, Father."

He should have known it wouldn't get past Harry. How best to explain hereditary issues to a boy of nine? "As much as I would like it to be spelled exactly like mine, they wouldn't let me because you or Bensey might want to be the earl someday."

"They aren't very smart, are they? Even me and Bensey know your true son will get to be the earl."

Lord, he didn't know whether to laugh or cry. "No, I don't suppose they are. It will still sound the same when you say it, however."

"Oh, Kensington, this is a wonderful thing you have done," his mother said. "I must go write your brother and sisters about this." She kissed him on his forehead before leaving.

"This is the grandest thing, Father, above all things."

"I am happy that you are happy, Harry."

"Harry Warron," his son corrected.

"I'm not going to call you Harry Warron every time I say your name."

Disappointment crossed Harry's face. "Then will you just for today so I'll know how it feels to be Harry Warron?"

The boy hadn't lost the ability to slay him. "For

today only, Harry Warron."

The pleasure on Harry's face at hearing his new name spoken was reward in itself for the effort and money it had taken to make this happen. Harry turned to Claire. "Will you call me Harry Warron for today, Lady Claire?"

"Of course I will, Harry Warron."

Bensey came and stood next to him. "I want to be called Bensey Warron for today, too."

Chase pulled Bensey between his knees and pointed to his cheek. "Give me a kiss right here, Bensey Warron."

His sensitive, artistic son kissed his cheek and then rested his head against his father's chest. Chase feared he might cry. "I love you, Bensey Warron."

Bensey grinned. "I love you, too, Father Warron."

"Come on, Bensey Warron, let's go tell Mr. Edwards and Anders our new name."

"All right, Harry Warron."

They left the room holding hands. Chase handed his handkerchief to Claire, and she buried her face in it. He thought he heard her say, "How could I not love you?"

****

An hour later, Claire impatiently waited for Chase and Lady Anne. A delivery had arrived from Madam Jacqueline and she had been ordered not to open anything until the two of them arrived. She walked to her bed and stared at the boxes. There were four dress boxes and several smaller ones. She was dying of curiosity and brought a hand from behind her back to touch the largest one. A knock sounded at the door, and she took a guilty jump back.

"Come in," she called.

The door opened and Chase walked in behind Lady Anne. "Did you peek?" he asked.

"No, but I must be honest and admit I was within seconds of doing so."

He chuckled as he came to stand beside her. Lady Anne moved to her other side. He pushed the largest of the dress boxes aside. "We'll save that one for last. Go ahead, choose one."

She lifted the top off the one closest to her, and carefully opened the tissue. It was a lovely day gown in pale blue and white striped muslin.

"Oh, I love it." It was the first gown a modiste had ever made for her. It was lovely. Growing up, her mother had made her clothes and when she married Thomas, the village seamstress had done so. Since Thomas never took her anywhere she had never had a need for many gowns, much less needed to be fashionable.

Lady Anne helped her take the day dress out of the box. "The color is perfect for you, Claire."

"I think you can thank your son for that, Lady Anne."

Chase grinned. "I am good, aren't I?"

"Don't let it go to your head, Kensington," Lady Anne advised.

The next box revealed the one thing she most longed for, a riding habit. It was military style in a deep blue color. "Oh, as Harry would say, this is splendid!" She held it in front of her. "What do you think?"

"Like I said, I'm good," Chase said.

Lady Anne shook her head. "Your head is swelling right before my eyes."

Claire laughed. She had never considered how happy beautiful clothes could make one feel. The third box was another day dress, this one in a lovely rose floral print. She held it up and raised a brow.

Lady Anne sighed. "Yes, Kensington, you are good."

"I know."

Claire carefully placed the day dress on the bed next to the others and eyed the last box. When she pulled the top off and removed the tissue, she stopped breathing. It was the last gown he had chosen when they had gone through the fashion plates. The satin ball gown was the color of a rich burgundy.

"Oh, my." She lifted it from the box. When she saw the back, she shook her head. "This is breathtakingly beautiful, but I can't wear it."

"Yes, you can," Chase said.

"Let me see," Lady Anne said.

Claire turned the gown to show the back. "I would feel naked."

"It is unusual, my dear, but not indecent. Don't decide until you try it on and then we will see. But I think you're going to look stunning in it."

"She will," Chase said. "You need to try it on before Saturday to make sure it doesn't require any alterations."

"What is Saturday?" she asked.

"The Duke of Westhaven's ball. I have accepted an invitation and it will be your debut into society."

Claire had an immediate desire to crawl into bed, pull the covers over her head and refuse to come out until Sunday. "I think I'm going to be sick."

He shook his head. "No, what you are going to be

is spectacular. Now, what else is in here?" He rummaged through the paper, bringing out a pair of silver slippers and silver gloves. "Perfect."

That was easy for him to say as he wouldn't be the one wearing a dress with no back.

He picked up a smaller box and opened it. "Ah, here it is." A corset the same color as the gown dangled from his fingers. "This is especially designed to go with the gown."

"Really, Kensington, you should not be looking at her undergarments."

He smirked. "Do you think I have never seen a corset before, Mama?"

"This is not a conversation you should be having with your mother. We like to think our sons are innocent little boys, even if said son stands two heads taller and seven stones heavier than his mother. "

He waved it in front of her face. "I love corsets above all things, Mama, so what do you think of your little boy now?"

Claire could see Lady Anne fight a smile. Their rapport fascinated her. Mother and son had a deep love for one another. Their open affection and the way they teased each other made her regret even more the stiff, remote relationship she'd had with her parents.

They opened the last of the boxes and Claire was thrilled with the three silk chemises and the plainer corset intended for the day dresses. Nothing further was said about Chase being in the room as they admired the fine craftsmanship of her new undergarments.

The next two days flew by. Before she knew it, Saturday arrived and she was sitting in her bath while Maggie washed her hair. Except for Friday morning when she had tried on the gown, she had managed to put tonight's ball out of her mind. The bath was the beginning of her preparations for the evening, and her nerves made an appearance. If only she could turn the clock forward and make it tomorrow. She dipped her head so Maggie could pour fresh water over her hair.

"There, my lady, all the soap is out."

Claire stood, and Maggie handed her the drying cloth. "Maggie, what if I do something to embarrass him tonight?"

"Embarrass your lord? I don't think that is possible, but what I do think is that you are getting yourself turned inside out for no good reason."

A knock sounded at the door and Maggie opened it, accepted a note and small black box from a footman. When she handed them over, Claire opened the paper and read.

> *C*
> *Wear no jewelry tonight but these.*
> *C*

Claire opened the box and gasped.

"Let me see," Maggie said.

Claire turned it to show Maggie. Nestled on black velvet was a pair of long, egg-shaped ruby earrings.

"Oooh," Maggie breathed.

****

Chase paced at the bottom of the stairs. He had never felt such anticipation over a ball in his one and thirty years. A swirl of red turned the corner and hesitated at the top of the stairs. Looking up, he stilled—his ability to breathe stolen by the sight of Claire.

The only word in the English language he could

remember passed his lips. "Mine."

Inhaling deeply, his eyes stayed on her as she descended the stairs. She was a diamond of the first water and his idiot self had spent the last two afternoons at his club dropping hints of a beautiful heiress who would be attending tonight's ball.

What the bloody hell had he been thinking?

She floated down in a cloud of burgundy satin, and if he never took another breath in his sorry life at least he would have lived to see this. Claire—his Claire—beautiful and sensual, looking back at him as if she would never have eyes for any man but him. He drank in every slow step she took.

Fool that he was, he had offered her up to every buck and dandy in London. All he had thought to do was give her a chance to look over the possibilities so he could be sure when...if she chose him, he could trust that she was sure of her heart.

Bloody hell, he would likely kill any man who came near her.

The dress came to an arc under her neck and hugged every delicious curve of her body, from her breasts to the curve of her hips before flowing down the long lines of her legs. He swallowed hard. The blood red ruby earrings dangling from her ears, her only adornment, made him want to slowly peel everything but the earrings off and then have hot, fevered sex with her. She stepped down, stopping in front of him.

"Turn around," he said gruffly—too gruffly. If she only knew how beautiful she was there would be no uncertainty in her eyes. She had no idea of the picture she presented—a goddess come to life. The vision before him was every man's fantasy.

She was his, dammit!

She turned and presented her back. Oh, the lady was too clever. Her hair had been pulled up in a mass of curls atop her head and then left to trail down her back, making the deep V of the gown almost hidden. But every man at the ball would be straining his neck to get a glimpse of what she had hidden under that glorious hair.

He was surely going to have to kill someone before the night ended.

With a gentle hand on her shoulder, he turned her to face him. "I knew you would look stunning in that gown, Claire. You steal my breath away, and I do mean that literally."

She smiled. "Please, don't leave me alone tonight."

Not a chance in bloody hell. "The purpose of this night is for you to see what you have missed in your life." He put a finger to her lips when she began to speak. "But I promise that unless you are dancing or wish me to the devil, I will not abandon you."

She closed her eyes and sucked his finger into her mouth.

"Stop that or, I promise, you'll go no further than my bed tonight." He pulled his finger away before he slung her over his shoulder and made good on his words.

"I wouldn't mind."

Neither would he, but was saved from doing something foolish by the arrival of his mother.

"Oh, Claire, my dear, you look lovely. There will not be an eligible man at the ball who will not want an introduction."

Chase gave serious consideration to following

through on his threat to keep her in his bed tonight. It would keep her away from all the bloody men his mother was determined to introduce her to.

"What is the reason for this new habit of growling, Kensington? It is most unusual."

He scowled at Lady Anne. Why had he thought it would be a good idea to ask her to chaperone Claire? As the carriage took them along the streets of Mayfair, he couldn't take his gaze away from Claire. How was he going to bear watching men vie for her attention?

"I haven't been able to decide whether to claim your first waltz, Claire, or the supper dance, so, I'm claiming both."

Lady Anne gave him a knowing smirk. "You do understand that by doing so, you will be announcing your interest in her."

Was that his intention? He had told himself he would give her two weeks, and he shouldn't be putting a do not touch sign on her on her first night out—even if he did want to paint *mine* in capital letters all over her.

"I know," he said tersely.

"Why is that?" Claire asked.

"Because, dear, one dance is just a dance, but two means he is courting you."

"I'm so ignorant of the rules." She grabbed Lady Anne's hand. "Please, don't leave me alone tonight."

"How easily I've been replaced," Chase teased. "It wasn't ten minutes ago you were begging me to stay by your side."

****

Chase claimed his waltz and for the first time since arriving, Claire relaxed. Swirling around the dance floor in his arms, all she felt was him, his gloved hand on the small of her back, his other hand holding hers. All she saw was him, and all she could think was how beautiful he was in his formal dress. Of course, he was beautiful without a stitch of clothing, also.

"What has you smiling so mysteriously?" he asked.

She shouldn't tell him, but she did. "I was trying to decide whether I preferred you dressed as you are tonight or not dressed at all."

His eyes turned dark and hungry. "You're courting danger, love. I haven't been able to touch you like I have wanted for a week, and my self-control is precarious at best. I may forget myself and kiss you."

"I'm counting on it, my lord."

He twirled her off the dance floor and was steering her toward the French doors to the balcony when Lady Anne stepped in front of them. "Going somewhere, Kensington?" Lady Anne asked.

Claire blushed guiltily.

"It's stifling in this crush, and I thought to get some fresh air," Chase said.

Lady Anne waved her hand toward the balcony. "Be my guest, but Claire stays with me."

He leaned toward Lady Anne. "You are an evil woman, Mama."

His hand pressed against Claire's back. Was he as disappointed as she to have been stopped from stealing a few minutes alone?

"I'll come to you for the supper dance," he said and walked out the French doors.

Claire envied the fresh air he was breathing. It really was stifling in the ballroom with so many people crowded together and all the candles burning. Lady

Anne had told her earlier that a crush was a good thing for the hostess, but other than dancing with Chase, she didn't see the appeal. She would much rather be at Hillcrest Abbey with Chase, the twins and her horses.

"Your partner for the next dance is Lord Summerton. He's a viscount and has twenty thousand pounds a year so he's considered a good catch. Especially if you like dogs, which is all he can talk about." Lady Anne leaned close and whispered. "I have it on good authority he wears a corset and his coats are padded."

Claire laughed. The things Lady Anne told her about each of the gentlemen who asked her to dance had helped. It was hard to be intimidated by a man who could only speak of his dogs and wore a corset.

"Ah, here comes just the man I've been looking for. Lord Daventry is an earl and every woman in the room sighs when he walks past. Of course, they do the same when Kensington walks by, but Kensington belongs to you, my dear, so that is neither here nor there. This is important, so do as I say. He will ask you to dance, and you will agree to the last waltz of the evening. He's a friend of Kensington's, but he is a rake and Kensington will be beside himself when he sees you waltzing with Lord Daventry."

Claire recognized the name. He was the man who was interested in one of her horses and wouldn't be against her training his.

Curious, she glanced at him. Oh my, he was almost as beautiful as Chase. But where Chase was all light and golden, this man looked dark and dangerous. She would wager Amira he didn't wear a corset. Except for his white shirt and cravat, he dressed in severe black—

no fancy, colorful waistcoat, no lace on his cuffs or jeweled stickpin. The attire suited him with his black hair, piercing eyes and chiseled face. The nerves she had put to rest returned.

Lord Daventry bowed over Lady Anne's hand. "Lady Kensington, it is indeed a pleasure to see you again. When you are not in town, it's as if all the lights in London have been extinguished."

Claire watched, fascinated, as Lady Anne giggled and tapped Lord Daventry's arm with her fan. "If you were a fox, Daventry, you would charm all the hounds to your side, I'm sure. Now, I would like to introduce you to my good friend, Lady Derebourne. This is her first time in Town, so be gentle with her."

Ink-blue eyes raked her from head to toe. Other than Chase, Claire had never had a man focus on her with such smoldering heat. It was thrilling, yet he was just another man she could easily say no to.

"Gentle is my middle name, Lady Kensington."

Claire returned his bow with a curtsey and held out her hand. He slipped his hand under hers and brought it to his lips. All the other gentlemen had kissed the air over her fingers. Lord Daventry touched his lips to her gloved fingers, and Claire realized she was having her first flirtation with a true rake. Although he wasn't Chase and never could be, she was fascinated by him.

"Do you believe in love at first sight, Lady Derebourne?" he asked.

Oh, he was a charmer, all right. Even so—and even though he was darkly beautiful—her butterflies didn't awaken.

"I do, my lord. The first time I saw my horse, Amira, it was love at first sight."

He laughed. "She is delicious, Lady Kensington. Where ever did you find her?"

Lady Anne glanced to her right and when she turned back to them, her eyes gleamed with satisfaction. Chase stood just inside the French doors watching them, a fierce scowl on his face. Claire swallowed a grin. Oh, this was going to be fun.

"I didn't find her, Kensington did."

"Oh ho, this just gets better and better," he said. "Lady Derebourne, you must grant me a dance."

"I believe I still have the last waltz free."

He grasped her hand and kissed it again. "I will be counting the minutes, my lady."

At that moment, Lord Summerton approached. "Lady Derebourne, I believe this is my dance."

"Daventry, I have a little favor to ask of you," Claire heard Lady Anne say as Lord Summerton led her to the dance floor.

What was Lady Anne up to? Claire wanted Chase to put an end to this silly game and if making him jealous would do it, she would go along. But her heart wasn't in it, nor did she want to hurt him in any way.

Lady Anne was right. All Lord Summerton could speak of was his dogs. Fortunately, they were dancing the quadrille and there wasn't much opportunity to talk.

Her next partner, Lord Easterly, was an earnest young man and she liked him, though she wasn't sure he shaved, yet. She lost track of the names of her dance partners by the time the supper dance arrived. Not one of them disturbed her butterflies.

Chase remained quiet during their dance and through supper. He made her and Lady Anne a plate of food before making one for himself, seemingly content to let her and his mother do the talking. Claire finished her glass of champagne and declined another. As they prepared to return to the ballroom, he finally spoke.

"Who are you dancing with now?"

Lady Anne answered for her, rattling off the list of names a dance had been promised to. When she arrived at Lord Daventry's name, he scowled.

"Don't give me that look, Kensington. Daventry is a friend of yours and was delighted to meet Claire."

"I'm sure he was," he muttered. "You seemed just as delighted to meet him, Claire."

He was jealous, and she felt guilty. She wanted to tell him Lord Daventry didn't disturb her butterflies, but she was going to trust Lady Anne knew what she was doing.

"He's interested in purchasing one of my horses. Before we left Hillcrest, I extended him an invitation to visit. I'm looking forward to our dance so we can discuss the particulars."

Lady Anne was right, he was developing a habit of growling. "He seems to be a charming man," she added.

"All the ladies think so," he said and strode away.

Lady Anne grinned.

"I hope you know what you are doing," Claire said.

"Oh, I do," she answered.

****

Chase prowled the ballroom, keeping an eye on Claire and her dance partners. He had danced a few times with the young ladies sitting against the wall. Unlike the beauties prowling about—sure of their allure and conversation skills—the girls he chose stayed blessedly silent allowing him to wallow in his misery.

Finding a wall where no one lingered nearby, he

leaned against it, crossing his arms over his chest. It gave him a perfect line of sight to glare at Daventry. Not that the earl took notice. The man was too bloody busy making eyes at Claire.

Did he have to put his hand so bloody low on her back? If he wasn't mistaken, and he was sure he wasn't, Daventry held her closer than was proper.

She laughed at something the earl said, and Chase wanted to plant the man a facer. Why the devil was he standing back and letting every buck in England have a go at her? She belonged to him. He pushed off the wall intending to end his farce of a plan.

"Don't you dare, Kensington."

He glared at his mother. He could bowl right over her if he wanted—and he very much wanted—but realized he had been damned close to causing a scandal.

"What the hell were you thinking to introduce her to Daventry? And then, a waltz of all things."

"Your language, Kensington." She turned to watch the couple dancing. "I must say, they do look nice together."

"Have I told you lately that you are an evil woman, Mama?"

She chuckled. "Yes, you have, actually. Now behave yourself."

After she wandered off, Chase turned his attention back to Claire. The waltz ended and he waited for Daventry to return Claire to Lady Anne's side. He watched in disbelief as the bounder led her out to the terrace.

How dare the rogue take the woman he loved out into the night?

Chase fell back against the wall when his knees

threatened to buckle. Bloody hell, he was an idiot!

He loved her.

That he'd been heading in that direction, he had come to terms with. When it had become a sure thing, he didn't know. She belonged to him, and that was all that mattered.

To the devil with his promise to give her two weeks. It ended now. He focused his eyes on the French doors and marched to them, heedlessly plowing past anyone in his way.

****

Lord Daventry glanced over her shoulder. "Here he comes, Lady Derebourne. From the look on his face, I fear I may be sporting a black eye tomorrow. Sadly for my pretty face, I can never say no to Lady Kensington. You can reward me by selling me that horse."

"If this works, my lord, consider Reckless a gift. I must warn you, he's a handful."

The earl grinned wickedly. "I adore feisty horses...and women. Are you sure I can't steal you away?"

"I'm sorry, my lord, but my heart belongs to the marquess."

Said heart pounded. She was tired of the games, tired of flirting with men she had no interest in, and her feet hurt. Daventry had confided that Lady Anne had put him up to stirring Chase's jealously. It was a calculated risk, and she prayed it would all end tonight.

"My loss." Lord Daventry smiled at her and slid his knuckles over her cheek.

"Remove your hands from my lady, Daventry, if you want to live to see tomorrow," Chase growled from behind her.

Lord Daventry gave her a satisfied smile, and Claire squeezed her eyes closed. Finally. When she opened them, the earl was gone and Chase stood in front of her.

"Am I your lady?" she asked.

He pulled her against him and slammed his lips over hers. "Does that answer your question?" he rasped when he pulled away. "Christ in heaven, Claire, I love you." He lowered his lips to hers again and this time his kiss was soft and tender, a kiss of love.

She had chased a dream and learned that sometimes, dreams do come true. Finally, she could say the words that had been in her heart since the night he'd told her how he'd saved two boys from the streets.

"I love you, too."

Chase grabbed her hand and led her down the stairs of the balcony. "Come with me, my love."

The path narrowed as they left the lights from the ballroom behind. "Where are we going?"

"Someplace my evil mother can't find us."

An hour later, Claire rubbed her cheek over his chest. Sated and content, she snuggled up to him. It had been wickedly thrilling to make love in a dark garden with hundreds of people mingling about in the nearby ballroom. And, oh God, had he ever loved her. Yet, it had been different tonight. His desperate need and passionate touches had consumed her.

The dark corner where he had dragged her was quiet now, the sounds of the orchestra gone with only their last note lingering in the air. As they made love, their bodies moving to the sound of the violins, Chase had asked her to marry him, and then caught her tears of joy with tender kisses.

Claire had no idea if they would have reached this point without her plan. Although she felt a bit guilty for using her training techniques on him, she wasn't sorry. She debated not telling him, but wanted to begin their life with honesty between them.

"I have a confession to make," she said, and then remembered the day she had spied on him at the lake. "Two actually."

He lifted his head. "What is that, love?"

She nuzzled his chest again. "Well, I want to confess that I watched you when you swam in the lake wearing only your...you know."

"My drawers? Yes, I know."

"You knew?" She narrowed her eyes at his pleased-with-himself smile. "How?"

"I saw you attempting, unsuccessfully I might add, to hide behind a tree."

"Why you...you..."

"Me what, Claire? Didn't you enjoy the show?"

"Oh, God, I did." His chuckle vibrated against her cheek.

"And your other confession?"

Warily, she confessed. "What would you say if I told you I used my training methods on you?" She held her breath and waited for his anger.

He stared at her for a very long moment. "You trained me like one of your horses?"

She nodded. "Remember how I would touch you, then retreat if you tried to touch me back, and the way I ignored you? That's all a part of my training methods, the way I get a horse to want to join my herd. I don't know why it works exactly, just that it does. I wanted you to join my herd, and I didn't know how else to make you want to."

Chase burst out laughing. He should be angry, but it was the funniest thing that had ever been done to him. His lady was bloody amazing.

"This is what I've seen your horses do at what you call the magic moment," he said and nuzzled her neck. She cried again, but he'd anticipated the tears and had his handkerchief ready.

"Where do you want to be married, love?"

Not answering his question, she asked instead, "Do you think the twins will want me as their mother?"

That she worried about his sons warmed his heart. "To quote Harry, 'we would like Lady Claire for our mother above all things'. Like their father, they love you."

"Forever and a day," she whispered.

He wrapped his hand around her hair and gave her a deep kiss. Lifting his head, he took her hand and pressed it to his chest. "Here is my heart, Claire. I trust it is safe with you."

Epilogue

And so, they were married in the courtyard at Hillcrest Abbey and had babies for older brothers Harry to protect and Bensey to draw. They loved each other forever and a day.

A word about the author...

Sandra lives in the beautiful Blue Ridge Mountains of North Carolina. Most days, you can find her with her fingers on a keyboard, her mind in the world of her imagination. It's a land where romance and happy endings exist, a land where anything is possible.

A few highlights of Sandra's life she fondly recalls are jumping out of a plane, flying upside down in a stunt plane, and riding her Harley in the mountains of Southern California and along the coast of Maine. She's managed a private airport and held the position of General Manager of a Harley-Davidson dealership.

Although those events in her life were great fun, nothing compares to the joy and satisfaction she gets from writing her stories.

Sandra is a 2013 Golden Heart® finalist. You can find her on Facebook and Twitter @SandyOwens1

www.sandra-owens.com

Thank you for purchasing
this publication of The Wild Rose Press, Inc.
For other wonderful stories of romance,
please visit our on-line bookstore at
www.thewildrosepress.com.

For questions or more information
contact us at
info@thewildrosepress.com.

The Wild Rose Press, Inc.
www.thewildrosepress.com

To visit with authors of
The Wild Rose Press, Inc.
join our yahoo loop at
http://groups.yahoo.com/group/thewildrosepress/

www.ingramcontent.com/pod-product-compliance
Lightning Source LLC
Chambersburg PA
CBHW070539260626
47161CB00002B/454

* 9 7 8 1 6 1 2 1 7 9 3 1 5 *